praise

Those Who Face Death:

"Vince Guerra's latest continues to be engrossing, realistic, and entertaining. Vince manages to weave an engaging tale, rapidly bringing personalities from throughout the series into focus on a new mission and a new set of problems.. The characters come to life with real life issues outside, and then inside, the nightmare of war. The action scenes were first rate. This package of being human in extraordinary circumstances comes together resulting in a read that is altogether realistic, fascinating, and entertaining."

— Dan Howe, CW3, US Army Special Forces (ret.)

"This book is the final chapter of *The Modern War Series*. The characters are compelling and if you've read the earlier books, you will love seeing how it all turns out. I could not stop. Wonderful. The scene at the end literally brought tears to my eyes."

— Chief Joe Paolilli, Firefighter

"In his fourth book in *The Modern War Series*, Vince ties together a brotherhood of warriors: men, women, and former enemies. Whether inside the cockpit of a frontline fighter or patrolling the dusty streets of a bombed-out village, your mind will race and your heart will pound due to Vince's articulate attention to detail in the prosecution of war against evil. *Those Who Face Death* is a must read."

— Bobby "Dicey" Wenzel, Lt. Col USAF (ret.), Fighter Pilot

The Modern War Series

Beyond the Golden Hour

The Stars and Their Places

Pegasus

Also by Vince Guerra

The Dread Pirate Roberts

Those

Who

Face

Death

Vince Guerra

Copyright © 2023 Vince Guerra

All rights reserved. No part of this book may be reproduced in any form or by any electronic or mechanical means, including information storage and retrieval systems, without permission in writing from the publisher, except by reviewers, who may quote brief passages in a review.

This is a work of fiction. Names, characters, businesses, places, events and incidents are either the products of the author's imagination or used in a fictitious manner. Any resemblance to actual persons, living or dead, or actual events is purely coincidental.

Cover by Copperlight Wood
Cover background image by Jeff Kingma, used with permission
Illustrations by Vince Guerra

Printed in the United States of America

Published by Copperlight Wood
PO Box 2980806
Wasilla, AK 99629
www.copperlightwood.com

ISBN 979-8-9887158-1-8 (paperback)
ISBN 979-8-9887158-2-5 (hardcover)
ISBN 979-8-9887158-3-2 (ebook)

Dedicated in memory of

Lieutenant Colonel Wm. Brendan Welsh

U.S. Army Special Forces

AKA

"Boss Mongo"

Author's Note

This is the final chapter of a four-book series following characters across the wars in Afghanistan and Iraq from 2003 to 2018.

As with every book in this series, true events have at times inspired and directed aspects of the story. While period-accurate units, battles, methods, and personnel have been incorporated, this series remains a work of historical fiction.

My goal has always been to honor the men and women who've lived the history, and to give the readers a greater understanding of the sacrifices they and their families have endured to protect liberty and our country.

Their courage is contagious.

Contents

Prologue

Mosul, Iraq 2014

Some veterans remain who can recall first-hand images of the armies of Germany, overwhelming in strength and sweeping over practically every nation they attacked. Storied forces — Polish, Belgian, French, or British — were routed before their commanders even knew what hit them. Those armies could only react to the onslaught in ultimately hopeless attempts to stave off disaster. History later defined this style of war fighting as blitzkrieg.

Neither Goriel Abdelhossein nor any of the five soldiers in the vehicle with him knew much about that history, or that a modern blitzkrieg was pouring over their forces across Iraq. All they knew was they were getting beat, badly.

"Left, here! Turn! Turn!" Goriel commanded.

But the driver didn't turn. He hardly even steered, crouching with his head barely high enough to peek through the cracked windshield covered in dust and blood, and to avoid getting his helmet smacked again by his commander. He simply put his foot on the accelerator and prayed.

Bullets peppered the front of the Humvee and continued to strafe its left side as they passed yet another horde of ISIS trucks, multiplying and popping up everywhere Goriel tried to go in his frustrated retreat.

"Faster!" Goriel shouted. "Mow through them."

The Humvee slammed through a gap and pulled clear of the heavy gunfire, running over a fighter in the street who tried to jump onto the hood. Goriel looked to the rear of the vehicle. One of his men lay dead against the left door, two others hid behind his body, lifting it up with their shoulders as a makeshift shield against the window, their weapons long silent.

"Get up and return fire!"

They ignored him. Goriel turned to the one Iraqi who still sat upright clutching his rifle.

"You, get on the fifty! We still have ammo for it. Do you want to die? Fight!"

The young soldier only blinked and hugged his rifle like a blanket.

Goriel turned back in disgust. "Stop the vehicle. Stop I say!"

But the driver didn't listen and Goriel was forced to reach his foot across the driver's body and slam the brake for him. The Humvee came to a wild stop as it glanced a broken brick wall and spun partially around.

"Get out!"

The driver lay down in the seat, eyes now completely closed, as he prayed frantically. Goriel shoved him out of the vehicle and the man curled into a ball on the ground, putting his hands over his head. Goriel climbed out the driver's side door.

"Get up!"

The driver just rocked and prayed.

Goriel opened the rear passenger door. "Out! We need to take that position!" The soldier who clutched his weapon nodded and stepped out of the Humvee slowly. Goriel looked at the other men now peering out from the safely of their dead comrade's body.

"What are you doing? Get us out of here!" one of them said.

Goriel pointed his rifle at his men. "Pick up your weapons and follow me or I'll kill you where you lay, cowards!"

The men slowly put down the body and searched for their weapons, each picking up a rifle before slithering out of the Humvee.

Goriel repositioned against an adjacent building. The three men followed, crouching, looking for threats. When they were huddled behind a partial wall, Goriel tapped two of the men on their helmets to get their attention.

"You two. Hold this corner and cover our six while we get a look down the road. We can assault them from behind." Goriel patted the other soldier on the shoulder. "You're with me." He moved off toward the ISIS position they'd just passed.

They went with their backs along the wall to the end of the street. Goriel took a quick glance around the corner and could hear the voices of the men who'd just shot up his Humvee, could hear their engine running less than a block away. If they acted fast enough, he could surprise them from behind and take them all out; all he needed was a couple more men.

"Hold here," Goriel ordered the soldier, looking back to the men he'd left at the other corner.

Both of them were frantically removing their uniforms. One made eye contact with Goriel and shouted to his friend, and upon realizing their commander saw them, they fled across the road.

"Where are you going!? Stand fast!" Goriel ran to their position but only caught a glimpse as they disappeared into the shadows of an alley. At his feet lay the discarded Iraqi military uniforms, along with two rifles and the rest of their gear. He simply stared at it and shook his head in disbelief.

How is this happening?

Gunfire interrupted his question, far off but intense. He stepped around the gear toward the Humvee, which sat with its driver's side door open, the driver also long gone. He looked at the dead soldier's body and briefly remembered seeing him crumple after getting shot less than an hour ago.

You still have one man left. It may be enough.

He swore and ran back to the soldier he'd left behind, relieved to find at least one who hadn't deserted him. He patted him on the shoulder.

"Come on, let's move."

The man looked at Goriel but remained crouched next to the wall.

"Say your name!" Goriel snapped, and smacked the side of his helmet. "Say your name, I said."

"Baravan," he said in a weak, confused voice.

"On your feet!" The soldier stood but his attention was drawn away to the sound of nearby gunfire.

"It's them. Right down there. They're killing our men. Our families. You hear them?"

The young man blinked and wiped sweat from his forehead.

"They're shooting at our men. Right down there, now follow me."

Goriel ran across the street, toward the gunfire, not bothering to see if the soldier followed and hardly caring if he did. He reached the buildings and quickly moved along the wall in the direction of the shooting. A few civilians ran in various directions, and nobody noticed him as he crept along, crossed another street, and went along another wall. Reaching the corner, he glanced around it and saw a truck twenty meters away, a heavy machine gun mounted in its bed with a man gripping it. He turned to his left and the soldier was next to him like an obedient puppy, and looking about as harmless.

Goriel retrieved a fragmentation grenade, pulled the pin, and heaved it toward the truck whose occupants shouted and turned their gun on him as he ducked behind the wall.

Bullets pounded the corner and he waited. Five seconds. The explosion rocked the street, sending dirt, concrete, and metal debris flying in all directions. He turned the corner with his rifle leveled at what remained of the truck, saw pieces of one man in the street and another not far away, rolling on the ground. Three shots stopped the body from moving and he scanned the street as civilians ran.

"Back to the Humvee. Let's go!" he yelled to the other soldier.

They moved together and were halfway back to their vehicle when two trucks laden with fighters tore out from another road, black and white ISIS flags waving from PVC flagpoles attached to their cabs. They spotted Goriel and his companion, shouting as they fired at them.

Goriel dropped to a knee and returned fire into the windshield of the nearest truck, killing the man behind the driver side, then stood and side-stepped rapidly, still firing with short, measured bursts into the windshield and the truck bed.

To his right, he heard the frantic cry of his fellow soldier.

"No! No! No!"

The man stood in the center of the road with his hands in the air, his discarded rifle at his feet. The ISIS fighters in the other truck unleashed their weapons on full auto and the surrendering soldier disintegrated.

Goriel sprinted around the corner in the direction of the Humvee as bullets flew all around him. He leaped over the abandoned gear of his men, climbed up the back and through the roof hatch as he heard a vehicle approaching. Grabbing the handles of the .50 caliber machine gun, he pulled the bolt as he swung it toward the oncoming truck, firing into the engine, the windshield, and then at the men scrambling out, mowing them down until movement ceased. Then he dropped back down into the vehicle, got behind the wheel, and fired up the engine.

After a few blocks, he passed two more ISIS vehicles going too fast to engage, and turned down another road where the street opened into a pavilion. He braked and grabbed the radio, tried several frequencies, but only picked up frantic and disjointed chatter.

Turning back to the main road, he went a few more blocks before coming to a roadblock, a smoldering and abandoned Iraqi troop carrier with a bloody body in the street a few meters away. He switched into reverse, but another truck boxed him in and fired at his rear. Goriel dove out as the Hummer's interior filled with bullets, and he crawled toward cover behind the hulk of another charred vehicle, and realized his rifle was missing. He drew his pistol and rose to his knee to get his bearings, heard more gunfire but couldn't tell its source or direction. He stood and pointed his pistol while side-stepping and saw someone shooting at the ISIS truck from behind a sandbag barricade he hadn't noticed.

"All clear!" A soldier's hand rose from behind the line of sandbags, waving Goriel over.

He stood still with his pistol aimed at the sandbags.

"Don't shoot!" the man said.

Goriel scanned the road, then sprinted toward their position and jumped over the barrier. "Thank you. Where is your commander?"

"Probably in his villa," one scoffed.

"We haven't seen any of them in days," the other added.

Goriel examined the area. The road was littered with Iraqi vehicles, some charred, others abandoned but in working order. *This is unbelievable.*

He spotted a tank and asked, "Where is the rest of your unit?"

"They left us."

"What? There's a tank right there!" Goriel seethed.

"Its crew is gone. I don't know where they went."

"So, it's just you two?"

"Yes sir."

Goriel tried the hand-held radio beside them.

"Nobody is responding to us. We tried," the soldier said scanning the street with his weapon.

He pulled out his smart phone.

"Where should we go, sir? Should we hold here?"

He ignored him and composed a text:

Mosul is overrun. Units fleeing and abandoning their posts. Please advise.

He sat down heavily with his back to the sandbags.

"Do you have any water?"

"Yes sir." One of the soldiers gave him a bottle, and he took a long pull from the canteen, then surveyed the men.

"Why didn't you run like everyone else?"

"We didn't know where to go. So we made this and hunkered down till we could make contact."

Goriel chuckled. "Right." His phone chimed a return text. He checked it, then stood.

"Gather whatever weapons you can, and let's find a vehicle that still runs."

The men obeyed. "Who did you text?"

"My father. He wants us to link up with forces that are still holding in Erbil."

"Your father is a commander?"

"Yes, and hopefully he'll be taking over from whoever is responsible for this disaster."

The men stared at him with awkward expressions, unsure how to respond.

"I don't suppose either of you know how to drive that tank?"

They both shook their heads. "No sir."

"Of course not. Well, there's an armored troop carrier down there too, probably several. Let's at least claim one of them before the enemy does."

Baghdad, Iraqi Combined Joint Operations Center
Two weeks later

"He's here, Sir."

General Abdelhossein looked up from the laptop he was standing behind.

"So?"

"He asked to see you specifically, Sir."

Annoyance was evident on the general's face and the subordinate averted his gaze, standing at attention.

Abdelhossein, or Ozzy, as the Americans who trained him used to call him, stepped out from behind his desk, passed a wall of maps and a bank of television screens. A small group of subordinates, all of whom had steel expressions and were dressed for a fight, watched him leave.

"Can't wait to see what this one has to say," Ozzy said.

He took his time making his way to the Ministry of Defense building, passed several soldiers who saluted him, and he noted that some had uncharacteristic smiles on their faces. A long-departed optimism buzzed in the atmosphere.

He entered the main conference room and saw all of the senior military brass in attendance, a semi-circle of them around an American officer of significant rank in camouflage uniform. The lead Iraqi commander spoke.

"Ah. Here is General Abdelhossein, of our Counter Terrorism Service."

The American had already started toward Ozzy the moment he had entered the room, ignoring the Lieutenant General's introduction.

"General Abdelhossein." He extended his hand but didn't smile. "You and your men have performed admirably, given the circumstances."

"Given what circumstances?" he asked, shaking the man's hand.

"Given that the rest of your country's forces folded like a cheap suit." There was an awkward exchange of glances between the other officers, but the American ignored them.

"I was here back when men wanted to fight. I helped train a lot of them. It's a damn disgrace how many of 'em cut and run at first contact." He turned to examine the room, noticing many of the officers avoided eye contact. He met the icy stares of those who didn't.

"How many tanks, armored personnel carriers, and Humvees did your men piss away last week in Mosul?" He looked around waiting for a response, but it came from behind him.

"Over a thousand," Ozzy answered.

"Twelve to thirteen hundred's more like it," the American scoffed. "Thirty thousand men ran from what? Five hundred?"

"We estimate that the enemy numbered considerably more than that," the Lt. General objected.

The American answered with a dismissive expletive.

"But your unit," he continued, now facing Ozzy again, "and maybe a few Kurds, stood their ground and kicked those fools' teeth in, albeit in limited areas." A slight smile cracked on the American's face.

"Are you here to contribute," Ozzy asked, "or do you just plan on standing around smirking? I've got a war to fight."

The American laughed. "Make no mistake," he said loudly, "I'm not here to pad your egos, pussyfoot around your sensitivities, or supply new underwear for your soldiers. If you need any of that, go see my subordinates. I'm here for one thing, to help you kill these—" he finished with expletives.

"From thirty thousand feet," Ozzy smirked. "It's hard to take back a city with a few bombs."

"That's right," the American nodded, "but it's the best my government is willing do at present…for now. I will be able to provide you with some of the necessary ground personnel to make sure those bombs hit the right targets; they'll be integrating into your unit soon. But for now, your men find 'em, my pilots will fry 'em. Deal?"

Ozzy nodded. "How soon?"

"As soon as you tell me who you want to blow up first."

Ozzy smiled.

Tel Tamer, Syria

Dwura pulled Hazail close. Huddled on the floor in the back bedroom, mother and daughter clung to one another with closed eyes, praying with other women. The bloodthirsty shouts of maniacal men outside were nearly as loud as the repetitive rifle fire from successive executions, and more frightening.

The pleadings of men she had known in her childhood, friends and family members who had tried to avoid it all, were silenced forever by bullets. She squeezed Hazail.

Lord, let us live, or else die quickly.

They heard the front door get kicked in, and men hollering, overturning furniture, and firing into the ceiling. The women screamed and backed into the far corner; others jolted upright from praying positions on their knees. Then, the men were there, in the back room.

One rushed forward and slapped mother and daughter apart. Another grabbed Hazail by the hair and dragged her up onto her feet. Dwura was kicked and beaten with the butt of a rifle before she too was grabbed by the arm and lifted to stand. The men laughed as they manhandled them out the door, across the courtyard, and finally deposited Dwura into a huddle of other women and small children.

She stood to look for Hazail, but a man struck her in the head with his fist and she fell in a heap, blinking. Her ears rang. The dust from the ground obscured her vision. A red stream in the distance, boots, and truck tires. A sickening metallic smell in the air. She lifted her head slightly and saw a long line of men in the distance, laying on the blood-soaked ground, dead.

A woman covered her with her own body and whispered in her ear. "Stay down. They will kill you."

Dwura sobbed and closed her eyes. *Lord, save her.*

1
Missions

Central African Republic (CAR)
2017

Aiden McCoy wiped the sweat from his brow with his right palm, smearing his forehead with dirt in the process before putting his sunglasses and hat back on.

"Someone coming up behind us," Porter said, driving.

Aiden lifted Porter's submachine gun, removed the magazine, then reinserted it and laid it on the seat between them.

"You're good." Aiden looked at the passenger side mirror. "I can't see 'em. How many?"

"About to pass us, don't know yet." Porter removed his 9mm M&P pistol from its holster and held it by his thigh, pointed at the floorboard.

A rusty SUV pulled alongside his window. Aiden leaned forward and met the gaze of a young man wearing aviator sunglasses and brandishing an AK-47 in his left hand while motioning for Porter to stop their vehicle with his right.

Porter avoided eye contact and kept driving with one hand on the wheel.

"Go ahead and stop," Aiden said.

"Gotta say, I'm not into that plan."

"Can't risk them shooting us off the road. Stay behind the wheel. Let me go first."

"You say so, boss."

They decelerated quicker than the SUV expected and stopped as the other vehicle zipped past them. It came to an abrupt stop also, its tires kicking up a cloud of dust and sand between them. The SUV's driver reversed and as the tailgate approached Porter's windshield, Aiden holstered the semi-automatic pistol he'd been holding.

"Be ready."

Porter parked, holstered his own pistol, and had the submachine gun in his lap before Aiden's shoe touched the road. Aiden left the passenger door open; Porter cracked his.

Aiden took three brisk steps toward the vehicle with his hands at chest level, closing the distance almost enough to touch the SUV's taillights when the first man stepped out.

"Hello, friend," Aiden said in Sango, one of the common languages of the region.

"What you doing here? What you carry in truck?" the young man with the AK-47 returned in English, pointing recklessly with his rifle.

"Nothing much. Just small cargo," Aiden answered in English.

Another passenger from the SUV exited and came up behind the man confronting Aiden. He was a little older than the other and held a lowered, long-barreled revolver.

"What are you doing here?" he asked Aiden, tapping his revolver visibly against his thigh.

Two additional figures exited the vehicle, one a scrawny teenager, the other a child not more than ten years old. Both held AK-47s that looked out of place against their small frames.

"Are you the Boss Man?" Aiden offered to shake his hand, turning his attention back to the oldest man. The gesture caused the Africans to holler in their own language, and the man cocked his pistol and pushed it against Aiden's forehead.

In a fraction of second Porter jumped from behind the wheel and leveled his submachine gun on the leader, and using the door for cover, stabilized his weapon in the open window frame.

Aiden extended his left arm to motion for Porter to steady, then slowly put his hands up to chest level as if to surrender. He still smiled. "No problem, friend. No problem."

The man pushed the end of the pistol deeper into Aiden's forehead.

"Don't move." He raised his voice to his companions. "Look in their truck."

Porter kept his weapon pointed at Boss Man but stole a glance to the left at the three young men with the rifles. He could see their hesitation, their focus on him behind the door. The child started to shake, and his weapon shook with him.

The steel end of the revolver was still against Aiden's forehead. The leader turned his head slightly.

"I said –"

Aiden seized the distraction. Still smiling, in a lightning move he slapped his assailant's inner forearm with his right hand while grabbing the revolver with his left, flipping it around and pointing back at it at him so fast the man was stunned speechless.

"Drop 'em. Drop 'em now!" Porter ordered the three young men, surprised at his friend's maneuver.

Aiden aimed toward the brush and fired off a round, then squared the smoking barrel on Boss Man's face again.

"You die first. They may get me, but you die first. Tell them to put their weapons on the ground." He was no longer smiling.

With a shaky voice, the leader waved his hand toward the SUV and barked something in Sango. The two teenagers obeyed, lowering their weapons, but the child continued to shake, gripping the AK-47.

Porter moved out from behind the truck's door. To the teenagers he yelled, "You two, on the ground now!" He then took careful steps toward the child and touched him gently on the shoulder, careful to make sure his rifle was aimed at the ground.

"It's okay, buddy. Set it down." Porter pointed to the rifle, then at the ground. The child obeyed and joined his comrades in laying face down.

"Clear!" Porter called to Aiden after confiscating and clearing the weapons.

Aiden had held the leader's gaze the entire time. He lowered the pistol, cleared the cylinder, and put it and its bullets in his cargo pants pocket. Then he put his fingers in his mouth and let out a sharp whistle.

"Guy!" he yelled.

An African man holding a rifle emerged from the back of the truck. He took in the situation then spoke to the other man in Sango.

"Just scavengers," Guy said dismissively after a brief interrogation. "We should go, quickly." Guy went to the child and knelt beside him.

"Stand up, please. We will not hurt you," he told the boy in his own language. "What is your name?"

"Jean," the child answered, standing.

"Do you know where your parents are?"

"They killed them."

"How long have you been with these men?"

"I don't know."

While they spoke, Porter inspected the vehicle and found a bag of mixed ammunition, a case of water, and another semi-automatic pistol. In the vehicle's cargo area were cases of cigarettes and water, boxed foods, and several gas tanks. He left everything but the guns and ammo, removed the keys from the ignition, and handed them to Aiden.

"Bunch of contraband. I took the weapons. Gonna stow 'em and get ready to roll."

"Go ahead, we're almost done here."

Porter went to the back of their truck.

"Get up," Aiden commanded the two on the ground.

They got up slowly and stood next to their humiliated leader.

"We're keeping your guns but you're free to leave," Aiden showed them the keychain, "as soon as you find your keys." He threw them far into the brush off the side of the road. "Go on now. You'll want to find them before dark."

"Would you like to come with us?" Guy asked the child.

"They will kill me if I leave."

"We're not going to let them harm you anymore. Come, let me show you." He ushered the child toward the cargo bed where Porter was handing out the water bottles and granola bars he'd taken from the SUV to several children of various ages.

"They are like you. They were soldiers but we are taking them to a new place to live," Guy continued. "You can get good meals. Sleep in a nice bed. You can learn to do things other than soldiering. We can try to locate your remaining family."

Aiden approached the boy and held out a granola bar, speaking what little he knew of the native language. "You're safe now." The boy eyes darted around the scene. One of the children stared at him while chewing.

"We won't force you to come with us," Aiden continued. "We don't do that like they do. You don't have to be a soldier anymore. Just like them." He motioned toward the other children.

The boy looked at the blank faces of the others. None had weapons. He nodded.

Guy helped him into the back of the truck, then followed and sat next to the tailgate with his rifle in his lap, speaking to the children as Porter dropped the canopy.

A few miles down the road Porter ceased checking the side mirror. He glanced over at Aiden, casually eating from a tube of Pringles confiscated from the SUV's cache.

"You die first," Porter said. "You got that from Unforgiven, huh?"

"Tombstone."

Porter nodded. "That's right. Tombstone…good movie."

"Great movie."

"I didn't figure the PJs taught you guys how to disarm like that."

"They didn't. My grandpa did."

"Grandpa McCoy must have been a badass."

"He was," Aiden said, finishing off the chips.

Porter thought for a minute.

"You know…you'd never be able to disarm me like that." He smiled, watching the road.

"Yeah I could," he looked at Porter, "and so could Grandpa."

Ginger heard the children clamoring in the courtyard before she heard the vehicle. She ran her hands under the faucet and hastened to dry them while peering out the dust covered window.

Walking outside she could see the truck slowly passing the opened security gate. Two armed men closed it as soon as the truck was inside, and a dozen small children ran to watch up close while many of the older adolescents remained where they sat but looked up from their books and other work.

Shiloh quickly came up behind her mother, but paused, still inspecting from afar.

"Did he call you?" the ten-year-old asked.

"No, not since they left last week. That must be them, though." Ginger gently rubbed her daughter's arm. "If something was wrong he would have called. Come on." Together they approached the truck, which drove slowly through the courtyard of excited kids. Ginger saw Aiden through the windshield; he reached out the window and waved.

"They look okay," Shiloh said as Aiden gave them a thumbs up.

Ginger smiled and waved back. "Yeah."

The truck stopped and Porter put it in park, turned off the engine, and let out a deep breath.

"Piece of cake," Aiden said, getting out.

"Yeah, sure," Porter muttered to himself, slinging his machine gun and readjusting his Red Sox cap. "Easy peasy."

"Hey," Ginger said as Aiden gave her a tight, long hug and a quick kiss, and then hugged his daughter.

"How we looking?" Ginger asked.

"Seven, all in pretty good shape, plus one we picked up on the road. Where's Allen?"

"Over there." Ginger pointed to a six-year-old in the distance playing with two other children. "Any action?"

"Naw. Got a little hairy but no shots fired. Well…maybe one shot. But hey," he reached into his cargo pants and pulled out Boss Man's stainless steel revolver. "I got you a souvenir."

"Oh, that's so sweet of you." She checked the cylinder and examined its weight. "Next time bring ice cream."

"Sorry, they were fresh out."

Porter came around the front of the truck. "Tell her how you got it." He gave Ginger a quick hug. "How's the fort holding up, sister?"

"Good. Welcome back."

Porter gave Shiloh a fist pound. "What up, dork?"

"You still stink, Froggie," Shiloh said, completing their standard greeting and giving him a side hug.

"Oh, stop," Ginger shook her head.

"How did you get the gun?" Shiloh asked her dad.

"Tell ya later. I'm gonna go say hi to your brother."

"How about *you* tell me later," Ginger said to Porter as they walked to the rear of the vehicle. "He'll just play it off."

"Hey, we didn't have to shoot at hardly anyone this time."

"Greeeat."

At the back of the truck, Guy and two other workers helped the children out and spoke reassuring words to the new arrivals, all of whom took in their surroundings with wide eyes and guarded composure.

"Welcome back," Ginger said, shaking Guy's hand.

"Thank you. We were blessed."

"I can see that." Ginger knelt beside a young girl and spoke to her in Sango. "Welcome. You'll be safe here. My name is Ginger, what's yours?"

"Kiminu," she said quietly.

"That's a pretty name. Are you hungry? We can have some lunch."

The young girl nodded her head.

Shiloh came up to another girl and smiled.

"Hello," she said in Sango, then switched to English. "Come." She offered the girl her hand.

They repeated the greeting with most of the children, switching languages when necessary, and soon all them were less guarded; the casual attitudes and smiling faces set them at ease. As the procession made its way toward the orphanage's dining room, Guy and Porter noticed a new arrival, the oldest boy, staring at the armed security facing outward toward the road.

"You can rest here," Guy said, and gently put a hand on his shoulder. "We are well armed, they will not come for you here. Go now, you don't want to miss your meal."

The boy followed the crowd into the building.

Porter looked across the orphanage courtyard which had resumed its normal state of orchestrated chaos. From a distance he saw Aiden holding the only white boy in the complex and spinning him in the air. The other children laughed, several of them tugging at Aiden's pantleg for a turn.

Porter went to the truck's cab and removed the duffel bag of weapons, their own and those they had confiscated over the week. Guy climbed behind the wheel and started the engine, then smiled at Porter through the window.

"Piece of cake, eh?" he said as he drove away to stow the vehicle.

"Yeah, piece of cake."

2
Tactics

Mosul, Iraq

Men scurried back and forth between the white 2012 Kia hatchback and the tables lining the garage walls, loading the car with explosives and loose metal objects. They filled the back seat, the passenger seat, the floorboards, and cargo hatch, until the only room left was the driver's seat.

"It's ready," the operational chief said. "Go and get him."

A bearded man knelt next to a younger man bowing in the corner, praying.

"It's time. Are you prepared?"

The young man stood from the small rug.

"Yes."

He walked to where the driver's side door would have been had it not been sawed off, along with the rest of the vehicle's front panels, hood, and windshield. In their places were sheets of metal plating welded to the Kia's frame, making the front end a look like a car children might have made from cardboard.

The young man slid into the driver's seat and two men immediately placed a sheet of metal shaped like the door panel over the opening. Another stepped forward, dropped a welder's mask over his eyes, and welded it in place. Inside, the young man strained to see out the narrow slit in the Kia's front armor. He set his cell phone in his front pocket, inserted the earphone with the attached microphone, and started the engine. It didn't take long before his phone rang.

"Yes. I'm ready."

"Drive out and to the left. We will direct you where to go."

Matt thought the noise was from a bug, and he swatted at his ear. But no sooner had he done so when it became evident the buzzing was from far overhead, and moving toward them.

"Drone," he said, looking skyward between the broken walls of bombed out buildings. "Does anyone see it?"

The Iraqi Security Forces soldier ahead of him turned back and searched the sky.

"Negative."

All five of them — four ISF Iraqis and Matt, the lone American — looked to the air with weapons raised, searching out the flying object they could still hear but not see.

Matt cupped his hand over his eyes to shade out the sun, his dirty ball cap on backwards. He caught a glimpse of something dart across the span between the buildings.

"There," he said, pointing his AK-47.

One of the soldiers fired a short burst as the drone disappeared again. The sound diminished as it ascended high into the air. It had fulfilled its mission.

The ISF squad leader spoke the obvious.

"We should move, quickly."

For the past hour their patrol had cleared this street, foot by tedious foot, taking care to locate and not detonate hidden IEDs. Now, knowing the street was cleared of mines, they ran back in the direction they had started from.

Matt's intuition kicked in. *Stand fast. Something's off.* But he followed the soldiers, not daring to stop for fear of being left behind. In seconds they could see the ISF Humvees they'd arrived in, still manned with the engines running, with four additional ISF troops dismounted and standing by.

He nearly cracked a smile until he heard the drone again, hovering somewhere. A vehicle engine revved. He turned and caught sight of the odd-looking, boxy grey vehicle on a collision course with the parked Humvees.

"Truck bomb!" someone yelled in Arabic, one of the few phrases he was now familiar with, referring to a vehicle born improvised explosive device, or VBIED.

Matt took three shots at the driver's side window and heard the rounds ping off the steel plate. *Armor, too late.* The former PJ ducked behind a chunk of broken concrete and curled into a ball, covering his head with his arms. At the last second he felt another soldier landing nearly on top of him.

The explosion rocked the street with such fury it lifted them an inch off the ground. The wave of dust, debris, and metal fragments washed over, sucking the sound out of the city intersection, leaving only a ringing in Matt's ears. For a moment he wondered if he was dead, then he heard screaming.

He tried to stand and instantly felt the sharp sting of shrapnel in his calf. He took a quick self-assessment – both legs still there, with deep red blood from capillary bleeding – and he removed his backpack med kit, wondering how much of it remained unscathed. The soldier who had jumped on him ran toward the carnage down the road, searching for targets and leaving a trail of blood in his wake.

Matt tried to reestablish equilibrium, feeling queasy and light-headed, and the shrapnel made him limp as he moved toward a slew of patients. The first was alive from the waist up, but mostly no longer existed from the waist down. The cold reality of triage set in and he shook his head.

"Sorry." It was all he had to offer.

He sized up the carnage and asked himself for the hundredth time why he'd come here. The answer, as always, reverberated instantly: That Others May Live. And whenever it did so, a change took place. Combat mindset kicked in. He was no longer a bored civilian deadbeat seeking former glory, as his ex-wife liked to smear him, but a combat medic, minus the uniform and the backup.

He set aside the AK-47 and focused completely on the next man in front of him. "I got you, buddy. Just lay back." He opened a package of combat gauze to pack the worst of several holes near the soldier's armpit, and as he did, he calculated the other casualties around him against the time he'd have to do something about it with the meager supplies he had. *Most of these men will die*, he concluded, *and Lord knows how many injured civilians will be pouring out of the surrounding buildings in a few minutes.*

He thought about his twelve-year-old daughter back in Arizona and wanted to text her to say he was okay for now. *Get your head in the game.* Matt shook the thoughts away and focused on the patient, hurriedly dressing his wounds enough so he could move on to the next guy and, hopefully, get some of them out of here alive. The same thought always nagged him. *We need more medics.*

Ozzy looked over the casualty report for the previous few days.

"We need to push, now. We need to get more aggressive." It was more to himself than to the men around him, and he went on in a louder voice.

"Perpetual planning is every bit the enemy as the daesh holed up in dark corners."

He cast the paper onto the desk and stood. Until the powers that be were ready, the push would have to wait, and casualties would mount, block by bloody block.

"We know they've reinforced and dug in here," his aid pointed to a three-story building on a tablet, "based on the sniper activity. I suggest we target it for an airstrike."

"Close proximity," Ozzy pointed to several other buildings near it, and turned to the American JTAC controller. "What do you say?"

"Given the density of the civilians, I recommend a helicopter strike. But if you want to be sure to bury all of them and their weapons cache and tunnels, you'll need to bomb it down to the foundations. Either way it'll probably be authorized on my end. Your call."

"We already tried assaulting it twice. And lost a tank in the process," another Iraqi officer chimed in. "And lost men both times. They've got clear fields of fire along with the sniper threat. I say drop a bomb."

Ozzy made up his mind. "Target approved. Drop the building."

He watched them leave the room and shook his head at how things had changed. When he'd taken command three years ago, the American air assets had stressed a policy of limited strikes against carefully selected and approved targets, approvals that had to pass the scrutiny of timid men in distant locations. As often as not the restrictive rules of engagement meant missed opportunities and a forever war. Now, with a new American administration came a new policy against ISIS: Annihilation; end it as soon as possible.

Isolate and kill them where they are before they scurry away; this was the informal and deadly efficient strategy in a nutshell, implemented a little more than a year ago to perfection. Eighty percent of the territory formerly claimed by the Islamic Caliphate was now back in coalition hands, the two major holdouts being Mosul in Iraq and Raqqa in Syria.

If it wasn't for the millions of civilians trapped in and between these cities, the task would be fairly straightforward. What made it even more difficult for Ozzy and his men was the fact that their families were somewhere out there — some free, some hiding, some enslaved by ISIS, and some simply missing.

"Sir," another aid rushed in. "A V-bed detonated a few minutes ago."

"How many?"

"We don't have a casualty count yet. Several."

"Find out."

"Yes sir."

Ozzy stared at the ceiling. He closed his eyes and said a short, barely audible prayer.

USS Dwight D. Eisenhower, Arabian Sea

Birdie Allen sat at the computer terminal in the flight operations center and watched the blips on her screen that represented a pair of F-18 Super Hornets turning toward the target. She also tracked several of the massive aircraft carrier's planes currently in the air, as well as coalition jets from various nations, U.S. Air Force fighters from bases in Turkey and Saudi Arabia, and a few drones piloted remotely from Nevada that were currently in the path of her Hornets. As usual, it was a crowded day in the air.

Her ship's aviators were going to drop bombs on the bad guys in a few minutes, and she wondered if any of those targets were the ones who had cost her family so much grief. She tried not to think of the brother they had killed and instead said a quick prayer for her other brother, somewhere on the ground she knew not where, hopefully nowhere near the target. Later on she'd probably need to repent for enjoying watching those bombs fall. But for now she merely did her job, and didn't mind at all.

The Hornets circled the vast city of broken rubble until they pinpointed the target building.

"Mac Two Eight, Taco Three," the JTAC spoke to the lead F-18 pilot, "tally your target building. No movement."

"Mac Two Eight, do we have friendlies? Over."

"Negative, Taco. Report if you see any."

"Confirm target. I don't see anyone," his wingman said.

"Taco Three, request you drop one Mark 82 dead-center with a delayed fuse. Request your wingman drop one Mark 82 in the same spot directly after."

"Taco Three copy. Four copies," the lead plane replied repeating the information, then relayed it to his wingman over the plane-to-plane intercom.

With their gloved hands they entered the necessary commands into the fire control computers as they turned again to line up with the target, inbound from directions thirty degrees separated from one another.

"Taco Three ready, Four's ready."

"Tacos, you are cleared hot."

"Taco Three in hot from the south, egress west." A few seconds later: "Taco Four in hot from the southwest, egress north."

Mosul, Iraq

The explosion shook the entire area, obliterating the building. Ozzy heard the roar of jet engines overhead and his eyes never left his binoculars as the clouds of dust dissipated, scanning what was left of the structure's foundation.

"Advance," he said to the man next to him, who relayed the order to another.

From a few blocks away, he watched a tank start driving along the road adjacent to the former ISIS position. A platoon of Iraqi soldiers followed it, encountering no resistance after days of delay. As the tank passed the wreckage, machine gun fire rang out.

"Where is that coming from?" an officer asked.

"Across the street from the north," Ozzy said.

Bullets pinged off the tank, and machine gun fire strafed the line of troops behind it. As they watched, the M1 Abrams tank stopped and returned fire. Its turret rotated as another line of fire hit it from the opposite direction and cut down several more soldiers.

"Civilians," Ozzy said, as two men, two women, and several children stumbled from an adjacent building. At first they seemed headed toward the tank, but hesitated upon realizing they were caught in a firefight and scurried near a wall, confused.

"Command the tank to move to cover those civilians. And send that squad to cover them now."

The officer relayed the message and Ozzy focused his binoculars on a young girl standing off by herself. Suddenly a man Ozzy presumed to be her father ran to her, grabbed her, and took two steps back toward the others but was cut down by ISIS machine gun fire, along with the girl he held.

Ozzy gripped the binoculars tighter as he watched them fall dead. He panned to the left and saw dust kicking up all around the others as rounds hit the other men, women, and children huddling on the ground. There was a pause, then more rounds hit the bodies again and again for what felt like an eternity. It was overkill of a magnitude Ozzy couldn't believe or understand. In a few seconds the entire grouping of civilians were dead, parents indistinguishable from the children they had held.

Ozzy wanted to fling his binoculars to the ground. Five years earlier he might have thrown up. Instead, he merely went about the business of war and watched as the tank and his squad addressed the threats on both sides of the road. The ISIS machine gun fire stopped as suddenly as it started; either they'd been killed, or more likely, had withdrawn to hole up a little further down the way.

"Should we still move to those civilians, sir?"

"Negative. See to our men," Ozzy said, walking away. "The civilians are all dead."

3
Logistics

Porter woke up with a gasp and looked around his room before laying his head back on the pillow. He closed his eyes, took a deep breath as his heart rate normalized, and tried to go back to sleep but he was wide awake. He reached over to the nightstand and picked up his phone. No texts. A dozen emails, some important, but none from Jen. He put on a shirt, slipped on his flip flops, and went outside. The sun hadn't risen but it wasn't far off and he'd have time to enjoy a cup of coffee before many others began waking.

He stopped by the security detail manning the back line of the compound on his way to the kitchen.

"Morning, Alain."

"Good morning. Up early. Everything alright?" the African asked.

"Yeah, couldn't sleep. Want some coffee?"

"No thank you, I plan on sleeping myself in an hour or so."

"Right."

"I believe Mrs. McCoy is up as well. I saw her headed that way not long ago."

"Thanks."

In the kitchen he found Ginger stirring cream into a mug.

"Got any left for me?" he asked her.

"What are you doing up already? Figured you and Aiden would be out for hours still."

"Couldn't sleep. What are you doing up already?"

Ginger smiled. "Same. Woke up thinking, and once the brain turns on it's all over."

Porter took a mug off the counter and wiped the interior with his fingers. "Dream woke me up." He filled it with coffee and took a sip. "You?"

"Doing travel logistics in my head. I thought I'd get up while it was still quiet to hammer out some things around here for when we're gone."

Porter nodded. "You guys still heading back home for a bit? Or are the fundraisers gonna take up all your time?"

"No, still booked to spend a week with Aiden's family, after Indiana."

Porter looked out the window at the growing daylight and said nothing.

"What was the dream about?"

He seemed to wake from a thought. "Oh, just this recurring one I've had a few times. I'm swimming in some decent surf toward a beach. No gear, just casual. As I get to the shore, I see some team guys lounging in the sand just lined up and chilling. I walk up to them and in the center is Gator…that's an old SEAL buddy, Chris."

"I know who Gator was," Ginger interjected quietly.

Porter took a drink from his mug. "Yeah, I guess that makes sense. Anyway, he's there kicking it with his head tilted back and big dark sunglasses on and he's laughing at me. That's it."

"Huh. Any idea what that means?"

"It's just a dream. Not sure it means jack."

"Not necessarily. Could be God is trying to get something through that stubborn skull of yours."

Porter thought for a moment. "Yeah, maybe."

"You tell anyone about it? Jen?"

"No."

"Spoken to her lately?"

"Just texts once in a while."

Ginger walked toward the open doorway. The sky was getting lighter by the minute. Porter followed her out and they stood on the porch together.

"Are you going to see her while you're back?" she asked. "Or just go straight up to your parent's place?"

Porter let the question hang in the air before answering.

"I hope I'll catch her. Her schedule is unpredictable."

"So, you're gonna pansy out again," she said innocently, the mug partly obscuring her face.

"Why do I even talk to you?"

"Because you know I'm right."

Later that morning, Aiden sat with his laptop at a patio table, sending off hurried replies to dozens of emails. He got to one from Matt and began reading it while Ginger and the kids finished their breakfast.

Aiden, thanks for writing me back so quickly. I don't know exactly where to start but here is a breakdown of the immediate needs:

1) Medics. We're seriously overwhelmed here. I've never seen it so bad (and you know we've both seen plenty), civilians as well as Iraqi and Kurdish troops are getting hammered every day and some of this stuff is just beyond me even.

2) Supplies. Water, food, medical supplies, clothing...pretty much everything.

3) Heavy weapons. I know this isn't something you can provide (I couldn't even bring in my own rifle) but if you have any sway with people who do, the Kurds especially need heavy machine guns, mortars, etc.

4) Documentation. We need people to film what's going on and get it out there.

5) Extra hands. Just to distribute food and stuff, help people get out to safety.

Sorry to ramble on bro but I could go on for hours. Anyway, if you know anyone who can lend a hand or forward this on to people who do, I'd appreciate it. To answer your question, yeah, I sent it to all the brothers we know.

They were all nice but they're all just done man, if you know what I mean. I don't blame them. We did our part and all. This is really not our responsibility, I'm just here because I know it's where I need to be.

Praying for you and your ministry. You have a beautiful family.

Matt

Aiden pushed the laptop slightly away from him and sat back in his chair. He put his hands behind his head and took a deep breath.

"You alright?" Ginger asked.

"Yeah," he smiled.

She took the dishes away. Shiloh started her schoolwork, and Allen helped his mother.

Aiden watched the other children across the courtyard in various activities. Younger kids playing, older ones studying. Through an open window to his left an instructor was giving a lesson on truck driving and basic mechanics to some of the older children.

He watched Shiloh write, waiting for her to pause.

"Did you get to know any of the new kids yesterday?" he asked.

"Not really," she said, twiddling with her pen. "They're always a little standoffish at first. Plus, they're…you know."

"Yeah, drugs in their system."

"Yeah. I can't speak with them as much as mom can. I kinda fumble through it."

"Me too. I rely on Guy," he said as Allen climbed into his lap.

"Dad, can you read this to me?" he asked, getting comfortable and handing him a floppy children's book.

In between page turns Aiden said to Ginger, "There's a reply on my screen from Matt, that PJ friend of mine I told you about."

"The guy in Iraq?"

"Yeah, you should read it."

Ginger leaned over and Aiden watched her face, recognizing sadness. He finished the last page of Allen's story and set him back on his feet.

"Alright, there you go. Good book."

"Thanks," Allen said, disappearing into the building.

"So, what do you think?" Ginger asked.

"I don't know."

"You know anyone else who might be able to go…or be willing?"

"He knows all the same guys I do. I can ask Porter. I don't suppose you want to start flying black market arms into Iraq anytime soon, eh?"

"Oh yeah, sure."

"Seriously. I know a guy in Berbérati who can give us a helluva deal on RPGs."

"Sure babe. Wave to my old buddies before they blow you out of the sky. I think I'll pass."

"Yeah, probably a bad idea."

"I can feel you thinking over there," Ginger said.

"Yeah. Just thinking through options." He stood and stretched, then kissed the back of her head before going outside.

"Options about what?" Shiloh asked, watching her dad chase after some kids in the courtyard, his prosthetic leg visible with his shorts.

"Your dad has a friend in Iraq who's asking for help."

"What kind of help?"

"Pretty much everything your dad is best at."

Porter, Guy, and three security guards stood talking by the fence line as Aiden approached. All five were armed.

"Afternoon, fellas."

"Guy told us about your altercation on the road yesterday," one of the guards said.

"Figured we'd up the alert level for a day or two, just in case," Porter said.

"Are you concerned?" Guy asked Aiden.

"I defer to Porter on that. Personally, not really, they were just kids mostly. Good to be cautious though."

"They were just preying on targets of opportunity," Guy added.

Aiden looked at him and Porter.

"You two got a minute?"

They nodded and walked a few strides out of earshot.

"I got an email from a PJ buddy of mine in Mosul. He's out now, went over as a civilian. It's bad over there. He's asking for help. Here." Aiden handed over his phone so they could read the email.

"Are you considering joining him?" Guy asked.

"I don't know. I mean, no, not at the moment. We have commitments stateside for the next three weeks and we're hoping to extend that if things here stay settled, so in any case we can't do anything for a month or more, but…I just don't know. Been praying about it since I read it. I wanted to hear what you guys think."

Porter took off his ball cap and ran his hands through his hair.

"I don't know man. Mosul? I mean —" He swore, then held an apologetic hand. "Sorry, but—" and swore again.

"I know," Aiden smirked. "Believe me, it's the last place on earth I'd want to be right now. And I can only imagine what Ginger's thinking."

"You haven't discussed it yet?" Guy asked.

"Just showed her the email. A lot of emotions for any of us heading over, but especially that region." Aiden looked at Porter. "You as well, I imagine."

"It's just a pile of rocks and dirt like any other. At least it's familiar, but for her? I don't know."

"Would your family go with you?" Guy asked.

"I don't know that either. I guess it's pointless to speculate until we know more. I just wanted someone to bounce it off of for now. That, and to see if either of you have connections that might be useful to them."

"I'm afraid I do not," Guy said.

"I can ask around," Porter said.

"Thanks guys."

Aiden turned and Guy watched him take a few steps away.

"Aiden!"

He looked back.

"If you go, I will go with you."

Aiden nodded and walked off.

After a long day of packing and coordinating, Ginger and Aiden finally got the kids settled into bed and collapsed on the sofa.

"So did you write your friend back yet?" Ginger asked.

"Yeah, I told him we'd pray and see what we can do. I didn't commit us or anything. I'm just not sure what that means."

"Right. What did Porter say?"

"He's checking but most of the guys he knows are either still over there doing stuff, or they're out and like, 'Nuh uh. No way.' You read what Matt said. It's a hard sell for guys who've been there done that already."

"Like us."

"Right. They've done their service over there. Hell, I'm with 'em on that, I guess."

"Yeeeah, not really," Ginger said, gesturing toward their surroundings.

"I just go where the big guy tells me to go."

"Same here."

Aiden put his arm around her. "And what is God telling you about this?"

"That there's no imaginable reason why we should take two kids into a warzone where they could potentially lose one or both of their parents, or worse. And yet…"

"Yeah." He pulled her closer. "We don't need to figure anything out tonight. Let's just keep praying on it. We've got plenty else to deal with for now."

4
Orientations

Manbij, Syria

Casey Allen watched the mortar spin thirty degrees and pause. He expected the gun to shake everything around him, but with its short and stubby tube this marvel of modern weaponry didn't look very impressive, nowhere near as intimidating as a large artillery piece. Yet all the American soldiers present had seen the weapon in action before, mounted on the top a Stryker vehicle. It held the Syrian Defense Force (SDF) members in rapt attention.

The round launched skyward, and for a second all eyes followed its ejection, yet before the first round was at its apex the mortar tube spun an additional twenty degrees in the opposite direction, and twelve seconds later fired again. The process was repeated a third time, and once all three projectiles were in the air, all eyes scanned the horizon. The rounds landed at separate targets: three, four, and five miles away.

The SDF troops chattered with obvious excitement, and Casey and Demarius Smith watched from behind dark, black sunglasses.

"How long you give it till they use it on our guys?" Demarius asked, "Two years? Three?"

Casey merely scoffed as the machine powered down, and then the fire control system operator addressed them through an interpreter.

"This concludes the demonstration. Feel free to have a closer look but please keep your hands off for the time being."

Most of the SDF troops were already inching toward the gun before the translation was complete. They combed over the barrel and peered down into it. They examined the sensitive and expensive hardware within the mechanism and grabbed everything too often and too comfortably. Casey listened to the American technicians struggle to give the tutorial to overeager subjects, and debated whether or not to raise his voice in dispersing them.

Before he could, a burly Syrian who looked forty years too old to be there snapped something in Arabic that caused them all to step back. One by one they all took another step backward as his gaze fell on each of them until eventually even the American techs felt uncomfortable.

Casey stared at the man with his arms crossed over his beefy chest. He could see the man's fierce eyes, like those he'd seen time and time again in ISIS fighters. He didn't make eye contact with any of the Americans, only the Syrians, and then walked off. The SDF soldiers went back to the gun but with more respectful manners.

"Ever see that one before?" Casey asked Demarius.

"Negative." The two Green Berets watched him disappear as fast as he'd come.

Mosul, Iraq

Chips of concrete and dust exploded, washing over Goriel as he turned away from the hole in the wall. His squad dropped down behind what was left of the interior walls, then raised their rifles between the gaps. Matt was six men to the right of him, watching the ISF troops firing to suppress the ambush. Most of them took short, controlled bursts, trying to decipher where the shooter's nest was located.

One of the soldiers shouted in Arabic, and the others responded with a barrage of shots into a second-story window across the street.

"Hold your fire." Goriel removed a grenade and tossed it into what was left of the window opening. The explosion sent plumes of concrete fragments onto the street below. Goriel gestured to a pair of soldiers and made a sweeping motion toward the ground floor entrance below. He repeated the gesture with two additional soldiers, then he followed and Matt sprang after him.

From a completely different direction they heard more gunfire as they ran into the building. Goriel went up the stairs, and two Iraqi soldiers kicked in doors on the ground floor, disappearing into other rooms. Matt hesitated, unsure whether to go up or stay on the ground level. He held his rifle pointed at the ground and waited. Soon he heard relaxed voices upstairs and ran up the steps. He found Goriel standing at the window examining the street below, the others sifting the remains of ammunition, weapons, and bomb materials that the grenade had damaged. One of the soldiers kicked over a dead ISIS fighter and crouched next to him, opening pockets on the dead man's tactical vest. He located a mostly empty package of cigarettes and stood to light one up.

A total of three ISIS lay dead in the room, four more in other rooms. Goriel moved away from the window.

"We're done here," he said in English. As they exited, Matt heard whimpering from a wounded ISIS fighter. He took a step in that direction but the sound was silenced by an ISF soldier who stepped over and put two more rounds in the man's head.

"They've pretty much abandoned that area."

"How do you figure? We can't move more than a street at a time without encountering sniper fire."

"You have plenty of armored vehicles."

"It's mined with IEDs they set while retreating."

"Then bomb the buildings."

"There are still civilians holed up in their homes."

Ozzy listened to the argument with growing frustration.

"Enough," he said, closing off his lieutenants' back and forth. "We're going house to house, block by block. None of them escape, and especially their snipers, who are somehow better trained than any of you."

The men absorbed the insult in silence.

Ozzy ran his finger along a street on the map. "Tell your men to continue along this line and keep moving until they reach this point. Once they do we can redeploy if necessary but I want every inch cleared. They have nowhere to go but north."

"Yes, general," the officers agreed, filing out of the makeshift command post.

When things had quieted down, Ozzy sat and closed his eyes.

"The SDF is moving fast," his remaining major said. "They're taking villages back every day."

"Good."

"Many civilians are returning to their homes."

"Twice as many were slaughtered." Ozzy's eyes were still closed.

The major took a deep breath. "Hopefully the Syrians will be able to identify the dead."

After a long silence, Ozzy opened his eyes.

"Where is your family, Major?"

"They're settling in with my uncle in Anbar. Constant threat from IEDs."

Ozzy rocked in the high-backed office chair and stared at the wall.

"Thank God they are safe."

"Yes, general."

Ozzy looked into his lap and smiled. "They're running, they're boxed in, they're taking losses they can no longer replace. Your family will have a safe country again."

"Yes, general." His major nodded. "God is great."

The major saluted, turned, and left. Ozzy closed his eyes again and slowly rocked in his chair.

USS Dwight D. Eisenhower, Mediterranean Sea

Mario looked out the small, circular window of the UH-65 Chinook and watched the carrier disappear into the distance. His men sat back in their mesh seats even as the Chinook made irregular, jinking course corrections. Most took the lengthy flight as an opportunity to sleep, knowing it would be scarce in the immediate future. Mario wasn't tired. Instead he studied the face on his rugged tablet. He scrolled to the next one, then the next.

The helo made another jink and this time hit some turbulence. He wasn't one to get airsick but the tablet strain on his eyes coupled with the load-up on carbs half an hour earlier was enough to make him turn off the device and gulp some air.

He looked at his watch. Roughly seventy minutes until touchdown, and the helicopter silently crossed into Syrian airspace.

In the dark of the moonless night, the lead F-15E Strike Eagle slid away from the refueling tanker. Rattler directed Dodge, his wingman, to fence back in and then he turned to an intercept heading for the new pop-up target the AWACS radar platform was yapping about.

The Weapons System Officer in the back seat of the lead plane was painting a group to the north, pressing south. The WSO noticed two hits on his radar.

"Group, bullseye three-fifty, forty-five, azimuth three," the lead WSO called into the radio.

An AWACS called to the F-15s, identifying the radar blips for them. "Darkstar ID's two-ship Fullbacks," meaning a pair of Russian SU-34 fighter bombers.

Here we go, Rattler thought. *Ivan's trying to hog the playground again tonight.*

Russian fighter bombers were in their way, something the Americans were encountering almost every day now. The

Russians came straight-on, leaving the Americans few options. Either they intended to intercept the F-15s and engage them, or they wanted to send some kind of message. Regardless, the Americans had strict rules of engagement with coalition air forces across the crowded skies of Syria: Do nothing.

Observe. Orient. Decide. Act. Rattler paused right there at the Decide stage of his mental OODA loop. *I don't want to have to kill you Petrov, but I will.*

He prepared to engage the bogies. "Target, two-ship azimuth three, twenty-five miles, close hold."

Rattler had the western Russian locked, his wingman had the eastern one. They could easily take them out with a pair of AMRAAM missiles but the ROE was clear.

"Get out of the way clowns, I've got bombs to drop," he said quietly out loud. *Decide.*

It was a reoccurring game of chicken for the Russians, a message about territorial hegemony where they never escalated nor blinked. Either that, or they actually didn't know the Americans were there, which Rattler doubted.

Maybe they're in line for a ground strike of their own? No, not in our sector. They've got their own half of the country to play with.

"Tally two-ship line abreast, one o'clock, fifteen miles, low," he said, "ready to fire."

"Number two, same," his wingman replied.

A few seconds passed and the Americans held their breath. The Russian jets pressed straight up the middle below and between the two Strike Eagles.

Rattler and Dodge checked west then hooked south and breathed a little easier as the Russian fighters turned back north and disappeared in the distance.

"Darkstar, two-ship Fullbacks are bugging out north," he told the AWACS.

"Jerks," said Rattler's WSO in the back radio.

"Moving on." *We're gonna dance with those guys one of these days.*

The ground asset directed them towards their mission. "Two, tac left, time on target four mike."

5
Propositions

Sarasota, Florida

Porter squirmed in his seat, tried leaning forward with his elbows on the desk, but sat back in his chair instead, tapping his hands on the armrest.

"Relax, bro," Teddy said, laughing. "What are you all hopped up about?"

"Nothin. I'm good."

"It's nice to see you out of your element for a change," Teddy smiled.

"You want this microphone up your butt?"

Porter heard the music in his headphones followed by the show's intro, then Teddy spoke into the microphone.

"Welcome back ladies and gents, and thank you for enduring another hour of disaffected type-A personalities shooting the stuff. I'm Ted McMasters and with me as always is Ray B. And today, friends, we have a special treat in store for you, right Ray?"

"That's right, because sitting here in studio is a man we've been dutifully waiting to have on for a handful of years."

"He was too busy fighting wars," Teddy interrupted.

"And he still is, though of a different sort, but we'll get to that. United States Navy SEAL, Peter S. Dawkins. Annapolis guy, retired as a Captain in 2014 with Navy and Marine Corps Commendation Medals, a Navy Presidential Unit Citation, Bronze Star with 'V' device, and a few dozen other awards, including a Silver Star and…the notable distinction of having been the man most responsible for getting my arm shot off, once upon a time. Thanks, jerk.

Known better among frogmen as Porter cuz he loves the suds. Captain, it's an honor to have your bottom in that chair today."

"Thanks, Ray, and you'd still have that arm if you'd been better at dodging RPGs."

"No doubt, no doubt. Captain, some of the missions you've been in have been high profile, the highest even. Some have been unsung and known by merely a few people, but I doubt many people know about the mission you're fighting right now, every day, over in the middle of Africa, and that's what I want to start with."

"That's right," Teddy said. "Believe me, our audience wants to hear about the Iraq and Afghanistan stuff and we'll get there, but how you got to what you're doing now is next-level service. Tell us about that."

"Yeah, absolutely. The short version is I was bored." Porter laughed. "You know I'd been fighting some really bad dudes all over the globe my whole adult life. So getting out of the military was a little surreal."

"You mean nobody was shooting at you?"

"That and I just wasn't that interested in finance reports and desk chairs, although I have to admit I could take a nap in this one right now for sure."

"Only the best for you, Captain."

"Yeah I mean, I had a great business opportunity with some generous contacts in the finance world, and for once was getting a pretty substantial paycheck. Like, I could afford stuff…for little bit. I tried to get settled there, you know, save up and shore up some personal relationships that I'd neglected…but it just wasn't who I am. Neckties…dudes with manicures…nuh uh. Nope. I felt like I'd lost my screw and was taking on water."

"How long were you doing that before the bug kicked in?"

"Less than a year, and I tried a couple different things but it always kept getting muddled. My dad's a retired Coastie and he said to do what you're good at. And if you don't know what that is, ask people you love. It was one of those heart moments that I thought maybe I was just gonna sink away and get depressed or something, so I had it out with a good buddy of mine who's always been able to challenge the stupid out of me."

"Let me guess, was it a one-legged PJ?"

"Bingo." Porter smiled.

Teddy spoke. "Friends of the podcast will remember when we had on Aiden McCoy. If you haven't heard his story, go back and listen to it."

"His wife's, too," Ray said.

"Well, yeah," Porter said, "it was actually her who got to me."

"Folks," Teddy said, "Chief Cooper — Ginger McCoy, that is — her story will knock your socks off. I think she could take the three of us actually, with or without the Apache."

"We need to get the McCoys on together sometime," Ray said.

"I'll see what I can do," Porter said. "Where was I?"

"You were a pathetic loser and Aiden was about to slap you."

"Right," Porter laughed. "Anyway, Aiden had just started this ministry in the Central African Republic, helping to liberate kids from forced military service with tribal warlords. Seriously evil mothers. Having spent time there with the teams, he really wanted my input and so I agreed to go—"

"Just as an *advisor*," Ray mocked.

"Yep, right, just in an advisory role, sure."

"Folks," Teddy said, "just know that whenever the government says there are American troops serving 'only in an advisory role', what they mean is they're getting shot at but if they shoot back we'll throw them under the bus."

"Right," Porter continued. "Well, there was plenty of advising on that first trip, but more than that it was the sheer gravity of what these monsters were doing to these kids that…you know, it sparked up that rage…that break-glass-in-case-of-war rage, and I just had to get involved. I mean, in many ways it's more dangerous, having none of that hi-tech hardware we were trained with, or air support or whatnot. But when you look at those kids' faces and hear their stories, you just can't *not* be spurred to do something."

An hour and a half later, Porter took a long drink from the glass of beer then set it down.

"Another round, guys?" the waitress asked.

"Yes please," Teddy said. Then he asked Porter, "So how long before you head back to Africa?"

"Three weeks to a month, maybe. It depends on Aiden. I've got a few fundraising appearances to do between here and Maine, and then depending on some other things Aiden and I will head back and probably stay there till who knows how long."

"So here's the million dollar question I couldn't ask you on the air," Ray paused, getting Porter's full attention. "What about Jen?"

"What about her?"

"We figured when you retired that you were gonna hook up."

"I thought they did," Teddy added.

Porter readjusted his hat. "I don't know, I mean I love her, but it's complicated. She deserves stability that I've never been able to give her."

"Pardon the bluntness Captain, but that's a load," Teddy said. "But if you're too stupid or too wuss to seal the deal…" he reached over and picked up Porter's phone, "…mind if I give her a call?" He scrolled till he found Jen's contact listing. "Oh here she is. Dang, she's beautiful. Think she's home?"

"Call her and you lose the other eye."

"It'd be an improvement," Ray said.

Teddy handed the phone back to Porter. "Seriously though. When was the last time you talked to her?"

"A few weeks ago. We email all the time."

"And she's still single?"

Porter nodded.

"And do you plan on doing something about that? Or would you rather piss away the rest of your life cause you're too scared to let her take a risk?"

Porter took another drink and didn't answer.

Teddy took out his own phone. "Alright, never mind then." He dialed a number and put the phone to his ear.

"Who are you calling?" Porter asked.

"Aiden, to ask him when you turned into a soyboy."

Virginia Beach, Virginia

Porter rang the doorbell and waited. He crossed his arms, then uncrossed them and put his hands in his pockets, rocking on his heels. Then he took his hands out again and clasped one wrist tightly with his opposite hand. He waited before slowly putting his finger up to the doorbell again, hesitated, then pressed the button a second time. He checked his watch, then rapped three stiff knocks on the solid wood door. He leaned back and slightly left to peer into the side window before catching himself and straightening up as he heard a noise from inside, followed by a deadbolt opening and the door cracked open.

"Hey! It is you," Jen smiled, releasing the latch and opening the door.

"Hi."

"Strange man knocking on my door in the middle of the day...I almost shot you," she motioned to her pistol now on the entryway table. "What are you doing here? I had you getting in on the twenty-third?"

"Yeah, that was the plan. Sorry to show up on a whim but I was driving north and just...figured I stop on over."

"Good timing, I'm off today. How much time do you have before your next thing?"

Porter hesitated. "A few days before I need to be in Louisville."

"Didn't you come into Florida?"

"Yeah."

"So…you drove six hours out your way?"

"Just a little hop," he waited. "Caaan I come in?"

"Yeah of course, I'm just shocked to see you. Way to be spontaneous for a change." She escorted him inside the small house, and he took in the decor, glanced at the titles on the bookshelves — medical books, Christian non-fiction, classics, more medical books — and pictures. He paused when he got to a photo of himself and Jen in the tropics, her hair in braids, smiling next to Porter who wasn't.

"Jamaica? Dang, that seems like decades ago."

"Anytime you want to go back, feel free to buy me a plane ticket, and book me a room, and pay for pretty much everything else," she laughed. "I could use a vacation and stat. Want something to drink? Water, tea, coffee?"

Porter, still staring at the picture, could feel his heart beating faster. He was a little nauseated.

"Hellooo, McFly?" she asked.

He took a deep breath and turned halfway around, forced the words out before fear pulled them back in for the hundredth time.

"Wanna get married?"

Jen stared at him.

"Um…what?"

He smiled. "Wanna get married?"

She continued to stare, then looked at the ceiling and shook her head slightly.

"Man, you're bad at this."

His smile vanished.

"I'm sorry I just…here," he walked up to her and took a knee.

"Oh, don't start that now. You already said it!"

"Just…" He put up his hand to silence her. "Let me try again. Jen, will you marry me?"

She paused, waiting to see if he would do anything else.

"Is that it?"

"Yeah, I guess."

"Do you have a ring or anything?"

"Um, no. Sorry. I didn't really plan it out. I just wanted to get here as soon as I could."

"Wow." She smiled. "Just…just, stand up." She took his hand, then walked him to a sofa and sat with him. "Why now? After everything, why now, and why like this?"

"I…I didn't want you to go through it all again, if I got killed, you know. That plus Gator and all, I just never felt like I was allowed."

"Peter, Chris died fourteen years ago."

"And you still love him."

"Of course I do, we both do. I always will, but why should that still bother you? We've been over this sooo many times."

"It doesn't bother me," Porter touched the back of her hand. "I've been having this recurring dream. I swim up onto a beach, and Gator's there with some other team guys all chillin'. I think maybe I've just been afraid to let go of him and you, together, you know. I'm not sure if that makes any sense."

She brushed a tear from her eye.

"Jen, I love you. I want to marry you, and I'm sorry for not saying that years ago."

He sat, waiting.

"This is where you offer me a tissue," she slapped his chest, "big jerk."

Porter grabbed a box of tissues and handed one to her.

"You haven't answered yet."

She smiled and laughed. "You haven't given me a ring yet."

"How about I let you pick one out. Whatever you want."

"Oh believe me, I'll pick it out, and you'll not say a word about the price."

"So, that's a yes?"

"Yes, God help me."

"So…" he admitted, "I don't know about the what and when and all. I imagine you'll want to plan something?"

"Nope, I've waited long enough for you to man up. Let's go now."

"Uh…now? Like right now, now?"

"Yeah, I've gotta work tomorrow. Let's get 'er done."

"I was kinda hoping to talk to your dad first."

Jen gave him a blank expression. "Buddy, that ship has so passed."

"There're other considerations. Your work, my work—"

"We'll figure it out. Now or never. Take it or leave it."

Porter smiled. "So, do we have to get a license or something? Is there a waiting period?"

Jen went to the kitchen counter and picked up her keys.

"Why am I agreeing to this?"

Louisville, Kentucky

The pastor drew the congregation's attention to the big screen beside the stage. An image went up of a muscular black man with a dour expression and sunglasses, his arms crossed in a tan t-shirt, standing in front of a line of Apache helicopters. A wave of comments and catcalls flowed from a few hundred people in attendance.

"Yup, that was me," he rubbed his stomach, "a few pounds lighter, as you can see. Now these machines I worked with are the smartest, most sophisticated, finickiest, and fiercest things ever to fly over God's green earth. The only thing more difficult to manage are the smart aleck pilots who fly them."

Ginger raised a hand to her chest and silently mouthed the words, "Who, me?"

"Now, folks," Eddie said, standing up straight and motioning to a new image of Ginger and her Apache arming team in Iraq. "I'm gonna be honest. The first time I met this lady I didn't think much of her. She was cocky…smart…and she had this little hair flip thing she did while smiling—" he mimicked it, "—that she'd give me whenever she jacked up something on my helicopter." He waited for the laughter to die down, frowned, and stared at Ginger again.

"I hated that." More laughter. "She also outranked me. I hated that too." Eddie then got serious. "But folks, I'm gonna tell you. That white girl can fly." Applause.

"And keeping her and the rest of our squadron primed was the greatest honor of my military career. Oh, and her husband isn't too shabby himself, but they'll tell you all about that. Please give a warm welcome to my friends, Ginger and Aiden McCoy."

The congregation clapped while they walked onto the stage, shared hugs with Eddie, and took the microphones.

"Thank you for letting us join you today. We're so blessed to be here to tell you about our ministry in the Central African Republic. But first I want to tell you that there was really only one person I feared in all of Iraq, or anywhere else for that matter. Your pastor may seem tame now, but Lord help the aviator who brings back one of his helos with unused rockets sitting in the tube."

"Amen!" Eddie shouted and nodded.

"He was a lot of bark though, and I loved him like a brother. Still do. Now, here's a question I think your pastor and I would both like to challenge you with today: Are you safe?" She paused. "I ask because when I used to sit in that cockpit, I thought I was invincible. How wrong I was."

Ginger spent the next fifteen minutes giving her testimony: growing up with a single dad and an absent, addict mother, life-altering regrets, her military career and its sudden, tragic ending. Through it all she was poised and confident, but Eddie frequently lifted his glasses to wipe his eyes.

"Afterward, for the first time in a long time, I'd felt like I was finally safe. I had this amazing husband, a beautiful daughter, and a young son just learning to walk. But God has a way of shaking us up when we get a little too comfortable." She handed the microphone to Aiden.

"When you hear the voice of God telling you to do something, do you do it?" He raised up his hand. "I'll be the first to admit that I don't always do it right away. It often takes some prodding and second guessing before I even get around to praying about it, but thankfully He's persistent and patient. Amen?" As the crowd spoke its approval, a series of ministry images in Africa went up on the screen.

"Not long into my first visit I met Guy, here. He asked me, 'What are we supposed to do with a one-legged American?' I assured him I could hold my own, but Guy was marauding by the age of seven. He grew up filled with rage at having watched his parents executed. As a child he was drugged almost constantly, and he didn't escape the warlords until a few years before we met.

"Here was one of the toughest and nicest men I've ever met, asking me if I had the guts to take on this mission alongside him. I prayed and told God, 'Yeah, no,'…but God just wouldn't shut up about it."

Aiden spoke for another twenty minutes about their ministry, and when the service was over he entered contacts into his phone while the family gathered their belongings and arranged plans with Eddie.

Aiden's phone chirped a new message notification, and as he checked it, Ginger noticed his expression change.

"Something wrong?" Eddie asked.

"No." Aiden put his phone away. "But dinner sounds great."

Once in the rental car, Ginger asked, "Who was it that texted you?"

"Jake." He handed the phone over.

I'm in. Get the details to you ASAP.

"Uhh boy," she said, handing Aiden his phone back.

"What's wrong?" Shiloh asked from the back seat.

"Nothing's wrong. Just a little news we'll need to pray on," Aiden answered. He glanced over at Ginger. "What do you think?"

"I think I need a drink. But I'll settle for a nap."

Boothbay Harbor, Maine

Porter opened the car door for Jen who took his hand as she stepped out.

"Ready for this?" he asked.

"Are you?"

"Yeah, they love you. Always have."

"I know, but it's…I guess we'll see what it is."

The air was salty and the modest houses were from a bygone era, most with attic windows and white-fenced front porches teeming with hanging flower baskets. Porter knocked on his childhood front door, still holding Jen's left hand with the other.

The door opened, revealing a woman with short white hair.

"Oh, wow!" Mrs. Dawkins pulled him in for a long hug. "What are you doing here so soon?! And you brought Jen!" She let go of Porter and hugged Jen. "What a great surprise! We didn't expect you for another week and you didn't say anything about bringing her."

Porter glanced at Jen to offer her a chance to reply, but her expression clearly indicated he was to do the talking.

"Well, there was something I wanted to tell you in person so we hopped on a plane real quick for a couple of days' visit." Porter lifted Jen's left hand, revealing the sparkling ring to his mother.

Porter's mom smiled wide at Jen, then looked seriously at her son.

"Well, it's about time."

Louisville, Kentucky

Ginger woke up startled, laid her head back on the pillow, and stared at the hotel window. An unusual silence she hadn't heard in years filled the room and she wondered if Aiden and the kids would barrel through the door at any moment.

When they didn't, she picked up the remote and began flipping through news channels on the TV, not finding what she was looking for. Opting for her phone instead, she searched "ISIS Iraq."

She perused YouTube videos for the most recent one and hit Play to watch a war correspondent with the ISF interview soldiers. Ginger's heart beat faster upon hearing the dialect. Sudden rifle fire interrupted the audio and the reporter's words were overlaid with images of civilians, including children, running for their lives. She turned the phone off.

Boothbay Harbor, Maine

"We're not heading to Mosul anytime soon," Porter said, "even if Aiden does. But it affects us both either way. Our team in Africa, both of our families…" He felt Jen squeezing his hand firmly but not anxiously.

"How do you feel about that?" Porter's mom asked Jen.

"I think…" she turned to face Porter, "that whether in Mosul, or in Africa, they're going to need nurses."

Porter was surprised by her confident assertion.

"We're not just talking about a mission trip," his dad said. "Mosul is a warzone. So is the CAR. Iraq these days is one of the most dangerous places on the planet. They're murdering men, women, and children indiscriminately. Taking women and girls as wives, buying and trading them as sex slaves at auction."

"It's not like that everywhere," Porter said. "If Aiden goes, or even if I hypothetically went with him, we'd be behind the Iraqi army front lines. They need medics, which is his specialty, and people with security experience—"

"Which there's almost nobody on earth better at than you," his dad said.

Porter took a long breath. "Yeah."

Louisville, Kentucky

"Wooooh," Eddie said and leaned back in his deck chair. "That's a big one. You sure?"

"No," Aiden spoke for them both, "but we feel He's nudging us that way. Not sure for how long or where exactly. And there are a hundred variables to consider but we've got a connection there."

"And we still need to check with the kids about it," Ginger said.

Eddie raised his eyebrows. "So you'd all be going? Whole family?"

"If we go, we go together." Ginger said. "They relate to kids in Africa in ways I can't. Only God knows how He can use them in Iraq or wherever we serve."

Aiden took Ginger's hand. "I know, it's not a typical family vacation spot…but it's what we do."

Eddie leaned forward and spoke to Ginger with the intensity of authority.

"And are you ready? Mentally ready…to go back there?"

Eddie's wife patted his arm. "She's a grown woman who knows her own business, baby."

"Hun, you're right but she knows what I'm sayin'."

"It's okay," Ginger said. "He's right. I've been wrestling with those fears since Aiden first mentioned it."

"And not just Iraq, but Mosul of all places? I'm sorry, you know I'd never disrespect you, but you won't be doing anyone there any favors if you're not one hundred percent dialed in for it."

"No disrespect. Believe me, I'm with you on that. Do the demons try and dredge up all that trauma at the mention of it? Absolutely. But does that give me a good excuse to tell God no?"

The question hung in the air. Eventually Eddie sat back and held his wife's hand.

"Well then, little sister. How can we help?"

Baltimore, Maryland

"How's it going?" Cynthia Lyons asked as she leaned on the back of her husband's office chair and read over his shoulder.

"I didn't imagine it would be this difficult to find a decent flight into Baghdad," Jake said. "Got your tickets all squared away though," he said, spinning a little to let Cynthia ease herself into his lap. He clicked on another tab and showed her the itinerary for one adult and three children to Arizona.

"That's a good price," she approved. "Nice job."

"Yeah, I'm just sorry I'm leaving you hanging, traveling with all them on your own."

"It'll be fine. It's not like I haven't done it before."

"Yeah, exactly."

"It's important. Really, I'm good. And Dad is already planning all the horseback riding and camping he plans to do with them. With any luck I'll get a few hours to myself for a change." She could feel Jake's uncertainty by his silence. "Having second thoughts?"

"No. I mean, it's not exactly the relaxing vacation I'd planned on spending with you guys. I just wanted to read a few books and not have my hands in a dude's chest cavity for a change. Freakin' Aiden."

"Is he going, then?"

"He hasn't said yet…but he is. I knew the second I read his email."

"Well, I don't imagine it'll be very crowded on your flight into there. Not many people seek out a vacation in a warzone."

"Nope, just borderline psychotic ex-military type doctors who don't know any better."

Mosul, Iraq

Matt felt his phone buzz. He wiped his eyes and tried to blink away the dust as he lifted himself up on his elbow to check the text:

Hey, Matt. My family and I will be honored to join you there soon and help out in any way we can. I'll give you the details when I know more but at this point just know we're praying for you. That others may live.

The soldier next to him noticed a smile on Matt's face. "You get a picture from girlfriend in America?" he laughed. "You show me?"

"No. It's from one of my brothers."

6
The Warfighters

Seattle, Washington

Josiah McCoy felt the slight bump as the jet's landing gear found the runway and he breathed a sigh of relief. The breaking clouds revealed a bright dawn in front of him and he was almost happy for the first time in days. A few minutes later they were parked at the gate, and on the other side of the door a flight attendant gave the summation that concluded Josiah's most recent mission.

"Ladies and gentlemen," she said, "we'd like to welcome you to Seattle. Local time is 6:45 in the morning. On behalf of myself and the flight crew we want to thank you for choosing to fly with us today. We hope you enjoy your stay in Seattle, or wherever your final destination takes you."

When the checklist was complete, the copilot unlatched his seat belt and stood.

"Good flight."

"If you can call that flying," Josiah said.

"Yeah, cruise, cruise some more, cruise some more," his copilot joked.

"Not like real flying. Don't mind the paycheck though."

"I hear that. Almost home though, right?"

"Yeah. Getting there."

"Spend much time in Seattle?"

Josiah smiled. "Not if I can help it."

As the yawning crowd in back moved forward, a first-class passenger with thick-framed, colorful glasses stuck her finger in Josiah's face. A small dog yapped from inside the designer carrier she held.

"I don't appreciate the manners of your flight crew," she said glaring at the nearest flight attendant.

Josiah made quick eye contact with the flight attendant who gave him wide-eyes and a forced, gritted teeth smile.

"Or your handling of this airplane for that matter. Shook us half to death on that landing. Didn't he?" she soothed the noisy little dog.

"Ma'am," Josiah said with a compassionate voice, "rest assured I take your concerns very seriously. Here." He pulled a business card out of his front pocket. "This is my card. As soon as you get settled in your destination, please reach out. That way you can provide all the details."

The woman looked at the card, surprised. "Well, thaaank you. I certainly will." She shouldered her massive handbag and shuttled out the door, glaring as she passed the flight attendants.

Josiah's copilot was aghast. "You gave her your personal phone number?"

"Hell no. It's just my name on the card. The phone numbers are random ones I pulled off the airline's website. I think one of them is the call center to apply for baggage handler jobs."

Mosul, Iraq

Goriel and his men exchanged fire with the enemies across from them, both groups using the ruins as cover. He stood, fired a burst, paused to line up an ISIS fighter in his sights, fired, and felt a grim satisfaction. He dropped behind cover, knelt, and put his hand on the ground, imagining the floor where he used to stand while waiting for his grandfather to finish helping customers.

Rage boiled and he stood again, fired again, and killed another one. This time he didn't drop behind the cover; he advanced, still firing. Images of his mother and sister fleeing in the night flashed in his mind. He could hear the laughter of his friends playing soccer, all blown to pieces by a bomb set by these monsters who killed indiscriminately.

They enjoyed the killing, celebrated it, and Goriel ran to repay what they'd laid on others, shooting until *click* – he released the empty magazine and loaded another while still taking quick steps toward them. His men came in behind, also shooting, all of them with similar hatred for the cursed daesh who did this to their country.

They never surrender. Good.

In the early days right after the Americans left, the daesh brazenly paraded through these streets, trucks teeming with disgusting humans waving their grotesque flag and taunting him. He'd wanted then to be here, in this day, killing them and watching their scared eyes turn back in their accursed heads. He never imagined he'd have to wait this long to enact his revenge, but now it was here. These men who'd taken everything from him and his father were finally running.

They won't get away. Not now.

One ducked behind a mound of dirt. Goriel paused to heave a grenade over the pile, and dirt and body tissue emitted skyward as he slowly side-stepped around three mangled bodies that remained to be spat on.

He kicked a few stones out of the way before lighting a cigarette. What remained in Mosul were the most hardcore ISIS fighters, the best snipers, and most brutal sadists. Opposing them were men like Goriel, also with nothing left to lose.

He took a drag and his breathing relaxed, his heart rate decreased, and his fury was satisfied for the moment.

Hammam Al-Alil, Iraq

"That's it," the exhausted doctor said in Arabic. "He's gone."

The scant medical team gathered up the equipment — some for disposal, some for sterilization and reuse — and quickly prepared the surgical room for the next patient. Renas pulled the blanket over the young man's body and then stooped down to gather up the pieces of his uniform they'd had to cut away.

Outside, she threw the soiled garments into a burn receptacle. She stretched her back and closed her eyes, savoring the momentary pause.

"Renas," a voice called to her from behind.

"Coming," she answered with her eyes still shut, then went back to work.

Chugiak, Alaska

"They still let this old guy fly?" Porter said to Josiah, shaking his hand and giving him a man hug. "How you doing, Captain?"

"With people, even," Aiden said, turning bratwursts on his parents' grill.

"Is this your family, then? Wow. I remember the boys when they were *little* little. And you," Porter said to Stacy, "were maybe just a baby then, right?"

"Hence why I have no recollection of the event," Stacy said, smiling next to her mom.

Josiah examined the grill. "Smells good. Where's Dad at?"

"Had to run to town to pick up something for Mom. Said he'd be back soon," Aiden closed the grill and gave Josiah's older son a hug. "Dude, you're huge."

"Aunt Alyse just got here," Stacy announced as more people poured into the backyard.

Alyse hurried up the stairs to the deck the moment she saw Aiden and gave him a long hug.

"Welcome back! How long are you guys in town?"

"Just a week," Porter said.

"Then you all go back to Africa?"

"Well…" Porter started to speak but paused and looked to Aiden.

"No," Aiden said. "We'll be making a little detour first, open-ended, as it were."

"Where to?" Josiah asked.

"Ah…Iraq, actually."

"Do you feel like you have to go too, since he's going?" Josiah's wife Abby asked in the kitchen as the women prepared side dishes.

"Yes and no," Jen said. "He said he wouldn't go if I wanted him to stay." She looked at Ginger. "But he knows that place inside and out. And I think Aiden needs him whether he knows it or not."

Ginger smiled. "He knows."

"And I've spent too many years waiting around at home for shoes to drop while he played Rambo over there. So that's how I figured it, anyway."

"I'm sure they can find a good use for a surgical nurse," Ginger said.

"They can probably use her more than the boys," Mrs. McCoy added.

Later in the evening, Aiden watched his youngest sister speaking with Shiloh and tried to remember the last time the whole family was together, wondering how their lives might be different if he hadn't relocated his family half-way around the world. He went to the fridge and grabbed a beer. The bottle cap popped, hissing triumphant.

Ignoring the laughter from the living room, Aiden walked through the hallway to his parent's study. He examined the walls and bookshelves full of mementos like discovered rocks and hand carved craft projects, photos of him and his siblings, his nieces and nephews, and friends. He paused at the case containing the folded American flag that had, a few years prior, draped Grandpa McCoy's casket.

Aiden perused the books on the shelves, many of which he'd read as a teenager, others he'd studied from while preparing to join the PJs. He looked out the window at the birch leaves shuddering in the wind, and the tall, rugged trunks of the spruce trees he'd climbed as a child, so different from the ones Allen was used to climbing in Africa.

He turned to the next wall and paused. In front of him was another glass case, holding a five-pointed gold star medallion featuring the head of Lady Liberty. Above the star were wings and arrows, and above them was the word VALOR. The medallion was held by a light-blue ribbon with a cluster of thirteen white stars at its base.

Aiden read the placard below the case:

Sergeant McCoy distinguished himself by conspicuous gallantry and intrepidity at the risk of his life above and beyond the call of duty. While conducting a search and rescue mission in Afghanistan…

"Here you are," Alyse said, behind him.

"Hey."

Alyse looked at the medal on the wall. "You alright?"

"Yeah."

"You sure," she said.

Aiden let out a chuckle. "I'll be good. Just uncertainty, you know."

"For Ginger and the kids?"

"Yeah."

Alyse put her arm around her brother's back and leaned her head on his shoulder, still looking at the medal. "You'll be fine. Just don't be a hero, okay?"

"Sure, no problem."

Alyse smiled. "I'm not sure I believe that."

7
Night Ops

Northwestern Syria

Casey Allen and his men watched the four Kurdish trucks firing as they approached a distant village and got peppered in return with large caliber rounds from a concealed gun. A rocket flew from the village into the cluster of trucks, the dust from the explosion obscuring the American's night vision. Another rocket fired and one of the trucks exploded.

The remaining three continued to advance toward the machine gun fire pounding away at them, closing the distance to the village. The Kurdish trucks stopped, their occupants quickly dismounted and ran toward the village, firing as they flooded the courtyards and entryways. Three more trucks entered the field to reinforce their comrades and exploit the breach. In seconds, fire from the village abated as more soldiers swarmed into the darkened buildings, sporadic rifle fire trailing off until the sounds ceased.

"Show's over," Demarius said, taking off his NVG's.

"Guess we'll be moving on tomorrow," another American said.

Casey still scanned the desert, the rest of his unit at ease around him.

"Relax, bruh, you'll give yourself an ulcer," Demarius said.

"Tired of always just sitting around watching other people fight. It's not why I signed up," Casey said.

"Me neither," he said, taking off his helmet and laying down behind the wall of sandbags. "But I'll bet they'd be happy to switch places with you." He closed his eyes.

Casey spat into the dirt. "I doubt that."

Ratla, Syria

Mario crept along in the darkness, seven additional SEALs following with slow footsteps through a grove of trees. When they reached the end, the point man paused, knelt, and held up a fist. Through night vision the team examined everything around them — the street, trees, nearby buildings, and finally the vacant lot across the way. Mario motioned that direction and two of the SEALs passed into the open as he kept his rifle pointed down the dark expanse to his right.

The team crossed the road and lined up within the shadows of a wall enclosing the courtyard on the other side. Inch by inch the team moved along it, and the first one to reach the edge stopped and pulled out a short stick with a mirror on its end. He angled it around the wall, and again toward the rooftop. There was nobody to be seen.

"All clear," the point man whispered into his radio.

"Proceed," Mario whispered in reply.

The SEALs moved in unison as they turned the corner, still against the wall like a silent snake moving in the darkness. Turning the corner brought them into an alley leading to a descending staircase. They crossed to it and four SEALs took a knee, two pointing weapons in the direction they'd just come from, the other two on the opposite side of the stairwell aiming downrange. The last four went down the stairs with Mario in the lead.

At the bottom, he keyed his radio.

"In position."

Josh, one of the two SEALs at the rear in the staircase, worked a handheld radio separate from the one attached to his right ear. He placed the receiver into his other ear and spoke.

"Cyclone Three to Griffin, do you copy?"

High overhead, a U.S. Navy Advanced Hawkeye command and communications aircraft replied, "I copy you, Cyclone."

"Griffin Two One Seven, Cyclone ready to receive."

"Standby, Cyclone."

"Copy, standing by," he said into the handheld radio.

Mario, his rifle pointed at the door, glanced over at him. Josh gestured with a raised fist, indicating *Hold*. Mario spun his finger in the air, silently communicating *Hurry up*. Fifteen seconds passed before the handheld radio chimed in Josh's ear.

"Griffin Two One Seven to Cyclone Three, you are clear to proceed."

Josh gave Mario a thumbs up.

"Ready," Mario whispered over his team's comms. He took a deep breath, trained his sights into the center of the door, and waited. After a few seconds the doorknob slowly turned, and a bearded, hefty Syrian of about sixty opened the door, wearing only a white tank top and canvas pants. He didn't flinch at seeing four SEALs with rifles trained on his chest and forehead, and he spoke in accented English.

"Good evening. Would you like to come in for some tea?"

"I'll take it to go," Mario said.

The man nodded. "Do come in." He turned and walked into the dimly lit room, careful to show his open and empty hands. Mario kept his rifle centered on the Syrian's back and examined his body language, noticing several scars along his bare arms and shoulders. Gunshot wounds, by the look of them.

Inside, the room was barely furnished with a simple radio station, a table with an HK submachine gun, a pistol, and several magazines for each. There was also a laptop turned on and an opened bottle of scotch, mostly full. Beside the table in a corner were two men hog-tied face down, bleeding onto the dirty floor.

"Cyclone Three and Four get down here, everyone else hold your positions," Mario said, lifting up his night vision optics and blinking. He lowered his rifle and followed the man into the room. "You already took 'em?"

"As you can see."

"They alive?"

"This one is." The portly man tapped one of the prisoners on the head with his left sandal. "His companion put up a bit of a fight. Not much use now."

"Who is he? Need us to take him, too?"

"No. I'll deal with it."

"ID?"

The Syrian went to the table and picked up two hard drives and three plastic holders, each containing a micro-SD memory card, and handed them to Mario. He then went to the dead man, removed his hood, and pulled his head back by the hair for Mario's body camera to get a good look at him, and one of the SEALs took a picture with another device.

"Looks like it was probably him. Let's get the other one up."

"Better carry him," the Syrian said. "Not sure his legs work anymore."

"Right," Mario said with a whiff of agitation.

The SEALs picked him up like a limp parcel and could feel he was either close to death or comatose. They moved him out the door and up the stairwell as Mario took one last look around. The Syrian sat down in the only chair and put his feet up on the table that his weapons lay on.

"Would've been easier on us if you'd made sure he could walk."

"Sorry," the man said dismissively.

"Should we bother taking him? Will he live?"

"Maybe. If you hurry."

Mario keyed his mic.

"Cyclone One, moving out." He nodded at the other man. "Thanks for the tea, friend."

The Syrian didn't answer, but merely nodded and leaned back in his chair.

Mario quietly closed the door as he entered the silent stairwell. Four of the eight SEALs carried the prisoner by his limbs, retracing their steps into the trees, and after that, into the adjacent desert and the moonless night.

In the basement room, the Syrian put his laptop in its satchel, slung his submachine gun over his shoulder, and covered it all with his robes. He placed the pistol in an appendix carry holster, then brought a twenty-pound propane tank from another room and set it next to the prone man's body.

The Syrian took a swig from the bottle and set it down on its side. As the liquid poured across the table and floor, he used the screwdriver extension of his multi-tool to give the propane tank's release valve a slight turn. It hissed as he peeked outside and exited quickly up the stairway, leaving the door wide open. At the top of the stairs he removed a grenade from his pocket, pulled the pin, and tossed it into the open doorway before running down the alley, keeping to the shadows.

The room exploded and fragments pierced the propane tank, erupting into a massive ball of flame the Syrian could feel even as he disappeared into the distance.

USS Dwight D. Eisenhower

Mario was the last man off the Chinook. His team shuffled their prisoner past the crew members and flight deck personnel who were careful not to see anything but the aircraft. The cargo was quickly below deck.

The ship's intelligence officer later met the SEALs in the debriefing room where they were freed of their gear and drinking coffee. Two additional officers filed in; the last one closed the door behind him.

"Gentlemen. Do you have any details to add to the video documentation of this mission?"

Mario spoke for his team. "Yeah. Whoever grabbed them off the street had him and another guy all packed up and ready to go. Looked like long before we got there. None of that was in the planning."

"The local asset handled that part of mission. There were circumstances."

"Yeah, well whatever happened, there was another guy he took out, too."

"Inconsequential," one of the other men spoke. Mario noted he wasn't in a Naval officer's uniform but wore a navy blue polo shirt, instead.

"Seems pretty consequential when the mission I planned is completely altered and a mystery guy gets whacked," Mario said.

"What can you tell us about the contact who handed him over?"

Mario and his team members gave each other quick glances without facial expressions.

"Not much. Why? He's your guy."

"Please answer the question." The man in the polo shirt sat down and looked at his watch.

Mario crossed his arms. "They all look about the same to me. Room was pretty dark. He seemed careful about avoiding eye contact. Didn't chat much, didn't tell us why he killed the other guy. In and out in less than two minutes. Can't say I'd recognize him if I saw him again."

The SEALs murmured their agreement, and the man in the polo shirt stood.

"That'll work. Excuse me, gentlemen." He opened the door and left, closing the door behind him.

8
New Arrivals

Northern Iraq

Ginger glanced out the window again, then back at her book. It was a repetition that Aiden noted the moment the plane had crossed into Iraqi airspace. He closed his own book and watched her, then leaned across Allen, asleep with a hoodie pulled tight over his head, and gave Ginger a slight tap on the shoulder.

"You alright?"

Ginger faced him, startled.

"Huh?"

"I asked if you were alright?"

"Yeah." She smiled, then looked out the window again.

Below them Iraq spread out on a cloudless day, the Zagros Mountains filling the horizon. Ginger and Aiden watched in silence, remembering them and so many other mountainous regions nearby in different circumstances.

"It actually looks beautiful from here," Ginger said softly.

"Most places do from up high. Kinda wish it was California instead, though. You know…a trip to your dad's. He's less likely to take a shot at me."

Ginger raised her eyebrows at him. "Not if you deserved it."

Aiden sat back, smiling, and reached over for her hand. To his left he noticed Shiloh in the seat across the aisle with Jen and Porter, inching up to get a glimpse out their window.

"Want to switch seats?" he asked her.

"Sure."

When they exchanged places, she took in the landscape below. "Huh, doesn't look like a warzone from here."

"What did you expect from 30,000 feet?"

"Bombed out buildings and stuff, I guess."

"It's not like that everywhere."

"Do you know any of them?"

"Who?"

"The people we're meeting down there."

"Just Gary and Linda, by email. One of the guys we'll meet is a good friend who served with your dad in Afghanistan. And Porter knows a lot of people here, including some of the Iraqi commanders."

"How does he know them, just from being a SEAL?"

"He trained most of them."

Erbil International Airport, Iraq

Porter cinched the shoulder straps on his backpack, picked up the duffel bag and threw its strap over his head, and instinctively felt for his pistol in its customary location. His hand touched his hip where the gun would normally be but this time felt only his belt. For the first time since retiring from the Navy he felt vulnerable; it was rare for him to be unarmed, even in his hometown.

Aiden was speaking with the customs officer as he repacked the additional leg prosthesis he'd brought with him. Two additional customs officers had gathered out of curiosity. He usually wore shorts when traveling through airports for this very reason. It saved on explanations, and he usually found that security personnel spotted him from afar and sometimes became more accommodating in getting him through quickly. He smiled and gave a mini demonstration of the artificial leg he wore. The customs officers smiled back, said a few things he couldn't understand, and stamped the whole party through with minimal questioning.

Porter nudged up to Ginger.

"Freakin' Iraq, eh? Never thought I'd be back in this place again so soon."

"Never thought I see it again, ever."

"Gonna need to procure some firepower," he said softly, "and soon. I don't like doing anything in this country without some way to protect ourselves."

"We'll get hooked up eventually," Aiden said as they walked through the terminal. "Gonna have to scrounge around for some body armor though, according to Matt. And it's not going to be cheap from what I'm hearing."

"Did you hear from him?" Ginger asked.

"No. But Gary and Linda have a family nearby who will accommodate us so we can rest for a bit and head out tomorrow with escorts. There're some security checkpoints we don't want to just drive up to, or at night. Plus he's got a laundry list of supplies he'd like us to purchase if we can find 'em."

"Define *nearby*," Porter asked.

"Twenty minutes by taxi."

"I don't like that."

"Not much we can do about it. They don't have anyone able to meet us here right now, and I'd rather stay moving than wait around for a ride. Be a good idea to start praying about getting into Mosul too, because from what I'm hearing they may not even let us in."

"What about Guy?" Porter asked.

"Flight was delayed, he'll be in tomorrow sometime. We'll just have to play it by ear when he gets here."

Porter noticed Shiloh listening intently to the conversation, a bit of worry evident in her expression.

"Don't worry," he winked. "It's just Iraq."

The taxi drove along the highway that circled the sprawling city. As they got further in, the lanes narrowed and power lines crisscrossed overhead streets lined with hatchback sedans and mopeds of various quality. The driver spoke to Ginger and she relayed the conversation to the Americans as best she could.

"Does he still have family in Ninevah?" Aiden asked.

"Yes, but he has not had contact with them in years."

The driver looked at Porter before speaking again in Kurdish, and Ginger laughed.

"What?" Aiden asked.

"He wants to know why Porter has a stick up his…you know. But he doesn't want me to tell him."

Porter scowled at the driver before looking back out the window.

"Tell him he just gets cranky when he hasn't had his juice box," Jen said.

"You mean beer," Porter said, still casing every person and vehicle in sight.

They slowed as they moved onto a rural street with sparse houses. In front of one stood two men in street clothes, eyeing the taxi as it approached. They spoke briefly to the driver, and then to Aiden in English.

"Aiden McCoy?"

"Yes, that's me. Are you Jamali?"

"Yes."

He addressed the driver, pointed.

"Please pull into that driveway."

A large plate of rice and vegetables made a considerable improvement in Porter's mood. He drank a cup of tea in the small home's modest parlor, sitting against a wall that afforded him a good look out the window. While Aiden answered emails from acquaintances all over the world, Ginger sat on the floor, poring over a map of Iraq with her children and the host family. She explained the geography and as much of the history of the region as she could remember, and the family joined in, filling in the gaps and telling stories about Erbil and Kurdistan.

Jamali's phone rang, and after a few words he hung up.

"Change of plans, please gather your belongings. They're on their way to pick you up now."

"Is there a problem?" Ginger asked.

"No, but we're needed in Mosul."

"You heard the man. Load up," Porter said, already at the door.

Two white Land Rovers entered the courtyard and two men wearing body armor and brandishing M4 rifles stepped out to survey the party before them.

"Tourists," Hozan said to Ehmed in Kurdish, shaking his head.

Porter did a five-second profile of the Kurds and noted immediately that they carried themselves as professionals, and with their hardened appearance, trigger discipline, and manner of speech he guessed they'd been trained by western forces at some point. They carried all the hallmarks of fighting men annoyed by a brief assignment away from the front, and Porter felt a slight relief as they divided up into the two vehicles.

Once they were on the road, Porter turned to Jen in the back seat.

"Not too bad for a honeymoon so far?"

"Yeah, lovely."

"A honeymoon?" Hozan asked.

"We were married a few weeks ago. In our country, folks usually take a vacation of sorts after they get married."

"It's actually a nice trip so far," Jen said. "Not likely to be a lot of sitting around the pool though from this point on."

The driver smiled.

"Actually there are a number of five-star hotels in Erbil. Before the daesh, Kurdistan was on the verge of becoming a great…tourism place, yes? Sort of like Dubai, with many investors, many improvements."

"Is that still the case?" Jen asked.

"No, and maybe yes. There are few tourists, but it's hard to get people interested in investing right now as things are. They see Iraq and don't understand Kurdistan. We stopped the daesh at this city's doorstep. The other parts of Iraq fell so quickly, but we stopped them here."

"Where are you heading after you unload us?" Porter asked.

"Mosul. The ISF and Federal Police are combining to clear northern neighborhoods, and we're going there now."

"I imagine we'll be right behind you," Porter said.

"You will need clearance to do so."

"Yeah, so we hear. Any chance of us picking up a few rifles like you've got there?"

"You will need an Iraqi ID card and plenty of cash, and then you can buy pretty much anything you want."

"Don't have either."

"Your contacts will have weapons they can provide you with. I'm afraid it may not be the kind you're used to, however."

"Anything that shoots is better than nothing."

Hozan nodded. "This is very true."

The vehicles slowed as they approached the high gates of the next house. Armed Kurdish sentries inspected the passengers and as soon as they recognized the drivers, they signaled for the gates to be opened and waved them in.

Aiden stepped out of the vehicle and was instantly greeted by a tall American with a southern accent and his wife, her blonde hair pulled into a messy bun.

"Mr. McCoy, welcome to Iraq. I'm Gary, this is my wife Linda. I can't tell you how much we appreciate you and your team coming."

"It's good to finally meet you in person." He and Aiden shook hands.

"And you must be Ginger?" Linda asked, extending her hand to her as well.

"And is this your family?" Gary asked.

"Yes, these are our kids, Shiloh and Allen. And this is my partner, Porter, and his wife, Jen." More handshakes and greetings.

"You said you also have two additional teammates coming separately?"

"Yes, another of our ministry partners, Guy, is coming in tomorrow. And a surgeon friend of mine, Jake, will hopefully be here in about a week. He's also a former PJ and served here."

"Great, great. Well, let's move inside out of the sun. You must be tired from all the travel. Are you hungry?"

"Oh, no. Our first hosts shared a wonderful meal with us not long ago."

"Alright. Well, come on in."

The two-story house had a table, a few chairs, and an old sofa, but little else. The first thing everyone noticed were cardboard boxes stacked in each room they passed through. The opened tops of some revealed first-aid supplies, clothing, boxed foods, and toiletries. There were also towers of bottled water.

"These are our storerooms," Gary said. "Pardon the mess but it can get a little chaotic with all of the turnover."

They passed into a kitchenette with a long table covered by books, manuals, papers, and two laptops. Pinned on one wall was a detailed street map of Mosul covered in sticky notes with scribbled writing.

"I guess you could call this the office." Gary opened the refrigerator and offered water bottles to his guests while Linda stacked up most of the books and paper materials onto a corner of the table.

"So," Gary began, "as you can see we've got supplies, a few weapons, and some security who come and go as needed. Hozan and Ehmed here often work as interpreters and security, but aside from that, we're it. There are also a few Americans and other westerners fighting alongside them on the front lines, volunteers from Europe mainly. They drop in from time to time to rest and refit, or to get situated if they get injured. Our main operation though, and our challenge, is getting this stuff to the people who need it, and helping them get out of harm's way if they want to leave. Pretty simple goal but an almost impossible task without folks such as yourselves. We appreciate you coming."

"Our goal is simple too," Aiden said. "We're here. That's it. Use us however you need us, and as long as God agrees, we're there."

Gary and Linda smiled. "Thank you. As for what role you can play…the needs are total. I guess we can start with getting a rundown on your skill sets? I know your story rather well, Mr. McCoy, but these gentlemen don't, and we know almost nothing about your companions."

"Alright, please call me Aiden. I'm a former Airforce PJ. Served in Afghanistan, medically discharged in '04. After that I went into trauma counseling. A few years back my wife and I started our ministry in Africa. The crux of the operation is going into the countryside and getting kids out of the militias and into vocational schools, or back to their families or tribes." He motioned for Ginger to go next.

"Go ahead," she deflected, "you do the bios better than I do."

"Okay. My wife is a pilot, helicopters and fixed-wing, Army veteran, Iraq." He paused, careful about how much to reveal. "She got out in '08. Her greatest asset is her brain. Taught herself several languages. She can either do or learn anything she wants or needs to. Does that about sum you up, babe?"

"Well, you brag too much. There's plenty of things I can't do and don't want to try. But like he said, we're here and ready to do whatever you need. These are our kids, Allen and Shiloh, who are both great help with us in our ministry caring for kids." Ginger looked at Jen for her turn.

"I'm Jen. I've been a trauma nurse for fifteen years. I spent some time in Syria doing field work about three years ago. And I'm married to that serious looking guy over there."

Porter uncrossed his arms and put his hands in his pockets. "Name's Peter, but everyone calls me Porter. I'm a SEAL. Retired from the teams in 2013. Spent time pretty much everywhere, including right here in beautiful northern Iraq." He looked at Ginger. "Conducted every kind of operation you can think of."

"What were your specialties?" Linda asked, and the Kurdish soldiers dialed in.

"Killing bad guys, mostly…and not getting shot in the process. I was an operational commander, planned and led counterinsurgency missions, and trained a lot of the ISF special operators. Trained as a combat medic…that's about it."

"He was a DEVGRU troop commander. A captain," Aiden added. "Now, he pretty much keeps me from getting killed."

"When did you last fight in Iraq?" Ehmed asked.

"Officially, 2011."

"And unofficially?" Ehmed pressed.

Porter pulled his hands out of his pockets and rubbed his wrists while looking at the floor.

"Let's just go with the official date."

"It'll be a Godsend to have your expertise," Gary said. "All of you."

"What kind of weapons can we procure?" Porter asked. "We'd like the ability to defend ourselves if necessary."

"That's a tricky question. Theoretically you're limited to what you can legally purchase. Realistically you can buy anything you can afford, but I would recommend against going on a spending spree in the local markets. You don't want to draw too much attention to yourselves and become a target. We can provide you with a quality rifle each, I've maintained them myself, mostly acquired from dead ISIS fighters. Various versions of AKs and Tariq pistols. Not my preference, but the better the gun the harder it is to find good ammunition for it. What we've got you'll never have a hard time getting reloaded. We've also got a few Chinese grenades that Ehmed and Hozan have provided in order to get out of sticky situations. As for tactical gear and med kits, everything is available at the local markets. Body armor, vests, night vision…you name it."

Aiden looked at Porter. "Perhaps when Guy arrives, you guys can head over there and get us outfitted. Guy is a medic, former militia fighter for the CAR, lots of combat experience. He's really cool, but a little short on pleasantries."

"Glad to have him too," Gary said. "And you also mentioned a doctor who's been in contact with the hospital in Mosul?"

"That's my friend Jake. Great doctor, former PJ. He's a trauma specialist. I'm not sure what the arrangement is but he's set to get in with the doctors in Mosul, so it's not likely we'll see him much once he gets his feet wet. But he's assured me we can text him anytime if we need him, and he'll make us a priority."

"He's going to be plenty busy there," Linda looked at Jen. "It might be a good idea to get you in touch with them as well. They need nurses everywhere but especially there. Though I'd hate to see you and your husband separated while here."

"Yeah. But whatever they need…" Jen and Porter exchanged looks.

"I've got a friend there," Linda said. "I'll give her a call."

Porter took off his Red Sox hat and scratched the hair behind his ears. He picked up the nearest AK-47, field stripped it, and examined every inch. After a thorough inspection he gave a slightly approving grunt.

"Well?" Aiden asked.

"Not bad, actually."

Aiden lifted the lid off a wooden crate, revealing a grid of boxed grenades.

"These are very dangerous," Hozan said.

"Yes, I'm aware," Aiden said, picking one out of the box to the fascination of Allen, who sat with his legs dangling on the table nearby. "I've never used this kind before."

"They're reliable," Ehmed said. Then he saw Allen. "You must not touch them. Very dangerous."

"Yeah, I know," Allen smiled and nodded. "We have some at home, but they're different. I've never gotten to toss one."

"You have those at your home?" Ehmed asked.

"No. My dad does."

"Where is this? In America?"

"No, at our compound in Africa," Aiden clarified. "When we run operations, we often confiscate all sorts of weapons, ammo, and drugs. There's always a mixed bag of ordinance we have to go through. Some of it we turn over to the government, some of it we keep for security purposes. You never know when a box of grenades may come in handy."

Ehmed and Hozan spoke to one another in their language, astonishment on their faces.

Aiden set the grenade back in its box and held up a Tariq pistol. "Ever use one of these?" he asked Porter, feeling its weight.

"Yeah. A few times, just out of curiosity. It's a Beretta clone. Kinda the national gun over here. Cheap, easy to find."

"So…" Ehmed interrupted, pausing as if still figuring out what he wanted to say, "you come here to help us…even though you do this important work in Africa?"

"Don't ask me," Porter shrugged. "I just go where he does."

9
Arms and Armor

Tal Afar, Iraq

A lieutenant looked around the room, trying not to stare at his general while wrestling with his own emotions. Framed pictures adorned the walls. Clear evidence of a hurried departure were evident, the remains of pillaged cupboards and the telltale scent of death emanating from a nearby apartment.

Ozzy turned about, trying and failing to stifle emotions that every square inch kindled. He was surrounded by the images of his bride, later a mother, and the two children they bore within these walls. It was a home once filled with the laughter of friends and conversation, a place of refuge nestled within a changing country where uncertainty was the rule, but God and family were the pillars that protected them in every storm.

Gone now, except for God, and the images in Ozzy's memory.

He went to the window. The street below, scarred but not yet destroyed by war and violence, wasn't much different except now the roving bands of angry fighters were gone, along with those they attacked. Yet war and violence still reigned, as evidenced by distant gunfire, directed at Ozzy's behest.

Goriel said nothing and merely leaned against the wall by the front door, his eyes averted to the ceiling.

Neither officer hurried the general, no matter how many flies they swatted away.

"Lieutenant?" Ozzy said at last.

"Yes, general," he said, straightening.

"Order them to advance."

"Yes, general," he said, then dismissed himself to relay instructions over the radio.

Ozzy paused and lifted a crumpled knit blanket off the sofa. He felt the fibers and frowned, realizing they were covered with dust. He tossed the blanket back and turned to Goriel.

"We'll return. Perhaps with them." He smiled. "Soon," he said, patting him on the shoulder as he walked out.

Only then did Goriel glance at his boyhood home. He wiped the memory of his mother and sister away and walked out, leaving the dead to bury the dead.

Erbil, Iraq

Jen watched Porter try on the tactical vest in the open air market.

"You know, this may be the first time I've ever seen you put one of those on."

"Yeah. Maybe. Sexy, huh?"

"Do you think I need one too?"

"That would be sexy."

"I'm serious."

"Probably not. Not in the hospital. Want to try one on though?"

"Suuuure."

Jen lifted the vest over her head and held out her arms while Porter fastened the Velcro. She smiled at Ginger.

"Is it me?" she asked, striking a runway model pose.

Ginger shook her head. "Not really."

Allen picked up a spotting scope and peered through the lens as the Iraqi merchant began trying to talk Ginger into buying it for her son.

"Heavier than it looks," Jen said, peeling it off. "No thanks. But you load up, buster. You've got too many holes in your body as it is."

"What are you talking about? I don't have any holes in me."

"Uh, yeah you do. Should I count the scars?"

"Those were nothin'. Besides, these vests are more for holding gear than for protection. Not much you can do against bombs and machine guns. Not with this crap."

Jen's smile faded and she joined Aiden, sifting through EMS gear and haggling through one of the Kurdish interpreters.

"Why would you say that?" Ginger asked Porter when Jen was out of earshot.

"What?"

"She doesn't need you casting mental images of being blown up."

"It's just reality, Ginger."

"No it's not. It's a possibility but not a fact."

"She thinks she knows what to expect. She's never been in it," Porter lifted off the vest, "not the way we have. She needs to know so she can be ready."

"Know what? That any second a bomb can go off?" Ginger looked around. "That lady over there might be hiding a suicide vest under her robe. Jen knows that. Do you have any idea how much time she's spent watching news and reading books and articles while we were over here? Waiting around for you to finally hang 'em up, and praying you'd do it still in one piece? She probably knows as much about all of this as anyone does."

Porter gave her a skeptical look.

"Not the door-kicking details," Ginger acquiesced slightly, "but the big picture, sure, she knows. I mean, she came here, for crying out loud. If you don't realize that by now, you should."

"I know that."

"Then act like it. And be a little more tactful. Cause we're gonna be out there, and once again, she's not."

Mosul, Iraq

Matt ignored the machine gun fire. His bloody right glove stained a corner of the package that he tore open with his teeth while his left hand pressed on the wound of the man in front of him. Next to him, an ISF soldier stood up from behind their cover and let out several three-round bursts from his rifle, the expended shell casings raining on Matt's opened med kit. He shoved the second bandage on top of the seeping others and hoped it would be enough to stem the tide.

He looked up for help but all around him soldiers returned fire while others nursed their own injuries as best they could. Matt knew there were civilians across the way he couldn't reach also bleeding out. He swore and lifted himself up into a crouching position to put some of his weight onto the dying man.

He looked at his patient's face and recognized the glazed look of life draining out of him, volumes of coagulating blood pooled beneath him; the barely-perceptible pulse garnered another curse from Matt, who knew it was all in vain. The heart, long since deprived of enough blood to operate, finally ceased, and the desperate eyes of its former host opened wide; the scant blood remaining within the body provided a hint of color, and that too slowly faded.

A soldier dropped down next to him. "He's dead?"

"Yeah," Matt said in disgust, and repacked his bag. He searched for others in need but saw only live soldiers gathering gear to retreat, some carrying dead ones they'd been unable to save.

"Let's move him," the soldier ordered. "We must move. Now."

"Copy that," Matt said tiredly.

They picked up the body as gunshots continued to ring out. One held the legs, the other the armpits, and they carried him back from the direction they'd just come, following a line of wounded soldiers who led the way.

Erbil, Iraq

"What's your plan for now, then?" Josiah asked on the other end of the phone.

"Gonna drive to Mosul and see what kind of access we can get. Then we'll just see where we're needed," Aiden said.

"And how's everyone so far?"

"Good. Raring to go, especially Shiloh. She doesn't like just sitting around."

"Takes after both of you. How about Porter?"

"You know him. Just waiting around for the shooting to start."

"Good."

"Glad he's here, for sure. Wish you were here too – up there, you know."

"Plenty of airpower flying around, from what I hear. You don't need a washed-up old dude like me."

"Yeah. You're probably right about that."

"I hate you."

"Love you too, bro."

"Yeah, yeah…just keep your head down."

Aiden heard commotion from outside and stood to look out the window. The gates were parting for a Land Rover caked in mud and peppered with bullet holes.

"I will."

"No you won't, but stay safe anyway."

"Copy that."

"Thanks for calling. Love you too."

"Welcome back." Gary wrapped his arm around the driver as soon as he stepped out of the vehicle.

"Thank you." The Kurd smiled as two more men exited, both sporting combat gear and well-used rifles. They leaned against the hood, exhausted.

"Glad you made it in safe," Gary said, surveying the men. "We have some reinforcements we'd like you to meet." He introduced Aiden and his team, and both groups exchanged friendly nods.

"Were you a PJ once upon a time?" one of the men asked Aiden.

"Yes."

"Pleasure to meet you," Mike said.

"Mike is a Marine, spent time here in Anbar," Gary mentioned.

"Were you together?" Aiden asked.

"No, I was riding a desk stateside nearly retired by the time Mike was getting his feet wet." Gary motioned to Aiden and Porter. "You guys may want to debrief with them before you all head out tomorrow. Let's head inside."

As they walked into the compound, the new arrivals hung back with Ehmed and Hozan, surveying the Americans — men, women, and children, clean, healthy.

One of the men asked Hozan, "You're taking all of them into Mosul?"

"I guess so."

"You seemed to know something about the one-legged guy."

"Most of our guys have heard of Aiden McCoy."

"What about the other one?" Ehmed asked, noticing Porter give them a backwards glance before walking inside.

"No clue."

Mike dropped his backpack on the floor with a thud, generating a small cloud of dust. He leaned his rifle against the wall and fell into an armchair, closed his eyes while removing his hat, and rubbed some sweat from his dirty forehead. He looked at Aiden and Porter sitting nearby on crates, waiting for him to collect his thoughts.

"When are you going in," Mike asked after blinking a few times.

"Tomorrow, hopefully," Aiden said. "I've got one more teammate coming in today and then we're going to Mosul as soon as appropriate."

"You were in Afghanistan, right? Anaconda?"

"Yes."

"Any intel?" Porter interrupted.

"Yeah, it sucks." Mike quickly sized up the men questioning him. "What's your experience in Iraq?"

"Not much for me," Aiden answered. "I was out before Iraq heated up, but I've been here a few times in non-combat roles."

"What about you?" he asked Porter.

"SEAL. Know it pretty well."

"Which team?"

"Six."

Mike nodded. "You here to train them?"

"Who?" Porter asked.

"The Kurds, ISF, volunteers, any of them?"

Porter leaned forward and clasped his hands. "I mean, I will if they need it…but it's not really why we're here. We're mainly focused on helping civilians."

"Good. It's…" Mike trailed off searching for words. He closed his eyes again, put on his hat. "It's more than just war, it's –" he swore, staring up at the ceiling, "genocide, man. Pure, demented heart-of-darkness stuff." He shook his head. "They're evil. Those insurgents we dealt with back in '04, ya know, they were tough but they weren't the same as these guys. These guys are good, real good. Excellent snipers, use terrain to their advantage, set traps and bait. And they just don't retreat…ever."

"We've seen that before," Porter said.

"Maybe you had but I hadn't. Not like this. This one dude. We killed a room full of them and went through their gear, found phones. He had picture after picture of civilians…and videos." Mike paused again. "Had all of these young girls just lined up…" He closed his eyes again and was silent for several seconds.

"It's alright, man," Aiden said. "You don't need to relive it unless you want to talk about it. We're here to help. That includes you."

Porter shifted awkwardly on his crate and looked away.

"Thanks," Mike said, "but I'm good. It just pisses me off something fierce." After reflecting, he added, "You're going in to get those people out, right?"

"We hope so," Aiden said.

"You know how in the Bible it talks about the Israelites wiping out whole nations. You know, the uncomfortable parts about not leaving anyone alive?"

"Yeah."

"I get that now. That's what needs to happen with these, man. It just comes down to that. They all just need exterminated like…I don't know, like vipers or something."

"Probably," Aiden said. "But vengeance isn't our responsibility."

Porter and Mike made eye contact, and Porter shook his head slightly.

"Yeah, well," Mike said, "see how you feel about that when ya get back."

Erbil International Airport

"I understand your concerns. I don't know what else I can say." Guy leaned on the custom officer's counter.

"What is the nature of your work in the Central African Republic?"

"As I told your colleague, and his colleague before him, I am a Christian missionary. I help run an orphanage and the security for it."

"So you are a trained mercenary?"

"No. I protect children from militias and help them find work. Good work."

Three customs officers continued to search Guy's single backpack for additional clues to the curious human standing before them.

"Can I see my phone please?"

One of the officers handed it over. Guy opened his browser and pulled up Aiden's ministry website.

"Here, see here?" Guy turned the phone to show the officers. "This is me with my ministry lead, an American, Aiden McCoy. He's supposed to be picking me up here now."

The officers began speaking in Arabic to each other. The most junior of them spoke to Guy.

"You're here to meet him, the American with the…ahh," he tapped his leg.

Guy cocked his head, confused.

"This American is here," the officer pointed to the ground with both hands.

"Yes, he came in yesterday. I'm supposed to meet him."

The junior officer spoke to his comrades who responded with head nods and less formality. The senior officer spoke to the others in Arabic, then turned to Guy and smiled.

"Enjoy your stay in Kurdistan."

The young officer stamped Guy's passport and handed it back.

"Thank you," Guy said, still surprised by the sudden turnaround.

"Thank you for what you are doing in our country."

Guy strolled through the terminal, eliciting stares from practically everyone he passed. He went through the glass doors and took in the long line of taxi cabs, checked his watch, and then heard a voice behind him which made him jump.

"What's a black African doing in Erbil at this time of year?"

Guy turned, relieved to see Porter, in sunglasses and armed with a pistol, arms crossed. Hozan stood next to him.

"Where is Aiden?" Guy asked.

"No hello, how ya doing, buddy?"

"Hello, how ya doing, where's Aiden?"

"Back at the compound. We're heading there now. What's wrong? You're all jumpy."

"I'm fine. Hello," he said, extending his hand to Hozan. "My name is Guy."

"Hozan," he said, shaking it. "We should be getting on. Come."

A few minutes later, seated in the Land Rover, Guy spoke. "Sorry for being short. It was a long journey. I thought they might lock me up."

"Probably should have for something," Porter said, dialing a number on his phone. "I got him, boss. On our way back to you now…alright. Yup, no worse for wear." He leaned back and asked Guy, "You solid?"

"Solid," Guy said, staring out the window.

"Copy that. Out." He hung up.

"Aiden?"

"Affirmative. And no time to decompress, I'm afraid. He wants to move out immediately."

"Fine."

"But here, I got something for you." Porter leaned back and handed Guy another one of the Tariq pistols in a Kydex holster, and three additional filled magazines.

"I would have preferred a hamburger right now," Guy said, setting the pistol aside.

"You'll thank me later."

10

Access

Syria

Hazail crouched in the corner on bruised knees, shaking and sobbing.

Behind her she heard the sickening thud of another woman getting punched, and all she could do was close her eyes and pray. A wave of shame washed over her as she realized she'd been praying that they would take someone else this time. She had wept for the women who'd been first, taken right in front of her when it all seemed a surreal nightmare she could maybe wake up from.

The nightmare never ended. It just shifted locations, for years now.

There seemed to be no order to it. Sometimes they took the older girls, sometimes the women, sometimes the young girls, as young as Hazail had been when she'd first been taken.

Something had changed, though she had no idea what. The men were angrier, more sadistic, more bloodthirsty, and all restraint was gone. They took them away sooner, fed them less, moved them more frequently. Sometimes they killed them on the spot. Sometimes they carted them off to God knows where.

All of them understood they were merely a product. Soon she would be sold, and then what? Forced into marriage? Killed? Worse? Maybe she had already been sold. Maybe that's what happened to her mother all those years ago. Was she already part of someone's harem? She expected at any moment to be grabbed from behind by sweaty, angry men and fed to the demons who possessed them.

Mosul, Iraq

Goriel brushed off his pants and straightened his uniform before walking out of the dingy room that had served for a few hours of sleepless rest. He made his way past men in various locations seeking better outcomes; some slept, others sat staring at nothing, a few spoke in casual conversation, and a small handful actually smiled. Goriel found a seat next to one of these latter groups.

"Good morning," one of them said. "Did you sleep?"

"A little," Goriel lied.

"We heading out soon?"

"Likely." As he said this, his phone started to vibrate.

"Excuse me." He answered the call. "Yes?"

Every soldier in earshot, even those who had been asleep, looked to Goriel and listened.

"Right away, sir." He hung up.

"The general wants to speak with me in person."

"I guess that means we're not moving out any time soon then," a sergeant said.

"Not with me, anyway."

Goriel stepped out of the Humvee and made a beeline for the command tent, where he found his father in conference with several officers. Ozzy stopped speaking, nodded to Goriel at the back wall, and then addressed the others.

"We'll discuss this later. Dismissed."

The men dispersed, a couple of them patting Goriel on the shoulder as they left, and in seconds father and son were alone.

"I got a reconnaissance image of our old street." Ozzy handed his son a topical printout of a neighborhood in Tal Afar, Iraq. Goriel took the image but only gave it a cursory glance.

"It's all still there," Ozzy offered. "The whole street looks relatively untouched. Minus the laughter and the smell of your mother's cooking, that is."

Goriel looked at it again, and Ozzy sensed a softening in his demeanor. He moved to his desk, flipped open a leatherbound book, removed a picture from between the pages, and handed it to Goriel.

"Here. I thought you might like to keep this with you."

Goriel took the small photograph. The image was of him and his sister when they were much younger.

"Perhaps one day you can put it back in the frame your mother used to keep it in."

"Thank you," he said, putting the picture in his chest pocket, "but I'm not interested in going back there."

"They will be…one day."

He stared at his father.

"You must not give up hope, son." Ozzy put his arm around his shoulder. "They're alive. I know it. I just do."

Goriel stiffened.

"Will there be anything else? I'd like to return to my men."

Ozzy backed away and went to his desk. "No, son. You are dismissed."

Despite the checkpoints and two-way traffic, the Land Rover made good time, and Porter could feel the impetus of battle as they neared the sprawling city. The vehicle slowed as they approached yet another checkpoint, this one manned and reinforced with a tank and two armored personnel carriers.

They stopped and Ehmed rolled down the driver's side window. Two Iraqis approached and peered inside while a third paced around the vehicle, eyeing the occupants.

From the vehicle behind them, Aiden and Hozan watched the exchange. "Tighter security than it has been,"

Hozan said. "I'm afraid you may have come all this way for nothing."

The guards shook their heads and made hand gestures instructing both vehicles to turn around. "It doesn't look like they're going to let us through. I'm sorry."

Porter tried to keep up with the words of the exchange but understood the body language of aggressive dismissal, universal to all authority figures expecting compliance. As Ehmed argued their case, Porter took in the details — weapons, uniforms, routes of escape, as well as the faces of the soldiers watching from a distance.

"Tell you what," Porter said to Ehmed, "tell 'em we'll turn around and park a few meters down the road till we can sort this out."

Ehmed translated, then performed a three-point turn, pausing next to Hozan's lowered window. "Turn around and follow us. He wants to wait for some reason."

An hour later they were still parked by the side of the road, not far from the checkpoint whose men now watched the odd assortment of people with curiosity instead of tension.

Aiden sent off another text before walking over to Allen in the shade of the opened rear door.

"Hey buddy. Getting tired of waiting around?"

"Yeah. Why won't they let us go past?"

"It's their job to keep bad guys out. They don't know who we are, so we need someone to let them know we're here to help."

"I can tell them."

"I'm not sure they'll take your word for it. You hungry?"

"No," he said, as Ginger, Hozan, and Porter returned from talking with the guards.

"Any change?" Aiden asked them.

"No, but they don't seem so antsy anymore," Ginger said. "We're not getting through unless they get some orders about us. Might want to think about trying again tomorrow, maybe with Gary this time."

"I already texted him but he said he's not getting anywhere yet. He'll let us know."

"Maybe you would have done better without me here," Guy asked. "Perhaps they think I'm here to join the enemy?"

"They don't know what to make of you," Ginger said, "but they're not worrying about it. At least, I don't think they are. I get the impression they just think we're tourists or something."

"You get anywhere?" Porter asked Aiden.

"Sort of. Got an American colonel who says he'll see what he can do. You?"

"Spoke with a retired admiral a little bit ago who said he'd make a few calls, but also haven't heard back."

"We should probably head back soon if there is no change," Ehmed said with a sigh.

"Heads up," Porter said, noticing two of the Iraqi guards walking toward them. "Maybe we're getting somewhere."

The guards carried water bottles and handed them out while speaking to Ginger and the Kurds.

"They say a lieutenant is on the way to speak to you," Hozan translated.

"That's a good sign," Porter said.

"Maybe your buddies got through to someone," Ginger said as the soldiers walked away.

"Pretty sure I would have heard back if they had."

"They say anything else?" Aiden asked.

"No."

"I dropped as many names as I could remember," Porter said. "Not sure if any of them are still alive though."

Thirty more minutes brought longer shadows and a dusty plume in the distance. A Humvee approached at a rapid pace and briefly stopped at the checkpoint before driving through and parking in the center of the road, facing the Land Rovers.

The passenger door opened and out stepped a much younger man than anyone expected. He looked the vehicles over, shook his head, and stepped up to the entourage.

"You are Americans?" he asked, obviously annoyed.

Aiden, relieved to hear clear English from the Iraqi officer, answered, "Most of us." He introduced his team and their guides. "We're here to distribute aid and help the people of Mosul any way we can. We've got medical supplies, food, clothing, and military and medical training."

The young officer scanned the faces in front of them, sizing everyone up, and lingering for a moment on Allen and Shiloh.

"You bring your children? Are you aware of what's happening in Mosul?"

"Yes," Ginger spoke. "There are children across Mosul as well. Ours would like to assist them."

"I understand we may be an odd assortment," Aiden said, "but let me assure you, we're well prepared and informed of what we're getting into. If we're able to help your people, that's what we'd like to do, but I understand your situation. We don't want to be in your way."

"I'm told one of you spoke of knowing General Abdelhossein. Who was that?"

Porter perked up. "That was me."

"How do you know of the general?"

"I trained him."

They stared at each other for several seconds before the officer pulled out his phone and dialed a number. He then spoke in Arabic, as he looked Porter up and down.

"Know what he's saying?" Aiden whispered to Ginger.

"He's describing Porter. Just mentioned his Red Sox hat."

"One moment," the officer said into his phone, then handed it to Porter.

Surprised, Porter took it.

"Yes?"

On the other end, a man's voice asked, "Captain Dawkins, will you ever quit?"

Porter smiled, instantly recognizing the familiar voice.

"No sir. If knocked down, I'll get right back up …every time."

"You never do. Please hand the phone back to the officer."

"Yes sir."

The officer took the phone back and listened for a moment. "Yes sir." He hung up. "General Abdelhossein requests that you meet with him personally. And I'm to take you to him myself."

"Absolutely," Aiden said. "We'd be honored to meet with him."

"I am lieutenant Abdelhossein," Goriel said to Porter. "The general is my father."

The vehicles bounced along the dusty, war-torn streets as their occupants gripped the handles to brace themselves during the sudden accelerations and turns. Every mile closer to their destination shifted the mood in the direction of sober disgust and prayerful conviction.

"I'm glad we're here," Aiden said quietly. "People need to see this."

Other than occasionally murmuring "Wow," or "Whoa," the McCoy children were silent. Porter, intimately familiar with the city that used to exist here, noted the changes in terrain and the demeanor of the civilians they passed. It was different, but some things were quite similar. Guy and Ginger took everything in without saying a word.

They turned a corner and the vehicles slowed to a stop, idling at an intersection. Allen looked out the side window.

"They play soccer here, too. I should have brought a ball."

Aiden and Ginger looked at the open courtyard surrounded by low broken walls and the stringing remains of long dead powerlines where four boys were playing.

"You're right. But maybe they'll let us play with them," Aiden said.

"When ISIS was still in control here, they instituted strange rules," Hozan said. "They'd cut western logos off jerseys. Made everyone wear long baggy pants, no shorts. It was often the little things that broke one's spirit. A simple thing like a game, taken from us…and they wouldn't allow the officials to use whistles," Hozan added.

"Why not?" Allen asked.

"They said it was because the sound would make the devils gather," Hozan scoffed. "Ironic, huh?"

The vehicles started moving, and Allen sat back against his seat.

"I hope we can play with them."

The Humvee halted in front of a building teeming with military personnel. The Land Rovers pulled in behind it while soldiers on both sides of the street stared at the civilian vehicles as the occupants got out.

Goriel approached Porter. "The general asked to speak with you, Porter, sir. The rest will need to wait here."

"I'm here because of him," Porter said, gesturing to Aiden. "Tell the general I'm not driving this boat. He's gonna want to speak with my boss, too."

Goriel nodded. "Fine, come with me."

"Try to make some new friends," Aiden said to the others. "Be back in as soon as we can."

"Make it snappy," Ginger said, as dozen sets of curious eyes inspected her family and friends.

Goriel led Porter and Aiden past guards and through a long corridor, and Porter was surprised to see American troops scattered around the headquarters. None made eye contact, and he didn't recognize any faces. They turned into a room full of officers and computer equipment. In the center stood Ozzy, watching a monitor.

"General, sir," Goriel said. "These are the men you asked to see."

Ozzy turned his head. For a moment he seemed confused, but as he surveyed Aiden and Porter his lips formed themselves into a smile. He tossed a pen he had been fiddling with onto a desk and walked to them. When they were face to face, his voice escaped him and all he could do was stand and smile. Ozzy placed his right hand on Porter's shoulder, took a deep breath, and smiled again.

"Welcome, friend."

"It's good to see you again. Let me introduce to you Aiden McCoy."

"Mr. McCoy." Ozzy shook his hand. "Welcome, as well."

"General Abdelhossein, thank you for meeting with us. And thank you for the escort."

"I'm sorry you encountered delay. Had I known you were here together I would have met you myself. Has he told you? This is my son, Goriel."

"Yes. He informed us," Porter smiled. "You've moved up in the world. Good to see you in charge."

"Promoted by default," he laughed. "Everyone else was dead. How about you? I imagined you'd be an admiral by now. You'll understand my confusion to see you here as a civilian."

"Retired a few years back. Hooked up with Aiden here. Been working in Africa with him and his family. They're here with us, along with a team of other loner military and medical types. Figured we'd hop on over and lend a hand."

"Sir," Aiden said. "I can see you've got your hands full and we don't want to distract you. I've got a friend, former PJ, who's been embedded with some of your guys. He said you needed help."

Ozzy nodded. "He's right. What did you have in mind?"

"Aiden is a PJ. Solid as they come," Porter interjected.

"And the others?"

"Extensive medical or military training, or both," Aiden said. "My wife is a pilot. They're all ready wherever you need us."

"And you brought your children here?"

"Yes, general."

"You do not fear for their safety?"

"Sometimes, of course I do. But we're here."

Ozzy examined Aiden for a moment before speaking. "We are blessed to have your family in our country."

"Thank you, General. How can we serve you?"

Ozzy paced the room. "We certainly need frontline medics, as your friend said. But you must go where you feel led on this matter." Ozzy turned and called to one of the officers. "Major!"

"Yes, general," his subordinate approached.

"See that these men and their associates are granted full travel access for wherever they need to go." Ozzy eyed Porter as he spoke. "They have my trust completely."

"Yes, general."

Ozzy turned to Aiden. "You said your wife is a pilot."

"Yes sir, Army. Served here till '08. Apaches."

Ozzy turned to look at Porter. "Apaches, you say?"

Porter nodded.

Aiden noticed their familiarity. "Is there something I'm missing?"

"Ozzy, here – sorry, General Abdelhossein here…was part of Operation Wonderland."

"I…I had no idea."

"He was right beside me," Porter said, "when we recovered her. The whole time, in fact."

Aiden was speechless as the revelation hit him.

"Cooper. She is…?" Ozzy asked.

Porter nodded. "Yes. Her name is Ginger…and she's right outside."

Tears began to well in Ozzy's eyes. Most of his men, Goriel included, exchanged awkward looks due to the uncharacteristic display.

"I would like very much to meet your wife, Mr. McCoy."

11
Priority Targets

Creech Air Force Base, Nevada

Around twenty remotely piloted aircraft flew at various altitudes above Northern Iraq. The MQ-1 Predators and MQ-9 Reapers had been in the air for hours, loitering, searching, and would remain for several hours more. They were the most effective means of penetrating the dense urban environment, and the American pilots who flew them — from one continent and an ocean away — were emerging experts at recognizing enemy movements and tactics.

"Target is moving again," the Reaper pilot said.

"Copy that, keep tracking."

He watched the small hatchback through the Reaper's powerful lenses as it wove through the city in the middle of the night with its lights off, and emerged from the cover of narrowly clustered streets.

"Coming into the clear. Vehicle slowing," the pilot announced, then muttered, "Where are you going, buddy?"

The vehicle came to a stop before a long flat building. A garage door opened and the hatchback slipped inside.

"Looks like we found his hobby hole."

"Mark the target. Feed it over."

"Yes sir." The pilot glanced at the clock on the wall. He and his sensor operator copilot had tracked this target across the city for five hours. With its current weapons payload and wingspan, his Reaper could sustain flight for twelve hours. He hoped he wouldn't be spending that much time watching the building they'd just targeted.

Northern Iraq

Forty minutes later, a pilot looked out the window of his F-16. The vast city sprawled below but from 15,000 feet he couldn't make out many details. Even the F-16's targeting pod couldn't attain the clarity he'd need to hit a target like this with such precision, so with gratitude for modern technology he relaxed as the RPA's multi-spectral sensors saw what he and his plane couldn't. He acquired the laser signal from the Reaper, and fired.

The pilot in his F-16 and the Reaper pilot in Nevada both watched the building evaporate in a flash on the screen. The satisfying conclusion to the mission would be short lived; neither pilot would be landing his aircraft anytime soon in such a target rich environment.

The American and Iraqi JTACs on the ground used at least forty aerial platforms in the sky at all times: twenty RPAs of all variety including Ravens, Pumas, and Grey Eagles, up to ten fixed-wing aircraft, at least four attack helicopters, and two manned reconnaissance birds, all stacked from 2,000 feet to 30,000 feet. It was a concentration of sheer destructive capability rarely seen in the history of warfare, even factoring the Second World War into the equation when it was arrayed against massive armies of nation states.

As the F-16 pilot turned into a new heading, he marveled that the multi-billion dollar air war of his day was being conducted against a few thousand men whose battlefield arsenal consisted of second-hand conventional weapons, and whose air force was made of little more than $80 drones acquired off eBay.

But, he supposed, they could still kill. And thanks to him and his friends overhead, there were a few less killers plotting on the ground in Mosul to worry about tonight.

Ozzy held Ginger's hands with both of his own. "Your husband has told me you are integral to his success in every area."

"Yeah, he has nooo idea," she grinned.

"I think perhaps he does." Ozzy smiled and addressed Shiloh. "I hope you will one day get to meet my daughter, Hazail."

"Thank you," Shiloh said, a little embarrassed.

Ozzy noticed Goriel slipping out of the room. "You have my personal number, Mr. McCoy," he said, releasing Ginger's hands. "Call on me if you need anything. I will do whatever I can."

As the groups splintered and Porter climbed into his vehicle, he hollered.

"Shiloh girl!" He pointed two fingers in a V-shape to his eyes then at her. "You keep eyes on your pops for me till I get back! You read me?"

Shiloh smiled. "Five by, Froggie!"

"Later, dork!"

She waved, and Ginger gestured to Porter, indicating he needed to be smacked upside the head. He winked as they drove off.

"It's just for fun, mom. He doesn't mean it." Shiloh said.

"Yeah, I know."

Mosul

"Good to see you, brother," Matt said, giving Aiden a handshake that morphed into a man hug.

"Glad to be here," Aiden said. He looked at Matt's clothes. "You look like you've been in it."

"In it deep." He turned to the others. "Glad to meet you all. Here," he motioned to the man behind him, "this is

Mohamed. He's an ISF medic. We've been operating together for a while now."

"Hello," he said in English.

"So," Aiden said, clasping his hands in front of him. "What can we d—"

An explosion ripped through the air, causing everyone to flinch and duck. All eyes darted around, seeking the source of the blast and expecting the worst as their instincts and training kicked into gear. The soldiers raised their weapons and scanned the street and rooftops. Ginger stooped to put her arms around Shiloh, who stood frozen in confusion. Allen had his hands over his ears, and Guy placed a hand on his little shoulder while he scanned the street. A cloud of black smoke filled the sky over the rooftops a few blocks away.

"Airstrike," Matt said.

A group of ISF soldiers moved in the direction of the blast. Matt and Mohamed shouldered their gear and joined them.

"May be civilian casualties, I gotta go."

Guy, who was geared up in little more than a t-shirt, cargo pants, small backpack, and a rifle, gave Aiden a brief glance, then followed the soldiers. "I will go with them."

"Wait," Aiden said, turning to Ginger.

"Go," she said, "we'll be alright."

Aiden nodded, quickly hugged his kids, and jogged to catch up with Guy.

"Where is Dad going?" Shiloh asked.

"To go and help. It's why we came." She turned to Hozan. "Where is the best place for us to be right now?"

"There will be people filing this way soon."

"Then I guess we'll stay here to meet them when they come. Let's set up a station over there."

"Whatever you say," Hozan said, holding his rifle at the ready and scanning the streets to the front and the rear.

Hammam Al-Alil, Iraq

"Here we are." Ehmed stopped the vehicle near the gates of a sprawling encampment of trailers, buses, tents, and people.

Porter and Jen surveyed the throng of activity before stepping out, and Ehmed led them through the gates toward an intake center.

As soon as they entered the compound, Jen was overwhelmed with urgency. Areas strewn with patients in various degrees of need seemed unending: children sat with glazed looks in parent's laps, waxen elderly men and women were tossed aside on chairs or gurneys. Cries from distant tents hailed for scant nurses, and overly busy doctors only gave passing glances in their work to and fro.

"You sure you want me to leave you here, alone?" Porter asked.

Jen, taking in the surroundings, spoke without turning to look at him. "You're not here for this. I am."

She gave his hand a quick squeeze before walking up to the closest nurse she could see, examining a young man with bandages around his head.

"Excuse me," Jen asked her.

"Yes," the woman spoke in English, scanning Jen for injuries out of habit.

"My name is Jennifer Dawkins. I'm a nurse. I was told I might be of use to you here."

The woman squinted and turned to Ehmed. He spoke to the nurse in a language Porter and Jen couldn't follow.

"She asks who assigned you here."

"I was asked by one of your generals to come here and lend a hand. He said you were overwhelmed."

Ehmud translated for the nurse who was already distracted with other patients.

"Sure. I am Renas," she replied, giving Jen a curt smile and gesturing toward her clothing. "You...change?" She elaborated to Ehmed, then walked down the hall.

"She says you'll get blood on your nice pants, and she seems annoyed. If you follow her she'll take you to a nurse's station, though."

"Thank you. I guess I'm all set."

Porter surveyed the environment, unconvinced.

"Get going," Jen said. "Aiden needs you."

"Alright. I'll be back as soon as I can." He kissed her goodbye and she walked away, instantly absorbed into the ether of the makeshift mobile hospital.

"What kind of security do they have here?" he asked Ehmud.

"Marginal. She is as safe here as anywhere. The most dangerous areas are the ones we're still trying to clear. Where your other friends are."

Porter nodded. "Then let's get there."

Aiden followed the others to the blast site as gunfire sounded in the distance. He caught up to Guy when the group slowed around another corner, revealing a cratered ruin and a burning structure.

The buildings across the street were badly damaged, walls partially destroyed. People seeped from street-level doors, some with wounds, some carrying children. Still more wandered, dazed, inching along the adjacent roads. Matt and Mohamed tended to a body lying in the street, and Guy ran to a woman who stumbled, blood streaming down the side of her head. Aiden noticed a man holding a child about Allen's age; the father's face and chest bled from dozens of lacerations and he swung around, pleading in a language Aiden couldn't understand.

"Sir! Sir!" Aiden put on surgical gloves as he ran to the man. As he got closer, he saw the child was peppered with cuts from the broken glass, but also wasn't breathing.

"Let me help you," he said, motioning for the man to lay the child down.

The father spoke frantically as they lowered the child to the ground. Aiden scanned the boy from head to toe in a fraction of a second, verified his cleared airway. No obstruction. He put his hand to the child's neck and assessed the pulse. No visible signs of life. He began chest compressions. After the first set of reps, he unclasped his cargo pocket and removed a pocket mask, pressed it firmly against the child's bloody cheeks. He blew into the opening twice, then paused and listened. Faint breathing. Faint pulse.

He turned an eye to the child's chest and it moved moderately so he went back to compressions, repeating these motions for another minute until the child's breathing became stronger and he opened his eyes a crack. The boy cried out and flailed his arms; his father grabbed him as the boy shook his head and wailed, then burrowed his face into his father's chest.

"Here," Aiden tore open a gauze package and worked it in between the child's wounds and the father's shirt. "Hold this against his face."

The man nodded and sank to the ground, holding his son.

Aiden then assessed the father's wounds for the first time. He had glass and grit embedded in his cheeks and neck, and caked, drying blood clung to him like a ghastly tattoo but he appeared otherwise healthy. Aiden took a quick survey of his surroundings in triage mode and saw more people, but none in dire stress.

He removed a pair of tweezers from his med kit and quickly removed the three largest pieces of glass. The father winced but still clung to his son.

"I'll be back to check on you, okay?"

The man nodded, understood, and Aiden quickly repacked his kit. Matt joined him a moment later, having given up on reviving a man who lay near the pile of concrete his body broke against on impact.

People dispersed from the epicenter. In the distance, Guy attended to less severe injuries and Mohamed joined him.

"What do you think of Mosul?" Matt scoffed.

Aiden shook his head.

"Where to next?"

Ehmed slowed the Land Rover so as not to run over anyone. People meandered all over the street and two ambulances blocked the road up ahead.

"Think they're still here?" Porter asked.

"Maybe."

Porter dialed Aiden's phone again and got no answer. He texted and waited. Then he tried Ginger's phone, and she answered.

"Hey, where are you?"

"How the heck should I know?" He lowered the phone and asked Ehmed, "Where are we?"

"A few blocks east of where we'd planned to meet."

"We're almost where you were earlier but there're ambulances blocking the road."

"We're still here. Got some casualties trickling in and we aren't going anywhere. I haven't seen Aiden though. He and Guy went off when the bomb exploded and I haven't seen him for about an hour."

"What bomb?" Porter asked.

"I don't know. Just get here, I gotta go." She hung up.

He swore under his breath. "Mosul."

"Where have you been?" Ginger asked, holding a case of water.

"Took a while to get here with all the traffic. Where's Aiden?"

"He still hasn't come back yet." She motioned with her arms full. "He went that way, with the others."

"You good here?" He looked around, noticing Shiloh not far away helping Hozan and some others dish out rice onto paper plates. Allen stood close to Ginger, holding four water bottles in his arms.

"Yeah, we're good. Link up with him if you can and let him know we'll stay put till he gets back."

"Right."

Porter and Ehmed got back in the vehicle and drove the short distance to the destroyed building, parked, and immediately spotted Aiden pacing by himself, speaking into his phone, and Guy ten feet away.

Porter examined the damaged street.

"Airstrike."

"Probably," Ehmed agreed.

"Sure as hell. This was one of ours. Probably iced a few jihadis with that blast."

"And some civilians along with it."

Porter walked toward Guy.

"You guys alright?"

Guy glanced at him briefly before turning his attention back to the young man he assisted. "We're fine. We were several blocks away."

"Who's he talking to?" Porter motioned to Aiden.

"Your general friend."

Porter surveyed the line of injured civilians. "How'd it go here?"

"Five dead at least. Found parts of some others."

He continued scanning the street. "You need anything?"

"We'll need to resupply."

"I'm gonna see what Aiden's talking about." Porter walked over and Aiden nodded at him, speaking louder to include him in the conversation.

"I don't think that will be a problem. Like I said, we're here for you."

Porter raised his eyebrows. Aiden shook his head.

"Alright. See you soon. Out."

"What's Ozzy want?"

"Us. He said he's got a need he'd like us to consider. Wants us to meet with him to discuss it."

"A need where? All of us?"

"He didn't say. I texted Matt and he had no idea."

"No idea about what?" Guy asked as he and Ehmed walked up behind Porter.

"I don't know yet exactly. The general we spoke with yesterday wants us with his frontline guys. No Ginger and no kids, though."

"Doing what?"

"That's what I don't know."

"What will Ginger say?" Guy asked.

"Probably plenty, to Ozzy."

A meal of flat bread, rice, fruit, and lamb was served in an undecorated house with no furnishings aside from a table, chairs and a large but mostly empty desk in the corner.

"Thank you for this," Ginger said, "and for taking time to meet with us."

"It is, unfortunately, the most I have to offer. I had hoped to share my next meal with Porter under better circumstances. Please, eat." Ozzy gestured to the food.

"I told her why you asked us to come," Aiden said, "but none of us know what exactly you have in mind."

"I thank you for bringing them here," Ozzy said to Matt. "I must beg your pardon however, as I have a great need I must ask of them."

"I didn't bring them, they came because they want to help."

Ozzy nodded politely.

"My units are slogging door to door. We fight for every block and can't afford to lose our best men. The noose is tightening. I think we'll cut them off soon, but the experience and capabilities Aiden and Porter bring are invaluable."

Porter thought he knew where this was headed.

"You want us to train your door kickers."

"No. My men are capable. I trained them myself. What I'd like is for you to fight alongside them and deal with the civilians they encounter. We have TACP's who can bomb just about anything I want but I don't want this city turned to rubble. I need my men to sweep out daesh without abandoning civilians in the process. They can't do both. You saw that today firsthand, yes?"

"Yes, we did," Aiden said, looking at Ginger.

"It would not be permissible to take your children into these areas." He turned to Matt. "And I would ask that you consider staying with your current unit in Mosul. There is great need all over, and they are grateful for you, as am I."

"I understand," Matt said, staring into his tea.

"How much time are we talking?" Porter asked. "And what's the chain of command? For us, I mean."

"You're here of your own free will. You'd be free to return on your own judgement. You will not be under anyone's command, in fact I intend to order them to consider you as the authority on tactics, and my son Goriel will convey that to everyone you work with. Nor will I expect you to participate in any action unless you deem it necessary. My hope would be that you," he gestured to Porter, "can advise militarily, and you," he gestured to Aiden, "can help minimize the casualty count, both civilian and military."

A silence followed as the company picked at their meals. Eventually Porter spoke.

"We're not here to fight your war, boss."

"Of course. You must go as God instructs you."

Aiden sat, thinking, and Ozzy ate slowly with his eyes downcast. Ginger eyed Allen, playing with his flatbread. She locked eyes with Shiloh, who gave her mother a weak smile. She looked at Porter as he sat to her left, and remembered the first time she'd ever seen him, pointing a gun at her in the darkness where she laid, naked and afraid.

The city smelled the same as it had then, the night Porter carried her broken, blanket-covered body out of a hell worse than death. On that night, the gunfire she'd once unleashed as an implement of war terrified her, and she'd clung like a child, praying to be as far away from this city as possible. And never return.

She watched Ozzy eat, and realized he had been a part of the huddle of SEALs who'd protected her with their own bodies. Men she'd never expected to meet.

She wondered what fate had swallowed Ozzy's wife and daughter, and she wanted so badly to ask him about it, and to pray with him. She recalled her younger self a few years before meeting Aiden, and how she would run her hands over her belly as Shiloh grew inside of her. The realization that something beautiful was about to come from the horror that preceded it had kept her going when thoughts of suicide and nightmares tormented her; she wondered how many women might be enduring the same hell, just a few miles away.

"You need to go," she said, patting the back of Aiden's hand. "All of you."

"What will you do?" Porter asked, staring at her.

Ginger looked at her plate, and clasped Aiden's hand.

"We'll be fine."

Matt saw the dour expressions across the table. "Come on now, guys," he said, digging in for another helping, "let's not let our hosts' food go to waste. Ozzy, we've got your back." He held up his glass to him. "Anywhere you want, anyway you want it."

Porter took a deep breath, and a slow bite of his food.

12
Boots on the Ground

Ar-Raqqa, Syria

"There's our boy again," Casey Allen said.

Demarius turned to see the Syrian wearing a black robe and white headscarf. "Yeah. Dude is one of them for sure."

"They're all the same. I'd rather bomb this whole country than give these guys more hardware to use against us."

"Whaaat," Demarius adopted his sarcastic voice, "you think we're not doing something strategically necessary to promote democratic principles and secure peace and tranquility to our allies across the globe, man?"

"No." He smiled.

"Yeah, me neither, but we get to blow stuff up. So there's that, at least. Still, you can't complain too much. At least we're getting to help cut down their numbers a little. Better here than at home."

Casey crossed his arms and stared at the man, who caught his gaze and stared back. "I'm more concerned with the ones we're arming. Gonna have to fight them too, someday." He spit his chewing tobacco into the dirt.

Erbil, Iraq

As soon as the airport wifi connected, Jake logged on. Cynthia's face filled the screen with two children vying for entrance into the frame – one beside her, while another sat in her lap and smacked her chin from below with her little head.

"Hi Daddy!"

Jake smiled. "Hey guys."

"Hi, just like normal here, as you can see. Where are you?" Cynthia asked.

"At the airport in Erbil. I figured this might be the last time I get good cell service."

"Won't the hospital have service?"

"I may not even be in a hospital. They're not sure where they want me yet. They've got some new mobile surgical system they're deploying so I may go there. Also there's talk of opening a new forward operating facility nearer the main fighting. Won't know till I get there. How's it going there? Having fun at Grandpa's ranch?"

"Dad, Grandpa took us horse riding. And he even let me SHOOT. HIS. RIFLE. It was awwwwesome!" His daughter filled the screen with her face. "And we saw a snake, and a bunch of lizards, too. Did you know that when you try and grab them, if you get their tail and they run off, it sometimes breaks their tail RIGHT OFF?"

"No, I didn't know that. Sounds bad for the lizard."

"No, Grandpa says they grow back."

"Oh, good. So how's Mom doing?" Jake asked.

Cynthia gave the overly toothy grin that moms make when they mean the opposite of joy.

"Peachy, just peachy." Another grin, but for real this time.

"Sorry I'm not there," Jake offered.

"You'll be sorry when you get back, that's for sure," she teased. "Just kidding, we're having fun. Mom's even been doing breakfast for them and letting me sleep. That's been pretty amazing." The kids slunk out of frame, bored with the adult talk. "It's fun to see the kids excited by all of it," Cynthia said. "How is it so far?"

"Haven't seen anything yet. Aiden or someone is supposed to pick me up here, but I'm waiting till someone comes."

"Okay, text me as soon as you get somewhere new, if you can."

"I'll try and call you tomorrow. I love you. Thank you."

"I love you too. Do you want to say goodbye to them? They're outside but I can round them up."

"No, let them play. I'll call them again soon."

Jake unplugged the adapter from the wall and wrapped it up while surveying the airport. He stowed his gear into his backpack and shouldered it, then walked to look out the windows. He saw familiar shapes and landmarks in the distance.

"Dr. Lyons?" a man said to his left.

"Yes, but please call me Jake. Are you Gary?"

"Yes. It's a pleasure to meet you."

"Glad to be here," Jake said shaking his hand.

"Bull," Gary laughed, "nobody's glad to be here. But we're tremendously blessed."

Jake smiled. "I guess that's what I meant. So what's the plan?"

"Well, are you hungry?"

"Not really. I'm kinda anxious to get settled."

"Good! Let's get you on up to Mosul then. You'll be scrubbing into surgery before teatime."

"I imagined there'd be some red tape before that."

"I doubt it. I know you said you're not hungry, but you might want to eat something on the way. It may be a while before you get another chance."

USS Dwight D. Eisenhower, Mediterranean Sea

Birdie Allen took her tray of food and sat by herself, as usual. Her brief prayer was interrupted by a small group of large, bearded men heading for one of the farthest tables in the corner. They each smiled and nodded to her as they seated themselves a table away, and two of them added a cordial, "Ma'am."

The last of them passed her by, then stopped, turned, and went back to stand in front of her.

"Good afternoon. Mind if I sit here?"

Birdie sat up straight, looked him in the eye, and said in a firm but not unkind voice, "Yes. As a matter of fact I do."

The men at the other table exploded with a litany of joyful insults.

"Burnt him to a crisp," one said.

"Good call, ma'am."

"You'll have to excuse him, ma'am" another said, leaning toward her. "He's not supposed to be out of his cage."

Mario smiled and shook his head. "Alright." He took off his NAVY cap and gave an aristocratic bow. "Milady. I'm gonna be right over there tending my wounds."

Birdie tried not to smile as Mario's razzing continued and increased in volume. She took a sip of her coffee and reconsidered.

"Sir?" she asked, turning to them.

"She speaks!" one of them said, laughing.

"Oh, no. Don't encourage him."

Birdie stifled a laugh and tried to speak eloquently. "If you'd like to join me you may, but you must first refill my coffee. The choice is yours." She sat the mug on the edge of the table and went back to her meal.

Mario stood. "To hear is to obey."

"You're gonna regret it," his friends said.

A moment later he returned with a fresh cup of coffee and pulled his tray over to her table. "I'm sorry for roping you into our juvenile world. I could tell you probably wanted to be alone. My bad. I'm Steve, but they call me Mario."

"Allen. Birdie Allen." She shook his hand.

"Birdie? That's about the hottest name I've ever heard."

She squinted at him. "You need to work on your lines. You're not very good at this, huh?"

He answered with a mouthful of food. "Nowt at awwwll." He swallowed and added, "You gotta admit I'm pretty cute, though."

She shook her head and forked her plate of food.

"Why on earth did I invite you to sit with me?"

"Dumbest thing you'll do today, I guarantee it."

Hammam Al-Alil, Iraq

Jen assisted the surgeon in finishing the fifth procedure of the afternoon. She struggled with the language but was relieved to find most of the doctors, nurses, and volunteers spoke English. It didn't take long for a Norwegian volunteer from Doctors Without Borders to deem her fully qualified to assist in the most complex surgeries, and from that point on she was scrubbing in, back in her element, and getting comfortable.

After an hour, Renas had stopped looking over her shoulder. After two hours, Renas was searching for words to ask Jen about procedures; the doctors, skilled as they were, hadn't the time or inclination to teach as they worked. Jen was the opposite.

The surgeon handed over the suturing of a middle-aged woman's chest to her. As he left, he stopped at the door.

"So, how did you end up here?"

"I came with my husband and some other friends to help out. We met an Iraqi general who sent me here."

"What does your husband do?" Renas asked.

"Well," Jen paused. "I guess you could say he's a missionary now." She chuckled. "He wouldn't like the sound of that."

"Why not?" the doctor asked.

"Eh, you'll understand when you meet him."

"You say so."

He took a last glance at Jen's work and walked out.

"Where are you from?" Renas asked her.

"Florida, that's in the U.S."

"I know. I spent some time in a medical school…in Pittsburgh," she said.

"Sorry. Where are you from?"

"Halabjah."

"Where is that?"

"Near the border with Iran. I came back in 2014, things were…um…prosperous?" she said, wondering if she'd used the correct word.

Jen squinted, focusing on her work. "Uh huh."

"Well, that was then. Now, here we are."

Jen finished the last stitch and they began covering and wrapping the wounds. She realized the other nurses were waiting for her lead.

"Okay, let's move her to recovery."

After they transferred the patient Renas asked, "How long have you been married?"

"Um, about three weeks."

Renas looked at her with wide eyes.

"It's been a long month," Jen added.

Renas took her hands. "You should join my family tonight. And your husband, too."

"I'd like that. But I have no idea where he is right now. Or even what time it is. Or even how long I've been here, in fact."

Renas smiled. "Yes. It's like that here."

The first thing Jake noticed was the smell. Being accustomed to the hyper-sterilized odor of surgical wards at top hospitals, the third-world staging area of a warzone encampment gave him pause. Both he and Gary scanned the area, wondering where to begin.

A woman sat under a canopy with a glazed expression and a dirty covering on her head. A pair of children sat on her lap, and a sudden pain showed on her face.

Gary spoke in another language to a volunteer holding a clipboard and Jake made eye contact with one of the children. He hurriedly buried his head into his mom's neck, causing her to wince again.

Jake turned his attention back to the conversation he couldn't understand.

"She says we should find the lead surgeon," Gary said.

"Great. Where is he?"

"She doesn't know."

The volunteer left and Gary shrugged. Jake turned back to the child who smiled back this time, head still glued to his mother. Jake took gentle steps toward them and crouched in front of the folding chairs.

"Hello," Jake patted his own chest. "I'm a doctor. *Hamil dukturah?*" he asked, almost to himself, unsure of the translation.

The woman opened her eyes wider and spoke rapidly. It became clear that she had something wrong with her side. Jake looked to Gary.

"She has very bad pain. She's been here for hours."

Gary translated a few questions from Jake, trying to diagnose her, but soon they were interrupted.

"Hullo?" a voice cracked behind them.

A man cloaked in surgical scrubs stood behind them, and they rose, Jake gently patting the woman's shoulder as he did so.

"Good day sir," Jake said. "My name is Jake Lyons. I'm a trauma surgeon. I was told you would be expecting me."

"Yes, yes, we are expecting you, Dr. Lyons," the man said wearily. "Come with me."

Jake followed him and exchanged a parting glance with the woman and her children.

"That woman is suffering from a kidney stone, I believe."

"Lucky her."

"Lucky her?" Jake asked, on guard.

"If her kidney was falling out, she'd be unlucky. You didn't come to help us administer drugs for non-life-threatening ailments, did you, doctor?"

"I guess not."

"Good. Because I need you to help me put a man's head back together."

13
Aid Stations

Mosul, Iraq

"Iron sights. Great," Porter grumbled.

"What, can't hit anything without your fancy optics? Getting old, eh?" Aiden asked.

"I got old when I was twenty. Never underestimate the value of overpriced hardware."

"Got too used to the good life of unlimited purchase accounts," Aiden said, handling the Russian rifle.

"Should've spent the cash to get some better rifles in Erbil," Porter sighed.

"It's reliable," Guy said, waiting for them to finish resituating their gear. "I prefer German ones. I'm not here to kill people, though."

"You may not have the choice," Aiden said.

"Count on it," Porter added.

At the aid station, Ehmed and Hozan shook hands with Gary before parting.

"You coming with us?" Aiden asked.

"Yes," Ehmed said.

"Nice." Aiden hugged his kids, then Ginger. "Should have cell contact, from what they say. If not, get us on the comms through Ozzy."

"Be careful," Ginger said.

"We will."

Porter gave Allen a hug, then turned to Shiloh.

"Don't go home without me, Dork."

"Alright, Froggie," she hugged him. "You still stink."

"I know," he said, standing. "That way you'll know when we're on our way back. You guys check in on Jen for me, will ya?"

"Of course," Ginger said. She looked at Aiden, walking away, and said quietly, "Porter…"

"I know. Don't worry, I've got him."

The four of them caught up with Goriel's squad as he was giving instructions to his men in Arabic. When he finished, he filled them in.

"We're moving out on foot, ten minutes."

"Copy that," Aiden said.

Goriel looked them over, and focused on Aiden's artificial leg. "The terrain will be rough, most of the city we'll be operating in is strewn with rubble…"

"Not a problem," Aiden said firmly.

"If you fall behind, we cannot wait for you. You'll be on your own."

"Not a problem."

Goriel gave a slow nod. "Ten minutes."

Deep within the city, the procession inched along a wall, thirteen men in all. Most of the ISF troops led while the civilians kept as close as possible without getting in their way. Two ISF soldiers brought up the rear.

Every chance he got, Porter turned back to check their six. Initially the ISF guys smiled at him; now they gave him annoyed looks, realizing that Porter didn't trust them. He ignored them and surveyed the terrain anyway. During one of these backward glances he spotted movement in a second-story window and paused. A figure darted to the left across the opened window and disappeared.

The ISF soldier spat a command to keep moving but was startled when Porter raised his rifle and aimed at the window directly to the left of the one he'd spotted movement in.

"Contact!" he shouted.

The squad stopped and leveled weapons in every direction. Aiden followed Porter's rifle barrel toward the opened but still vacant window across the street. A tense five seconds passed. He looked at Porter and was about to speak when Porter fired three rounds into the building.

"Move!" Goriel shouted. The line of soldiers hustled down the street, knowing they were now exposed.

Porter and several others advanced while firing and in seconds the squad reached the end of the street, taking cover around a corner.

Goriel shouted orders to his men and several rushed across the street to assault the ground floor. Porter fired three more rounds.

"What was it?" Aiden asked.

"Guy with a rifle," Porter said.

Across the street, shots rang from Goriel's men. As they subsided, Aiden took a few steps toward the building.

"Cover us," he told Porter, crouching with his rifle pointed at the nearest doorway.

"Go," Porter said while he and Ehmed scanned windows and doors across the street, seeing an occasional ISF soldier pass through with raised weapons. One of the soldiers quickly pointed at something with his left hand, and the wall, window, and upper portion of the building exploded.

Porter winced and averted his eyes from the flying concrete that peppered his sunglasses. Smoke and dust swallowed Guy, still in the street.

"Aiden!" Porter yelled, running to where he'd seen them seconds earlier. He held his breath to avoid the smoke and dust, and found Guy laying against a wall, coughing.

"You alright?" Porter took a knee beside his friend, looking him over.

"Just winded…and dizzy," Guy said. "Did you see what happened?"

"Dude probably blew himself up inside. Where's Aiden?"

"I don't know. Go find him."

"You sure you're good?"

"Yes."

They heard voices shouting from inside the building. More shooting. Guy got himself to a wobbly stance and Porter put his arm out to steady him.

"I'm gonna look for Aiden. You should wait here."

"Go, go. I'm fine."

Porter and Ehmed stepped through the entrance and swept the lower floor with their guns. Porter moved left, toward the shouting.

Aiden straddled the arm of one of the ISF soldiers, leaning down with his ear to the man's chest and listening.

He stripped his pack off and laid it open on the ground, then lifted the soldier's arm to expose his armpit. He separated the Velcro of his chest armor to get more room before cutting open the man's undershirt along the ribs, and his left hand felt along the soldier's chest as his right hand opened a pocket from the med kit and pulled out a cannister resembling a large marker with a red lid. Starting in the center of the chest, Aiden worked his fingers to locate the third rib, then he walked his fingers below it and down the right toward the man's back until he found the axillary line he wanted. He took the lid off the cannister with his teeth, turned it over, removed the decompression needle inside it, and inserted the mechanism into the soldier's side all the way to the hub. Then he waited five seconds, listening before removing the needle.

He bent over and listened to the chest again, examined the man's face. Seeing him breathe, Aiden was satisfied enough to start looking toward the next patient. The entire procedure had taken less than a minute.

"Here! Here!" Another soldier under blood-soaked clothing motioned for Aiden as Porter and Ehmed entered the room. The soldier took labored breaths and winced.

"Let's get his armor off, gently," Aiden directed them. "Here, lean him up just a bit."

Porter scanned the room while Guy knelt to assist Aiden. Dark red blood seeped from several wounds but Aiden focused elsewhere. He ran his hand along the man's chest and as he did so, Aiden's expression soured.

"What is it?" Guy asked.

Goriel approached. "How is he?"

"He's got a collapsed lung."

"We should expand it then." Guy said, confused.

"Can't. He's got several broken ribs," Aiden kept feeling along the damaged side, "maybe all of them on this side."

"What does that mean?" Goriel asked.

"It means there's not much we can do for him." Aiden muttered a barely audible word to himself. He took a round canister from his pack and opened it to expand a breathing bag. He placed the mask over the soldier's face and squeezed the bag to administer air.

"What do you mean? He's as good as dead?" Goriel whispered.

"No, but he needs a hospital and surgery, fast. He's got sharp bones cutting into his lung and even moving him might just make things worse." Several gunshots rattled in the distance but it was impossible to tell where they came from. "Can we get a medivac?"

"I can call up an ambulance. But it may take a while to get here."

"Call for it. We'll just have to try and manage his breathing and pain." Aiden looked around, made eye contact with a soldier who was holding his friend's bloody hand. Aiden smiled. The soldier gave a weak smile in return and spoke quietly to his friend. The injured soldier's grip slowly crushed his hand.

Guy patched up the lacerations with light bandages and Aiden gathered his gear, surveying the corridor. Porter removed the partially used magazine from his rifle, tucked it into his back pocket, and reinserted a fresh one.

Porter noticed Aiden examining his bloody hands and forearms.

"Welcome back, buddy. Miss it?"

Aiden removed his gloves and opened a plastic bottle, pouring water on his arms to rinse them, wiping them off on his pants to dry.

"No."

"They gonna live?"

"We'll see."

Porter merely nodded.

Hammam Al-Alil, Iraq

"You're not going to close the amputation site?" Renas asked.

"Not on the first surgery," Jake answered, assessing the pressure cuff. Jake finished the amputation but left most of the intact but damaged tissue in place.

"Why didn't you trim the excess? Clean it up for an even stump?" Rena asked.

"With an umbrella effect blast we have the benefit of additional tissue to draw on. If we just remove it straight, we get a shorter limb with limited function. We may be able to use some of this, so we want to keep all potentially viable tissue, and hopefully restore a larger range of motion. If we discard it now, there's no going back. At least this way we preserve options. There'll likely be several debridements later on."

Rena examined the patient.

"So he may get to use this leg again."

"One can only hope…and pray," Jake smiled under his surgical mask.

Renas' eyes revealed a smile as she looked at the gentleman still under sedation.

"Yes, we will do that."

Jen recognized Jake, sitting at a counter examining a large book.

"Doctor Lyons, right?"

Jake looked up, quizzical, trying to recall the face.

"Yes?"

"I've been meaning to catch you with a free moment. I saw you yesterday and meant to introduce myself."

"Hello," he started to stand.

"I'm Jen. I believe Aiden McCoy mentioned me."

"Jen, that's right. Sorry." He offered his hand. "I'm Jake."

"Good to meet you, Dr. Lyons."

"Please, just Jake. At least, when it's just us, anyway."

"I don't think informality will play too well around here."

"Yeah, maybe," he smiled. "So how do you know Aiden?"

"It's a long story," Jen paused. "But I've known him for a long time. He and my husband, Peter, are friends."

Jake nodded, trying to recall Aiden's military buddies.

"He goes by Porter," she smiled, "but I knew him as Peter first. We just got married a few weeks ago, actually."

"Right. Yeah, I know who Porter is, but we've never met. I know he and Aiden go way back." A look of recognition came over Jake's face. "Afghanistan, actually."

She averted her eyes, took a breath.

Jake bit his lip, wondering.

After a pause, Jen answered. "Aiden saved my first husband's life. On the battlefield, that is. Porter was there. He died later on from his injuries, at home, with me."

Jake nodded. A long silence.

"Aiden saved my life as well," he said finally, "in a way."

"Yeah," Jen smiled, "he does that."

Mosul, Iraq

An hour later Aiden watched the ambulance pull away. He, Guy, and Porter hung back while the ISF soldiers vented their frustrations in various ways, eventually settling on angry silence.

"Saved one of them," Porter offered weakly.

Aiden said nothing. He turned around with his hands on his hips, slowly taking in his surroundings, pausing at each new direction. After a minute he turned and faced them, he shook his head at the ground, but then met their gaze with a different expression.

"We did what we could. Lotta people here who need us."

Guy nodded, and Porter removed the magazine from his back pocket and started refilling it.

14
Two Days Later

Ginger sat on the bed with Shiloh once Allen was finally asleep.

"Are you alright?"

Shiloh gave a small nod. "Yeah."

"Are you sure? It was a hard day. I'm sorry you had to see some of those injuries."

Shiloh nodded again. "Yeah."

Ginger waited, knowing there was more.

"There's so much…" Tears cut off her words, and Ginger hugged her tighter.

"I know. You were so strong today."

"I don't feel strong. If I were strong I wouldn't be here blubbering."

"No, it's because you're strong that you can talk about it. Some people bottle it up. It's good to let it out."

"You don't seem to be bothered by it."

"I am, trust me. I just have more experience with handling it."

"Was it like this when you were here?"

Ginger closed her eyes, took her time in answering. "Yes and no," she said finally. "Honestly, even though I know this country pretty well, I don't think I ever walked the streets or met the people face to face. I always flew over it, watched it through instruments and the windows. And every broken down or bombed out building we pass, I can't help but wonder if me or my friends fired the shot that destroyed it."

"Is that why you retired from the Army?"

"No." Ginger closed her eyes, wondering if this was the moment she'd feared all of Shiloh's life.

"So why did you retire?"

Her heartbeat accelerated. A cold sweat began in her forehead and worked its way down her spine.

"I was medically discharged. That means I got injured and had to retire."

"How did you get injured?"

Ginger put her hand on her forehead, thinking, praying.

"I was on a mission, pretty close to here actually. My helicopter got shot down. I got hurt pretty bad."

"And you couldn't fly after that?"

"Not for a long time."

"How long ago was that?"

Ginger stroked her daughter's hair. "Ten years ago."

Shiloh was silent for a moment and Ginger knew she was doing the math.

"So I was born around that same time?"

"No, you were born later. I got pregnant with you…" she continued in a whisper, "around the same time as my accident."

"Oh." A long pause. "Is that how my birth father died?"

She weighed the question, wondering if a ten-year-old could ever understand the answer. *Is she ready? Will she ever be ready?*

"I don't know how he died, but I believe he did die around the same time." It was technically true.

"I…I think I'm going to go to sleep now," Shiloh yawned.

"Good," she said, stifling her relief. "Let me know if you need anything."

"Okay."

She watched Shiloh take the cot beside Allen, and considered trying to sleep as well. But she knew it would be hopeless for many hours to come.

Machine gun fire had them pinned down in one direction. Goriel crawled over to Aiden.

"You wait here. We're going to advance around the right and flank them."

"Copy," Aiden answered. He and Porter slunk down with their backs to a wall.

"We good here for now?" he asked.

"Not for long." Porter searched the area across from them, listening to the brief interludes between gunfire.

Nearby on the left they heard a man shouting, followed by the frantic voices of a woman and child crying. The man shouted again. Aiden got up instinctively and moved to look in the direction of the voices. Guy followed him while Porter and Ehmed hung back, seeking targets. A few feet away the wall ended; Aiden and Guy had gone as far as possible.

The voices grew louder, more desperate. Suddenly the man emerged from behind a pillar with the woman and three children following, all crouching from the noise of battle around them.

The man made eye contact with Aiden and was terrified, but his expression changed to relief and he spoke to the woman, pointing to Aiden, then ushered his children over the natural barricades.

Aiden held out his hand.

"No, no!" he shouted, shaking his head.

The man picked up a child of around four or five years old and put him on his hip as he took the next oldest child's hand. The woman paused, seeing Guy and Aiden waving them away. She hurriedly turned to her husband as another volley erupted. The walls near the family flaked from the impact of high caliber rounds, cutting down the mother and the child with her. The remnant of her family disappeared behind the wall.

Aiden locked his eyes on their position, his body poised and ready to spring toward them like a dog straining against his leash.

"Porter! Get me some covering fire!"

"Stand fast!" Porter commanded.

Aiden obeyed, seething. Time inched past as he heard children crying. Different caliber gunfire rang out in a coordinated precession, then silence.

From far away they heard Goriel call, "You're clear." He stood on a second story ledge and waved down to Porter. "We've got them."

Aiden darted from his position and in seconds was into the carnage. The woman's body still cradled her child though both were long gone. The older children lay on top of their father, all of them blood splattered and pawing at their father who was breathing heavily, his eyes staring skyward, his weak voice speaking rapidly.

Aiden peeled away one of the boys whom Guy took aside to assess. Aiden did a quick blood sweep confirming the shots had penetrated the father's back, leaving the other boy unharmed by the bullets he had shielded him from.

Porter came up behind Aiden and took the boy in his arms, trying to comfort him while giving Aiden room to work but they all knew immediately it was probably a hopeless task. Aiden stuffed combat gauze into the worst of the many holes as the man's breathing grew fainter. He paused, debating if he should waste one of his few chest seals, thinking, searching for any advantage he might use to save the man's life. *Maybe if I could get him some blood? Maybe if we can just keep the man's heart beating a little longer.* He recalled how long it had taken to get an ambulance out here previously, for a critically wounded special ops soldier. Aiden placed his ungloved hand on the man's forehead, gently moving a strand of hair from his eyes.

The father turned his head slightly, noticed Aiden, then saw Guy bandaging his son. The boy scooted away from Guy and over to his father, took his hand, and wept. An attempt to speak failed, his last breaths insufficient to even speak the boy's name. He died with his eyes fixed on the oldest of three sons, the last of a family suddenly whittled down to two.

Still on his knees, Aiden slumped and closed his eyes. His hands hung at his sides and for a long time he said nothing. Then slowly he gathered up his gear, repacked his med kit, stood, and shouldered his rifle. He looked at Porter holding the boy who now stared into space, his head resting on Porter's chest.

"Let's…" Aiden paused, watching the boy. "Let's get them out of here. Maybe…perhaps they've got some family left…somewhere."

Porter watched the first stars appear after the sun had surrendered the day. He drank from a cup of tea one of Goriel's men had provided and took a silent accounting, just like he'd always done on nights following days like this.

A short distance away, Aiden was talking on his phone, running a hand through his hair; Goriel and one of his officers each ate from an MRE, probably settling down for the night, Porter judged, though he knew neither would sleep much, if at all.

Guy sat in conversation with three of the Iraqis and Ehmed. Porter had been half listening to it for several minutes but now he walked over and sat with them. He leaned back against his rucksack next to Guy as both sipped their tea.

"Where is that exactly?" the Iraqi interpreter asked.

"Right in the center," Guy laughed. "Here," he pulled out his phone and opened the map. The start point was already on Mosul and Guy typed in *Central African Republic*. The Iraqis crowded to see the screen and the image zoomed out from the Middle East, changed the positioning of the Earth, and zoomed in again on the center of the African continent. He zoomed in further with his fingers.

"Our facility is here, near the southeast. We often operate in the rural areas and neighboring countries, southern Sudan, Congo."

Guy waited for the translation to pass through. One of them brought up the map on his own phone and Guy put his away. They continued through the interpreter.

"And you do this work currently? You were doing this right before you got here?"

"Yes, all three of us."

They glanced at Porter and Aiden, and spoke among themselves. They asked Ehmed questions and he mostly nodded, sometimes shaking his head in bewildered reply.

"And what do you do with them after you rescue them?"

"We try to reconnect them with family," Guy explained, "but many have none left. Sometimes they've been brought too far, or it's too dangerous for them to return. Most end up in our care, or with other orphanages like ours. They'd have little hope otherwise."

"Have you been in many fights? With these militias?"

"I have been fighting for them or against them almost my entire life. Yes, many fights."

They addressed Porter. "And you? Many fights?"

"Not as many as him," Porter shrugged. "Done most of my fighting here, before ever going there."

"And him?" they gestured to Aiden in the distance.

"Yeah, he's been in a few."

"And he is your leader?"

"Yeah, but we were friends before that. He roped me into it." Porter smacked Guy on the leg. "Could have retired on a beach if it hadn't been for these clowns."

They laughed but seemed confused in the translation. Porter noticed and continued.

Porter nodded toward Aiden. "Yeah, he's been in fights. We met in one of the worst ones I've ever been in. Afghanistan early on. It's how he lost his leg."

"We've been wondering how he lost his leg. Our commander didn't seem to know."

"Ask him," Porter said.

They nodded again.

"Actually, he'll probably just blow you off with a joke." Porter set the tea down and leaned forward. "That guy over there…he's good in a fight. He may not look it, but if stuff starts hitting the fan, get near him…and keep him alive." Porter waited for the translation then he continued. "He lost his leg saving my best friend's life. And saved a truckload of other dudes along with him." He leaned back and picked up his tea again, and silence ensued until the translator addressed Guy.

"You, he, all of you… why do you come here to help us? You risk your lives to help us defeat daesh?"

Porter looked away.

Guy nodded. "We are all going to die someday. God will decide when and where."

The Iraqis smiled, talking among themselves. One of them reached over and patted Guy on the shoulder, speaking in his own language before excusing himself from the group and walking off alone.

Guy asked the interpreter, "What did he say?"

"He says, 'You are like us.'"

Jen sat on the torn loveseat and for the first time in what felt like days, checked her phone and was relieved she had no messages. Years of loving soldiers had taught her that no news is good news. She put it away and let her eyes shut for however much time fate warranted.

Sometime later, she awoke to the sound of a spoon quietly stirring in a cup.

"Sorry," Renas said softly. "I didn't mean to wake you."

"Oh no, I didn't mean to fall asleep. I was just…taking a break."

Renas smiled. "Yes." She motioned to the seat next to Jen. "May I sit?"

"Yes, of course." She shifted slightly to make room for her, the way people do even when it's unnecessary. She forced herself to break the awkward silence.

"You are a great nurse. Have you been doing it long?"

"Thank you. Yes," Renas said quietly.

"I'm so sorry this is happening to your country." Jen felt it a weak attempt at camaraderie and wished she hadn't said it.

"I grew up with it."

Sensing Renas didn't want to discuss war, she wondered what to say next.

Renas noticed. "Let me apologize. That was rude of me."

"Oh no, don't worry." Jen sat up straighter. "I didn't mean to pry. Just making small talk, I guess. I know you're as tired as I am."

Rena's patted her hand. "Thank you." After a pause she said, "I was a little girl when I first saw injuries like this. The war with Iraq was always there. Then it got worse."

"Where was that?"

"Halabjah, where I am from. Sadaam's attacks were frequent, he vowed to wipe out the Kurds and worried always about the Iranians allying with them. Bombs were dropped frequently, sometimes soldiers would swarm us, but then one day Saddam's forces just seemed to give up Halabjah. The Iranians shelled their positions but there was no fight, really. The Iraqis left and the Iranians came in. I was twelve years old and I remember clapping when I saw them. I asked my mother if the war was over, but she and the men were uneasy. Nothing seemed right about it. I went to sleep listening to my parents argue about whether or not to leave but we had nowhere to go.

"The next morning I woke to bombs falling. We ran to our basement shelters but the bombs were not falling on the city, they fell around it. All day the bombs fell and yet there we sat, unharmed. Eventually we heard other sounds and saw smoke, a dirty brown smoke that fell instead of rose. It smelled different too, like rotten fruit or garlic."

Renas paused and closed her eyes briefly before continuing.

"I saw the smoke envelop a playmate down the street. He screamed a scream that still haunts me, and then fell dead. It was gas. Mustard, sarin gas and others, I later learned. It sank and filled the low-lying shelters. Everyone it touched burned and convulsed as the gas attacked their nervous systems. My father lead several of us running for our lives. We climbed a hill and prayed. Some people were instantly blinded, others burned as if tormented by hellfire, some people who breathed it, their lungs liquefied. I didn't know any of this at the time. I just tried to help them but it was pointless, and my father forbid me from touching them. He was right though. There was nothing to be done."

"I'm so sorry," Jen said.

"It was a day that I hope I will never see again. The gas is terrible."

"And now they're using it again…in Syria."

Renas nodded. They sat for another ten minutes, sharing less ghastly conversation. Slowly they both rose, hugged, and went back to work.

Goriel glanced at Aiden's leg. "My father told me about you and Porter. He said not to underestimate you, that you are your nation's best warriors."

Aiden shifted uncomfortably. "Well, maybe Porter is."

"My father is mistaken?"

"No. Don't get me wrong. Guys like Porter, and Guy over there, and probably you no doubt, have ten times the experience I have. I was only in it for a few years. And lost a few guys in the process."

"He said you are both highly decorated."

"Yeah. It's just part of it."

They sat in silence and Aiden wondered if he was being rude. "Still, one nice aspect of it is that my older brother has to salute me even though he always outranked me. He hates that." Aiden grinned, but Goriel looked at him, confused.

"It's just a tradition." Aiden tried another track. "So, what do you want to do when this is over?"

"I don't see it ever being over."

"Well, what would you rather be doing right now? If there was no war?"

"Killing daesh is all I want to do." After a tense pause, Goriel rethought his answer. "I would rather be in my mother's kitchen. Listening to my sister laugh. How about you?"

"I'd rather be with my family."

Goriel nodded. "Then thank you for being here with us, instead."

15
Goods and Services

Incirlik Air Base, Turkey

The Syrian stood in the shadows of the aircraft's wing and stomped his feet on the concrete, watching the last pallet fork-lifted out of the chartered airliner. He checked his watch, calculating the remaining time before the sunrise. Three hours at least, plenty to get airborne and complete the next leg.

He craned his neck to shake off the sleepiness. He'd soon be able to grab a desperate hour of shut eye, but not until he was in the air on the next aircraft. Stacks of cargo moved up the ramp of a U.S. Air Force C-17 and the portly man made his way to it, moving in the shadows of the floodlit tarmac as much as possible.

Air Force crewmen secured the cargo with impressive speed and minimal communication, and in minutes the plane was ready for takeoff. He stepped onto the ramp and quickly found a seat inside, making zero eye contact with the crewmen who worked as though he wasn't there. He briefly stared at the Bulgarian and Serbian text on the crates while watching in his peripheral vision for the ramp to close.

The pilots completed their pre-flight checklists, and after confirming with the tower, the captain checked in with his crew. Lastly, he asked his loadmaster, "And is our passenger accounted for?"

"Affirmative."

"He say anything?"

"Negative. Just sitting in the back. I didn't go near him, thought we weren't supposed to."

"We're not. Let's get rolling."

The Syrian waited until the ramp was closed before looking around. The huge machine lurched forward and soon picked up speed, and he felt the lift as the wheels left the runway. He finally closed his eyes, asleep before the aircraft made its first bank, but he would be wide awake the second the landing gear touched down in Syria. It would likely be the only sleep he'd get for the next few days, but it would suffice. It always did.

Northwestern Syria

Casey examined the crates secured to the truck beds. He strolled around, making a mental note of the caliber designations on the pink invoices attached to the crates — heavy weapons, mortar shells, tubes, grenades, and rockets…lots of rockets. Disgusted, he walked back to his vehicle and saw that stocky, scarred jihadist again and was surprised he had a different look. Gone was the hardened, hateful gaze of the traitorous scum Casey had taken him for; this was an angry but tired face bordering on despair. The man quickly averted his eyes, and Casey almost felt sad for him.

The man disappeared and hatred again spoke sweetly to Casey, comforting him with the hope that he'd one day meet his suspected terrorist leader on the other end of a rifle, and soon.

The man climbed into the passenger seat of a Syrian military vehicle. "Go, now," he commanded the driver.

"I am supposed to follow the convoy."

"Drive. Now. Ahead of them," he said firmly, then lowered his voice. "Do not make me repeat this."

The driver checked his mirrors and pulled away from the group of vehicles.

When they were alone on the road, he closed his eyes and spoke again to the driver.

"Keep your foot on the gas. Stop for nothing until I tell you."

"You want to speed ahead? Not to keep the convoy in the rearview mirror? What about the weapons?"

His eyes remained closed. "They'll get there. I have somewhere else to be." After a moment he added, "Don't speak to me again."

Circling overhead, an armed drone noted each vehicle and assigned them numbers. They and other aircraft watched as the trucks laden with weapons quickly made their way unimpeded across Syria. A lone vehicle traveled far in another direction and was removed from the target list.

Soon the U.S. aircraft were ordered to sever their tracking. The American vehicle escorts stopped and let the trucks continue on their own. With these parallel actions, any knowledge of where the many tons of weapons just smuggled into Syria disappeared along with them.

"Our tax money at work," Casey scoffed.

"Yeah," the driver said. "Hope they know how to use it."

Casey glared at him. "Who?"

"You know. The Kurds, or the rebels, or whoever gets to use them against Assad and all."

"You think they're going out to arm the good guys? Not like there are any."

"Damn, Allen. Why you gotta always be like that? Look, I get it. But I gotta believe some of this will do some good. They're fighting our enemies too, after all."

"Half that stuff will end up in ISIS's hands within a year. Watch."

"ISIS ain't gonna exist in a year, Bro. That's the point. What do you think all these bombs are for?"

After a short pause Casey asked, "Can you name me one war in the modern era that was about winning? Vietnam? We had that in the bag till they pissed it away. Gulf War? Left Saddam in power. Iraq, Afghanistan? How many buddies we lose, and still the rockets are flying at a hundred grand a pop. My brother used to get reamed for not using all of his rockets on a mission. Seems to me it's just a lot of pretext to keep the fireworks flying with a lot of us dying."

Chugiak, Alaska

Abby heard a noise from the bedroom and followed the sound: a news report from Josiah's laptop as he sat up in bed. He looked at her without pausing the video and she slid next to him.

The reporting bounced between maps of Iraq and Syria with videos of military jets followed by gun camera footage and interviews with civilians on the ground, all underlaid by narration Josiah had heard plenty of times before. A bold red script at the bottom of the screen read, "DEVASTATION IN MOSUL."

After the standard six-minute clip, the talking heads moved onto other matters and Josiah muted the player.

"I thought you'd gone to sleep," Abby asked. "Don't you have an early flight tomorrow?"

"Yeah. Just got sucked in."

"That happens pretty easily since Aiden went over. Have you heard from him?"

"Just his email update a few days ago."

"What's wrong?" she asked, raising an eyebrow.

"I'm not sure. I just feel like we could do more."

"More how?"

"Not going over," he assured her. "Just…I don't know. It's hard to sit here and see all of that," he gestured to the screen, "and I just don't know how to do anything about it."

"You mean flying missions, right? You miss that part of it?"

"No. I got my fill, believe me."

"So, flying a 737 with over a hundred passengers isn't enough responsibility to carry?" she smiled. "Captain? Need a bigger challenge?"

"The computers do most of the actual flying. I just sit there like a dummy and try not to spill coffee or food on my shirt."

"Hardly. But I imagine it doesn't compare. So, you're bored?"

Josiah closed the laptop, set it aside. Abby took his hand.

"I'm just tired. Gotta get up and put on that fancy captain's hat soon anyway."

"You better."

Abby got up and walked past the kids' rooms, only one of which was still occupied; the others had become storerooms for kids who'd already flown the nest. She shut the windows, and in the quiet shadows cast by a sun that didn't really ever set in the summer she heard the sound of a single engine aircraft passing overhead. It was probably a puddle jumper, ferrying fishermen to a remote camp somewhere; the sky was always filled with them. She sat in a chair by the big living room window and remembered all the times such planes would prompt her to pray for the man who now slept in a safe bed a few meters away, a man who once dropped bombs and unleashed a 30mm auto-cannon for a living.

She prayed he would be happy, but knew he was unsatisfied. And like him, she had no clue what to do about it.

Northern Syria

"Up."

Hazail heard the quiet command and opened her eyes, along with the other women and young girls. Their slowness to rise elicited a wall-shaking command.

"Get up now! Up! Up!" The barking was punctuated with kicks at the closest girl, who scrambled to her feet and attempted to move to the far corner.

The man grabbed her by the hair and yanked her backward, cursing, and then spat on her face. "You want to leave, yes?" He smiled. "Good. You shall leave…and we shall find you a husband today." He laughed and threw her at the feet of the others.

"Now out, into the truck." He waved with his gun for them to leave.

As Hazail moved past, he leaned in close and grabbed her arm so hard it made her wince.

"Maybe I will purchase you for myself." He smiled again before releasing her to continue with the others.

In the back of the truck, Hazail clutched the hand of an older girl who whispered to her.

"Tell me. What does your God say will happen to us now?"

Hazail blinked away her tears. "I don't know."

"Will you ask him for me?"

She nodded and whispered, "Yes. Always," she said, trying not to sob.

Raqqa, Syria

The Syrian walked through several corridors past armed men before finally entering a warehouse filled with orchestrated chaos. He searched for his contact and was quickly recognized by a large man with a long grey beard sitting on a riser, flanked by security, who nodded to him and waved him up.

He made his way boldly past security and was met with an embrace from the elder, who kissed him on each cheek.

"Welcome. Come, come. Sit," he said, waving a less important acquaintance out of the chair next to him. He gestured to tables of food and drinks. "Enjoy. Please."

The Syrian helped himself to the food and sat. "Thank you."

"You look terrible. You must learn to relax more."

"I work much."

"Too much. But the need is great."

The area below them was crowded with mostly Syrians but also eastern Europeans and westerners of Anglo descent, and it was clear that an auction was about to commence. A young woman was thrust forward by rough hands to stand between two drum barrels. The crowd erupted in bids and counter bids.

The Syrian followed the bidding for a moment but turned to his food and slowly ate. His host noticed his disinterest.

"Do you see that young beauty down there?" he asked.

"Yes. Very beautiful," he said dismissively. "That's not why I came."

The elder leaned back and smiled. "Yes, of course. But you can mix some pleasure with your business, no doubt."

"Yes, perhaps I will." He turned his attention back to the sales floor.

They watched the slave auction move much faster and cheaper than the Syrian expected. He took greater interest as the elder watched him closely.

A teenage girl's price rose sharply beyond the others and the hollered bids grew louder. She began to cry and her handler pulled her hair, causing her to yelp and drawing laughter from some in the crowd. Others argued and raised their bids.

"You like that one?" the elder asked, leaning forward. He stared hard, waiting for a response.

"Too old for my taste."

The elder laughed. "Just wait, there will be more to come."

"Are you pleased with your shipment?" the Syrian asked, getting down to business.

"Not exactly what we were expecting."

"You got what was promised."

"They're almost entirely Eastern European designs."

"Easier to use and acquire than the top-shelf American hardware. And easier to replenish," he answered, still watching the auction. "Are you disappointed?"

"Not at all. But keep in mind we are fighting both Russians and Americans now, along with the others."

"What you've been given will kill just as efficiently. Ask the Bosnians…or the Yemeni."

"What else can you provide?"

"It will depend on what you want."

"Heavy machine guns, artillery shell, and surface to air missiles."

"The Americans will never supply you with SAMs directly."

"Then get them for someone else they do deal with. We will acquire them indirectly afterward. Can you get them?"

"Perhaps. How about Russian SAMs?"

"Less reliable."

"Less expensive."

"How long? For either."

"A week at least to set up a meeting either way. Perhaps a month after that."

"I can acquire them from the Russians through other suppliers sooner than that."

"Yes. There are plenty of outdated and faulty weapons available through other suppliers."

The elder folded his arms and stewed, but soon smiled again.

"Fine. Contact me when you have a price."

"Certainly."

Hazail was kicked from behind. "Now! Go." The man prodded her from a dank room out into the warehouse, and her eyes darted desperately for any sign of comfort.

Lord, help me. What am I to do? She made unintentional eye contact with several men; a cold shudder that began in her scalp washed down to her toes, and her legs shook. She gasped for air and turned to face her handler, seeking a direction she could breathe in.

With a hand like a plank he slapped her, and the crowd was angered. Another man grabbed him by the collar.

"Don't damage her!" The older handler shoved him aside and pulled Hazail to the front with almost equal violence.

The slap reset Hazail. Her panic remained but she did not show it as her legs found they could support her. She tuned out the voices and the faces, let them blur and she prayed.

God. Please help me.

Like everyone else, the Syrian's attention was garnered by the slap. He examined the young woman as she stood, staring blankly before her.

"That one you like. I can tell," the elder teased.

The Syrian looked at her feet, her once colorful but now soiled garments, and eventually settled on her innocent, beautiful eyes; a red blotch highlighted the slapped side of her face.

"Yes," he said softly.

"Then…" the elder stood, "she shall be my gift to you." The older man's voice boomed out a bid so large it silenced the crowd as all eyes turned to him.

Hazail looked up to the man who had just silenced the room. She averted her eyes to avoid looking at him directly and noticed a man beside him with a large scar on his neck staring at her with eyes that she'd not seen yet in any of her captors. It wasn't like the same angry looks she feared for so long and so often. This was markedly different — more determined, directed…passionate.

Hazail shuddered and tears welled up in her eyes.

God no. Please, no.

Rough hands took the girl and handed her over to two armed men. The Syrian stared, watching as the security guards took her out of sight and a new woman was placed on the auction block.

"Consider her a down payment, friend."

The Syrian stared, mute and nearly trembling, at the elder.

"And a bonus for you. I shall wait, anxious to hear what you are able to procure."

He took his cue and stood.

"Yes. I will contact you very soon." He descended the risers and commanded himself not to run after the guards who temporarily possessed his precious cargo.

16
Calculations

Porter rose from the surf wearing only his khaki UDT shorts. He stood and wiped the tropical water from his eyes and forehead. On the beach lay seven men dressed like him, soaking up the sun and all wearing sunglasses. Before he could speak, the sound of a jet engine screamed out.

He opened his eyes to the sound of passing aircraft and blinked himself further awake. Most of the ISF soldiers were still asleep but Aiden sat on a crate, keeping watch alongside two of Goriel's men. Porter rolled onto his knees and rubbed his eyes, then slowly got to his feet, feeling achier than he was used to.

"Morning," Aiden said.

He merely grunted.

A jet passed overhead, followed by a pair of explosions that jarred those on the ground watching through binoculars. Porter double-checked his gear and readied himself to move.

"Let's go," Goriel ordered as the dust cleared.

At first light they'd hooked up with a larger force of ISF and American Special Forces, including the JTAC team currently directing air support into the ground targets. The squad now worked its way down from that position toward the street level of the neighborhood just hit. It didn't take long before fire from concealed machine guns punctuated the waning morning hours.

"Take cover!" Goriel yelled.

After a few minutes it was clear they could advance no further in that direction, and Goriel's men double backed, frustrated at having to wait again.

"I'm gonna go check in with our guys," Porter told Aiden, and made a brisk trot over to the Americans.

"Right behind you."

Aiden and Porter listened in as the JTAC communicated with two F-16s circling far in the distance.

"Copy. Out," the JTAC officer said into the handset. "Damn."

"Hey brother," Porter said. "Anything we can do to help?"

"Yeah, go kill 'em."

"Rather you do it."

"Trying, man."

"What's the problem?"

"They're getting real good at suppressing their muzzle flashes. It's nearly impossible for our guys overhead to pinpoint which building they're operating from."

"We know they're in that one." Porter gave a five-finger point. "Can't you just hit it?"

"By the time we get it relayed in and approved, they'll already have moved."

"They're using tunnels, too," the American next to him added. "Practically the whole city is connected underground so they're moving from here to there. We walk 'em in on a target but by the time the bombs release they've already displaced. That last place we hit was probably already empty. Been hitting 'em all week."

"Maybe we can signal the jets directly somehow while they're still overhead?" Aiden suggested.

"Yeah sure," the JTAC said with a chuckle, "go stand in front of it and wave a flag around for the pilots."

"I'll see what I can do," Aiden said. Then to Porter, "Looks like Goriel's moving out."

"Gotta go," Porter said to the Americans. "Stay salty, brothers."

"You too."

The afternoon heat was nearly unbearable. Aiden took a drink of water and heard screaming nearby, then sporadic gunfire farther off in a different direction. He crouched, listening, and moved toward a trash heap behind a torched vehicle. The screaming continued, then gave way to panicked voices.

"There." Guy pointed to a low wall.

Goriel and his men moved the other direction, focused on the gunfire. They took up a defensive position several dozen meters away, waiting for what they hoped was the approaching enemy to reveal themselves.

"Run up and tell Porter we're going to check that out," Aiden told Ehmed, "then come back to us."

"Okay. I'll be right behind you. Be careful."

Aiden and Guy crouched lower and crossed the street, taking cover next to a destroyed Iraqi Bradley on its side.

"Wait here," Aiden said, darting across another street to a pillared entrance of an abandoned corner store. Just as he moved out of view, Porter and Ehmed caught up to their position.

"Where's he going?" Porter asked.

"There was screaming over there. We don't hear it now."

"Come on," Porter said, annoyed. They went in that direction, keeping their rifles pointed toward buildings down the road, the most likely place for concealed snipers.

As he turned the corner, Aiden saw a man laying in the road, bleeding in the shadow of an abandoned vehicle. His chest rose and fell with heavy breaths. Near him lay the bodies of several others, including an older woman whose clothing blew gently in the hot breeze, her eyes fixed open in Aiden's direction. Two uninjured men hovered in a nearby shadow, just beyond the clearing; with them stood a boy about ten years old. One of these noticed Aiden but his attention focused on the bleeding man, giving him instructions that Aiden didn't understand.

Aiden backtracked a few paces, making eye contact with Porter and Guy and waving them over.

"What's goin'?" Porter said.

"Not sure."

Ehmed hollered over to the man across the way, who answered with shouts and frantic gestures.

"Sniper. He doesn't know where."

"Hard to tell from the bodies," Porter said, looking around. He settled on a second story balcony and an open window. "That balcony at eleven o'clock," he said to Guy. "Probably from there."

"Alright. Give me some covering fire into there," Aiden said, setting aside his rifle.

"What are you going to do?" Porter asked.

"Run out to him."

"Like hell."

"He could also be in that other one, near two o'clock," Guys said, lining up the sights.

"You see anyone?" Porter asked Ehmed, the only one of them with optics on his rifle.

"No, but I agree, it's probably from either or both of those balconies."

"Covering fire," Aiden said pointing. "Both windows simultaneously. Should catch him off guard so I can get to that guy."

Guy looked to Porter for approval.

Porter shook his head and swore softly to himself. "Alright. Ehmed, you take two o'clock. Guy and I will hit eleven o'clock. On my cue. Ready?"

They agreed.

"Three, …two…one…Now!"

The three men stepped out and hammered rifle fire into their assigned windows. Aiden shot across the expanse and slid beside the bleeding man, immediately noticing another dead woman next to him, shot through the neck. He realized how little concealment they had, and guessed that was why the man continued to lay flat on his back. Aiden did likewise as Porter and Guy ceased fire, taking their own cover. They reloaded their weapons and watched Aiden.

"I need to move you. Do you hear me?" The man merely shook his head, speaking only to the clouds in the sky overhead. "Hey," Aiden tried again. "*Hal tasmaeuni?*" No response.

To his left Aiden could see the Iraqi men and the child, watching him with anxious interest. To his right he saw Porter and his friends, waiting for his next move.

"Alright, friend. We'll do this here."

Aiden rolled and turned so his face was almost touching his patient's pelvis. He swept his hands over the man's neck, back, and midsection, looking for the source of the blood, finding a single impact that blew out a chunk of the man's thigh but fortunately missed the artery. Aiden immediately threw a tourniquet high on the man's thigh, pulled the tensioner snug, and cranked the windlass down tight, securing it with the Velcro strap.

The man moaned as blood loss rendered him nearly incoherent. Aiden rolled him onto his chest, and with the wound now exposed he shifted, reached into his pocket, and retrieved a large rolled bandage and tore it open. The Israeli-style combat dressing had a plastic mechanism for greater pull-down tension and Aiden had it wrapped tight in seconds while continuing to slither as low to the ground as possible. When he was done, he grabbed the man by the shoulders to pull him to better cover, a few feet closer to the waiting family members.

As he struggled to get leverage, he raised himself a few degrees higher and felt a whisp nick his ear, followed by the single crack of a high caliber gunshot. He hit the deck, sweating, his heart racing, grabbing the ground with both palms.

"Stay down, Aiden!" Porter screamed.

"I need to move him!" Aiden shouted back.

"Okay, two o'clock only, guys. We'll keep a constant barrage till Aiden's clear. Understand?"

"Got it," they said.

"Again, on my mark. Aiden, get ready!"

"Ready!" Aiden said.

Another shot rang out, pinging off the car near Aiden's back.

"Three, two, one, go!" Porter yelled as they sent forth a steady burst of fire.

Aiden got up and tried to drag the man but stumbled and fell. He tried to get up and lift him but the dead weight was too awkward to leverage. He lay back down.

"Cease fire!" Porter commanded.

"Do you see the sniper?!" Aiden asked Porter.

"No. You need to get outta there!"

Aiden paused and looked into the man's eyes, not more a few inches from his own.

Alright, God. Alright.

Porter held up a finger. *Wait.* He huddled with Guy and Ehmed.

"Two of us need to lay fire on fast and heavy, one of us needs to run over and help Aiden move him to cover."

"I'll go," Ehmed said.

"Okay. Guy, keep it up till they're clear."

Ehmed handed over his rifle to Porter. "I want that back."

"Then get him and get back quick, otherwise I'm keeping it."

Guy changed to a full magazine. "Ready."

"On my mark," Porter said. He nodded to Aiden while Ehmed got ready to run.

Aiden grabbed hold of the man's chest.

"In three...two...one...go!"

Guy and Porter erupted fire again.

Aiden took the man by his shoulder, scooping him from underneath. In less than a second Ehmed grabbed the man's other shoulder and together they quickly dragged him to cover, dropping into the shadow of the concrete walls.

Panting, Aiden gave Porter and Guy a thumbs up.

Porter shook his head and slumped down, his back to the concrete.

"Has he always been this hard to temper?" Guy asked.

"Always."

"What about the sniper?"

"Wanna run over and assault his hide?"

"Not really."

"Yeah. Let's have Goriel's guys take him out."

Aiden finished bandaging up the older man and gave him a more thorough evaluation. He also examined the two men and the child, bandaging a few superficial injuries. They were dehydrated and grateful beyond words for the water Aiden and Ehmed shared with them.

"He needs blood," Aiden said. "But I don't think it will be too bad as long as they get him to a hospital soon."

Ehmed translated and the two men picked up the injured man as if making ready to carry him down the street.

"No, wait. We can call up an ambulance to take care of him."

The men nodded and Aiden made a phone call.

"Be here pretty soon. Hopefully."

Ten minutes later Guy and Porter rejoined them.

"Hey, how'd you get over here?" Aiden asked, taking his AK-47 back from Guy.

"Went back and checked in with Goriel to feed him that sniper position," Porter explained. "Then we took a roundabout path a block east. Goriel's moving over to take that sniper's position now."

"Hand it over," Ehmed said, extending his arm to Porter, who gave the rifle back reluctantly.

In the direction of the sniper's position they heard shooting, followed by a grenade, then a few more shots.

"Sounds like they got him," Aiden said.

"He doesn't look too bad," Guy said, referring to the injured man who was almost standing on his own, attempting to fashion a crude crutch from a discarded board. "What's the prognosis?"

"Bullet took a chunk out of his thigh. Lost some blood but he'll be fine if we can just get him outta here. Still waiting on an ambulance. I called Ginger, she said they'd try and get someone on the way."

Another twenty minutes passed, and the men were visibly impatient to get moving.

"How many days have we been out now, anyway?" Aiden asked.

"Six, I think," Guy said.

"Yeah, six," Porter agreed.

They sat in relative silence with only occasional gunfire to be heard.

"Too quiet," Porter said. "And I don't hear any ambulance."

After several more minutes, Goriel and two of his men joined them.

"I just heard over the radio that the ambulance you requested has been routed to another location," Goriel said. "If he's not critical, he'll need to be carried out."

"Yeah, we can do that," Aiden said.

"I need to push forward. We can't escort you if you go back alone."

"I understand," Aiden nodded.

"And there are certainly more seriously injured people farther in," Goriel cautioned.

"Copy that."

Aiden thought it over, and addressed Ehmed. "Will you tell them? Ask them if they think they can move him by themselves."

Ehmed relayed the information, and the civilians nodded, making ready again to leave. After a few heartfelt bows they picked up their elder, now laying on the collapsible stretcher one of Goriel's men had provided for them. Goriel and his squad proceeded quickly in the other direction.

Porter stood aside, growing impatient as Aiden watched the Iraqis depart. They made good progress and kept as under cover as possible, lifting the old man over a barricade. As they did so, the child turned, and seeing Aiden still standing there, he smiled and waved. A torrent rang out from the second story of a building next to them and Aiden watched all four disappear in a ghastly cloud of bullets and blood.

"No!" Aiden's eyes followed the muzzle flash of the machine gun and he sprinted to the building as Porter caught movement in another balcony. A man popped up and starting shooting at him as he knelt to return fire.

"Aiden, you…!" Porter took several shots. "Damn it, stop!"

Aiden sprung ahead so fast he almost tripped when his prosthetic toe caught the edge of a discarded windowpane lying in the road. His anger at misjudging the terrain was dwarfed by a new hatred that propelled him forward, and he used his arms to vault over obstacles that his engineered foot wasn't suited for.

He pointed his gun in and to the left, then toward the right, and saw two men scrambling for their weapons. He fired two controlled bursts, spraying and killing both before they got their weapons raised. Seeing a staircase, Aiden stepped over them and silenced another shooter halfway up.

The dying man dropped, and Aiden shoved him aside and down the stairs as he passed. He slipped on the blood but caught himself, still clutching the rifle with his right hand, and got his footing to continue his frantic climb.

At the top of the staircase an enemy was hurriedly reloading a belt-fed machine gun, mounted to shoot out of the window behind him. The man was dumbstruck by the rifle pointing at him, and Aiden fired two rounds that caught the man's robes in the back before his AK-47 went dry. Seeing his chance, the gunner frantically finished loading his weapon. Aiden removed his rifle's magazine to reload but couldn't feel a replacement.

The world was in slow motion as Aiden calculated where his spare mag could be. He dropped the weapon and drew his hip holster pistol, moving right and forcing his adversary to swing the heavy machine gun even farther.

Aiden fired three times, a classic Mozambique grouping of two to the chest and one to the head, and the machine gunner fell backward. Aiden saw the image of the boy waving him goodbye, and he pulled the trigger again, shot four…five…six…seven. The gunner's body bounced from the bullet impacts.

Cease fire and clear the room, there may be more.

He could see the grateful elder kissing him, and he pulled the trigger again – eight, nine, ten – and he continued firing until the gun went dry. He threw the empty gun at the disfigured body, picked up the machine gun and held it with bloody shaking hands. The weight made him pause and he slowly turned around the room, seeing nothing but smoke and destruction, smelling blood and cordite and sweat. He saw the vantage point out the window where the family had been.

He dropped the weapon at his feet.

Porter crested the final stair just as Aiden dropped the machine gun.

"Aiden, we clear?" Porter looked around. "We clear?!" He lowered his rifle slightly as he turned the corner and looked down the hall.

Aiden answered softly, staring at his last victim. "I don't know."

Porter took careful steps. "Wait here." He left the room, clearing the floor.

Aiden watched out the window as Goriel's men fanned over the street, searching for other enemies.

Porter returned. "We're clear, boss. You alright?" No response. "Aiden?"

"We can't do this."

Porter looked over the bodies.

"We can't keep doing this," Aiden said, rubbing his forehead. "What we've been doing. They're just too many. We can't help these people this way. The math doesn't work."

Voices in the lower floor called to them.

"Copy! We're clear up here!" he shouted down to Goriel, then took a seat on an upturned crate, removed his dirty Red Sox ball cap, stained with the dust and grime of thousands of days of combat in Iraq and elsewhere. He wiped the sweat from his forehead before putting it back on.

"It's just war, man. Doesn't ever change….but we don't have to be here. It's okay if you want to bug out."

"That's not what I mean," Aiden said. His voice had a different inflection, one Porter had grown to know after years of battles together, small and large, physical and psychological. "We have to kill all of them." He picked up his discarded pistol from the dead man's lap, reloaded it with a fresh magazine, and holstered it. "They're never going to stop. That guy we met back in Erbil was right. There's nothing else to do."

Porter stood and crossed his arms, staring at his friend. "There's that look again. The one you had when we were chasing Josey."

The former SEAL turned away and paced the room, considering the years he'd spent training to do exactly what Aiden was now proposing. He thought about the snowy, windy battlefield high on a mountain in Afghanistan where he and Aiden had fought and bled together. He thought about the years in Iraq, Somalia, Yemen, and a dozen other places — hunting down, capturing or killing America's most wanted enemies. He considered the elite operators like Aiden and a hundred others he'd trained; some were high ranking leaders like Ozzy and Mario, others were long-dead friends. Porter stared at the Islamic Caliphate's two most recent casualties.

Goriel reached the top of the stairs with a couple of his men.

"You cleared it?" he asked.

"Did a quick sweep." Porter said. "Couple of dead dudes down there you should check out. Didn't look for weapons caches, though."

Goriel nodded, and he and his men left to complete a thorough check as Guy and Ehmed stepped in the room, surveying the scene, saying nothing.

"Okay," Porter finally said. "We can do that…I can get with Ozzy and get us outfitted for war instead of what we're doing now. We can spend the next three weeks or however long you want killing them, day and night, as many as Ozzy will let us. He'll jump at it. Probably give me a field commission or however the hell it works over here.

"You'll end up with ten times more kills than saves. And you'll be satisfied you did your part here as much as you were able. But you'll never think you did enough, not that way, because these monsters always come back. Different places, different languages. Here, Africa…hell, Boston for that matter. It don't matter. You can't ever kill 'em all. But you can protect a few people, get 'em the hell out of here, give them a chance. Small chance, but a chance."

Aiden turned to face him.

Porter continued. "I thought that's what we came here for. Wasn't it?"

Goriel returned, watching the exchange beside the others.

Porter leaned against a wall and broke the cap off a fresh water bottle. "But you know me. Whatever." He took a swig. "I'm good either way."

"Good with what?" Goriel asked.

Aiden paused, looked at the dead ISIS fighters, then turned to Goriel.

"I need to talk to your father," Aiden said. "In person, immediately."

17
The Masters We Serve

USS Dwight D. Eisenhower, Mediterranean Sea

Mario stood at the front of the small briefing room that contained his SEALs and a few of the ship's officers. A split-screen image appeared on the screen beside him, showing a modest but modern fenced-in building on one side, and an overhead view of it on the other.

"We'll touchdown here," he tapped the screen, "in this parking area inside the wire. Move into the facility in two groups. Me, Derrick, and Sean as the assault element will hit this entrance, leaving the security element for this receiving area. Doors should be wide open and there should be – note, *should* be – no resistance. Alpha will clear the target building and link up with Bravo at the receiving dock. If we encounter anyone inside, we'll detain them and bring them along. Should all be civilians except for the two CIA field officers who should already have them stacked up and ready to leave before we get there."

Another graphic of fifteen photos went up on the screen.

"The official count is 15 personnel, all employees…and again, *should* be grouped in this receiving dock waiting for us. We ID them — you've got their profiles there – and then load them up in the Chinook. Once they're all accounted for and loaded, they're off."

"We'll have fighter and drone cover for the duration of the op. If everything goes according to plan, our Blackhawk will be there right after the Chinook clears off, and we're done. The lead CIA officer will escort the civilians wherever the hell he's taking them. The other one will be catching a ride out with us to the FOB to debrief and await orders. Total time on the ground should be less than ten minutes. Any questions?"

They shook their heads.

"Once we're clear, we give the green light and our guys take it out from above."

The men nodded. One asked, "How we gonna know it's clear to bomb if we don't sweep the entire facility?"

"That's on the case officers on the ground. Remember, this is a suspected chemical weapons facility. We don't enter beyond the target building and adjacent receiving dock, and nothing leaves that place but the folks we're there to get. If people aren't all accounted for, don't go looking around for them and risk stumbling into a roomful of VX. The agency spooks will make the call, it's their rodeo."

A hand went up. "A chemical weapons site with no private security? Really?"

"No clue. Maybe they bolted, maybe they weren't paid enough. Remember, a lot of bad people want to capture this facility. If they want it intact, we can expect opposition, so be ready for action. We've got good air support if we need it and should have plenty of warning before touching down."

The men all sat with expressionless faces as Mario looked around.

"Good deal. Topside in exactly one hour. Dismissed."

Birdie Allen was walking with a shipmate when she saw the SEALs on their way back to their gear room. At the back of the line, Mario made quick eye contact with her and nodded.

"Ma'am."

Birdie glanced back to watch them leave.

"Looks like they're heading out," her companion said. "They've got that game face on."

"Yeah," Birdie agreed. "Wonder if we'll see them again."

Syria

Hazail sat in the rear of the vehicle, too terrified to cry. All she could do was stare at the back of his head through the thin black veil covering her face. She had tried initially to signal vehicles to her left through the tinted windows but it seemed pointless. He seemed unconcerned with her feeble attempt to free herself from the zip-tied wrists the other man had secured when he had sat her down and rubbed her head mockingly, laughing, before closing the door.

She'd learned from a hundred slaps that one dare not ask them anything — where he was taking her, why they were alone, or what was going to happen next. She guessed the answers to those questions anyway, didn't want to hear a lie any more than the truth, and worried that hearing his voice would be worse than silence. Beatings and other violence had trained all the captives not to speak. They'd been forced to watch the punishments inflicted on those who spoke out of turn, or the sadistic executions of those who dared to resist. The images, the screams, and the smells still haunted her.

He hadn't spoken yet. Not to the men who handed her over, nor to her. She only knew it was him from the brief eye contact they'd shared earlier; he was a nameless, scarred terror with eyes indicating a familiarity with death, and hatred, and Lord knew how many other demons.

Father in heaven…

Hazail called out to the only family she had left in the world. Not for rescue, or for endurance, or strength; she had long since given up hope. She merely asked for the only thing she believed was still possible.

Please let me die before he touches me.

But God was silent.

The midday sun blazed overhead as the SUV pulled into a darkened garage. An isolated building on an even more isolated road absorbed the man and his cargo, and not a soul saw them since no human existed for dozens of miles in every direction.

The man stepped out and opened the rear door. He still refused to speak but motioned for her to exit the vehicle.

Hazail slowly slid out, her hands were still bound, and the Syrian put his hand out to steady her. His heavy, weathered grip made her tremble. In a flash he opened a large and deadly looking knife whose snapping sound upon locking open made her gasp.

He leaned in and took her arm, raised the point of the knife to her wrists, and cut the zip ties, more carefully than she expected.

He wants me…untainted.

The man closed the door and removed her shroud so he could look at her. She avoided his gaze and stared at the ground.

Never look them in the eyes. They always beat those who look them in the eyes.

"Come," he said, and led her from the garage and into the house. She rubbed her wrists, searching the garage for a weapon, but aside from the SUV it was completely empty. She followed him into his lair.

He stood aside as she passed and motioned her to continue down the corridor. She smelled nothing but him, saw nobody else, heard nothing else. A few feet in he directed her to a small room on the left. She paused at the doorway, staring at a twin bed holding a thin, sheetless, and heavily stained mattress. A bare nightstand and a corner chair were the only other furnishings. But there was a window — she was surprised to see a window, and was even more amazed it wasn't barred, and had a latch one could open from the inside.

She had not slept in a room with a window since she was abducted. Even from this distance she could tell it had a perfect, elevated view of the roads, two of them, and she could see for more than a mile down both in each direction.

I could escape. Maybe after? Maybe even before?

She sensed the man nudging up behind her; she stepped into the room as far away from the bed as she could manage while still getting a few feet away from him.

"Sit, please. I will return momentarily. Do you need to use the bathroom?"

Hazail shook her head no.

Now? Can I get out the window in time? Before he returns? Lord, help me.

"I will be back." He turned and closed the door behind him.

She jumped to the window and examined the barren landscape. There was nowhere to go, nowhere to hide.

Perhaps I could hide somewhere in the building. The roof? Till he leaves?

She reached for the latch. It opened. But her legs refused to move. Her feet stuck fast to the ground as if planted in concrete. Her arms were equally paralyzed.

In a nearby bathroom the Syrian splashed cold water on his scarred face and stared at himself in the mirror. He stroked his long beard and wiped the water from it. Slowly he straightened and removed his robe from over his head. Underneath he wore a white tank top, stained with sweat, and cargo pants with bulging pockets. On the tactical belt hung a holster securing a 9mm pistol, a double magazine holster filled with additional rounds, the knife, three grenades, a small med kit, and a phone case. He removed the gun and placed it on the bathroom shelf, then removed the belt and placed the heap on the back of the toilet. He took another look at his twenty-pound overweight frame in the mirror, stared at his own reflection, then turned and walked back to the bedroom.

Not far away, a Chinook flew high over the desert with a Blackhawk escort on either side. Most of the six SEALs on board closed their eyes for the flight, waiting for the signal to prepare to disembark.

Mario studied the images on his tablet, running over the mission template they'd practiced again in his head. Land, secure the site, grab the civilians, leave. *It doesn't get much simpler than that.*

The doorknob turned and Hazail jumped, her legs unfrozen as she scuttled away from the window and into the far corner, her eyes gauging the space between him and the opened door, her heart accelerating as she noticed his bare arms and the multiple scars up and down the left side of his body.

He entered slowly and closed the door behind him.

All hope of overpowering him vanished as she saw his physique. He had a beer belly but also muscular arms that looked as if they could rip a person in half, and may have done so.

God help me.

He gestured to the chair. "You may sit."

She obeyed, gingerly sitting on the very edge, visibly shaking.

"I'm not going to hurt you."

The words were but an echo and she said nothing.

"I said I'm not going to hurt you. Do you believe that?"

She lied with a nod.

"What is your name?"

"Ha..Hazail," she offered weakly.

"Hazail, I know it is hard for you to trust me, and you're wise not to. I'm sorry I couldn't explain this to you earlier but you must understand that neither of us are safe right now."

She nodded again.

"We don't have much time. I must depart soon and we don't have many options."

She stared, confused and afraid to speak.

"Do you know where your family is? What is your father's name?"

The mention of her father stirred an even greater trepidation. He had warned her all those years ago.

Never tell them about me, her father had warned her, *or your brother. They will use you or me to blackmail others. Do you understand?*

She had not understood then, but she did now.

"They're gone. He…"

Don't lie to him, a voice said in her head.

She meant to say her father was dead, but the voice was so prominent, so authoritative, so unlike any she had ever heard.

The man waited and it became clear Hazail meant to remain silent.

"Where are you from?"

"From…Iraq."

"Do you know where you are now?"

She shook her head.

"You're in northern Syria. How did you get here?"

"We fled across the border. When they attacked our home. My fa—" She stopped speaking and stared at the floor.

"Your father told you to flee?"

She nodded.

"It's okay. I said I won't hurt you, or him. Do you know where your mother is?"

"We were separated, years ago, maybe."

"It's okay to be scared, Hazail. I'm scared too."

She looked up at him. No man had ever admitted being scared.

"You are very brave. I can see that in you. Does Allah make you brave?"

A firmness overtook her small frame and her hunched shoulders straightened. Old images of her father came rushing back, images of him in uniform commanding troops, images of his smile radiating on his infrequent home visits, images of his passionate instructions to her and her brother about standing firm in the fires of hell, like the prophets, saints, and their lost family members.

She recalled her mother standing up to the other women in the village they'd fled to, her parents reiterating the warning to never deny God, to always trust in His protection no matter the circumstances. Supernatural strength was loosed as fear vacated and for the first time since fleeing Tal Afar that terrible night, she intentionally looked a grown man in the eye. She spoke with the conviction of a warrior.

"Isho gives me strength."

A small smiled passed his lips at hearing the Syriac pronunciation of Jesus. He stood and looked out the window.

General Abdelhossein's daughter was prepared to die. She did not hang her head.

He sat down again in front of her. Her eyes fixated on his, peace in her countenance.

Now his hands were the ones shaking in the cauldron of uncertainty of a decision he'd been wrestling with for years since his first days in combat as a Marine, throughout decades of spilling blood and wrecking nations across the globe, and especially since he'd last seen his daughter and grandchildren while recovering from his previous action in Syria, many years prior. He'd wrestled with this decision after every shady encounter with America's supposed enemies, after every clandestine transaction, and whenever he looked at himself in the mirror, as he did moments ago.

Dominic Reyes watched Hazail, shook his head in disbelief, and leaned forward.

"That is a very good answer. Hazail…I follow Jesus as well."

A thousand thoughts coursed through her mind as she struggled to understand what she'd just heard. Then she began to sob.

For a long moment neither said anything, then the veteran CIA officer ventured into territory dangerous for both of them.

"If you tell me who your father is, I may be able to find him."

"You serve Isho?"

Dominic looked at the floor, searching for words.

"Why? Why are you with those men?" she asked.

"It's complicated." He struggled to make sense of it, for both of their sakes. "I must work with them to fight them. I am not one of them."

As Hazail absorbed this information, the other voice spoke to her again.

Tell him your father's name.

She resisted.

Tell him your father's name.

"My father's name…is…Zayno Abdelhossein."

The name sounded familiar, and suddenly recognition flashed in his mind.

He asked slowly, "General Abdelhossein?"

She nodded, and Dominic rubbed his hands through his beard.

"I know of a General Abdelhossein. I've never met him. Can you describe him?"

Hazail shrugged, thinking.

"Wait." He left the room and returned a moment later holding a rugged tablet. He scrolled through some pages and then turned the screen to face Hazail. "Is this your father?"

Hazail reached for the tablet but he held it back, only allowing her to see the screen which showed Ozzy in an AP article from a few months prior in Mosul. The page was in English but she could clearly see her father in the frame.

"Yes," she said, beginning to cry again. "That's him. Oh, please don't hurt him!"

Dominic set the tablet aside.

"Hazail, I hope you believe me when I say this. I think I can get you to your father. At least, I will try to. But…I cannot do it right away."

He checked his watch and frowned. "I have somewhere very important I need to get to. I must leave soon. I would prefer to leave you here but there is almost no food, no electricity, and should someone stumble upon you they would likely take you back to them. And I have no idea how long it would be before I could get back to you."

He paused, thinking out loud. "I could take you to a refugee camp, but I could not be seen with you…and its unlikely they would be able to get you to him, anyway." He sighed and sat up straight, speaking to himself in English. "And it's just as likely someone there might sell you out to them at some point."

Hazail wondered at that last statement. Dominic was lost in thought for another minute, then stood.

"Okay. You can either come with me or stay here on your own and risk being left here. If I die, no one will ever come back for you. The nearest village is twenty miles, and the daesh can be anywhere. I could leave you only a few days' worth of food and water."

"If I go with you, where will we go?"

"I'm afraid I can't tell you that. You're just going to have to trust me. And we need to leave right away."

Hazail weighed the options.

"I will go with you."

18
Reunions and Partings

Mosul, Iraq

The squad reached General Abdelhossein's command tent and Goriel went inside to speak with his father.

They were a mess. Aiden noticed for the first time how much battle wear he and his friends had accumulated. On the way back to friendly lines none of them had spoken.

"How about you two take a break," Aiden said to Guy and Ehmed. "Contact your loved ones, rest, eat or whatever. We can plan on meeting back here in an hour and reassess our next move."

For his part, Porter had spent the last few hours in planning mode. He'd gone over his laundry list of needs to present to Ozzy, and after getting firsthand intel on the terrain and tactics of both Ozzy's men and the enemy, he'd formulated a strategy he wasn't terribly confident about. They'd need time to equip and train, time he didn't think Ozzy had and would be disinclined to agree to. And above all of that was Jen. *Should I ask her opinion, ask her permission, or not even bother mentioning it? And what will Ginger say?* They sat in the shade outside Ozzy's tent, and Porter wondered how Aiden would address the matter of offering their services for full-on war.

Aiden unscrewed a water bottle and used it to wash the dirt and blood smears from his forearms. Porter removed the magazine from the AK-47 and reloaded another, tossing the empty one into the disorganized backpack loaded with medical supplies. He looked at the weapon in his hands and longed for something, anything else. He sighed and slung the weapon, resigned to make do with what they had.

"Come on. I've got an idea," Aiden said, picking up his own AK and walking into the General's field headquarters.

Inside, Ozzy was giving directions in Arabic to a number of subordinates, and paid them no mind.

"What are we doing?" Porter whispered, wondering how long they were going to stand around.

"I'm just pondering the best way to ask him."

"Ask him what?"

"If we can borrow a tank."

"A tank?"

"Yeah."

"Aiden, I know it's not your area of expertise, but a tank won't do much for us in the kind of counterinsurgency ops you're planning on."

"Oh, I think it will." Aiden smiled and approached Ozzy when he paused his instructions. "General Abdelhossein, sir."

Ozzy looked Aiden up and down. "Yes. Goriel briefed me already." He turned to Porter. "You see what we're up against, yes?"

"Sir," Aiden interjected. "I have an idea I would like to run by you. I think there may be a way you can get the airstrikes on target faster and more efficiently before the enemy displaces."

Porter screwed his eyebrows, confused, and Ozzy looked at him.

"How?"

"Don't ask me," Porter said, looking back to Aiden. Several of Ozzy's officers looked up.

"We spoke with some of the American JTACs on the front lines. They explained the problem with getting actual kills on targets. The problem is in the relay, correct?"

Ozzy looked to one of his officers, who nodded in agreement.

"Yes," one of the American Air Force officers spoke up. "They disperse too fast through the tunnel systems so that by the time the target is relayed to the strike aircraft, the position is already abandoned."

"That was the JTAC's complaint as well," Aiden said. "I think I might have a solution." He now had their attention. "If you can assign a tank to us, we can take it back to the advance units on the front lines and let it act as a scout."

Aiden took a pen out of his pocket and laid it on the map. "Say this is the tank's turret. When our guys start taking fire, the tank can point its cannon at the target while maneuvering in another direction. When your drones see that, they can direct their sensors to confirm ISIS ground fire directed toward friendlies. Correct me if I'm wrong, but wouldn't that be an overt verifier to confirm an ISIS position? You can tell the pilots this constitutes visual confirmation, and then they can go weapons-free without the relay."

The officers nodded in agreement.

"Muqaddam," Ozzy called his lieutenant colonel.

"Yes, Mushir."

"Get these men a tank."

Outside the tent, their eyes readjusted to the bright day.

"So," Porter asked, thinking out loud, "what about what you said earlier? About going house to house, kicking ass and all that."

Aiden sat on a crate. "Spent a lot time praying about it on the way back. God told me to stay in my lane. It's not why we're here."

"I know. But it doesn't change the math. You still want to get back out there? Still want to deal with the kinda crap we saw today?"

"No. But when has it ever been about what we want to do? It's about what we *can* do. And right now we can get out there and help people…and leave the vengeance to others."

"Fine by me." Porter unstrapped his vest and sat down. "I was kinda hoping to be there when you told Ginger, though." He smirked.

"Hell no. I was gonna make you tell her."

Jen listened to her phone ringing as she fumbled with equipment, and picked up after several rings.

"Hey," Porter said. "Do you have time for a quick catch up?

"Yeah, of course," Jen said, holding the phone between her shoulder and her ear. "Sorry I missed your last call. I've been assisting almost non-stop."

"No worries. How are you doing there? Any issues I need to be aware of?"

"No, we're good. Just missing you a ton. What have you been doing? Is everyone okay?"

"We're solid. Same old war. Aiden doing Aiden stuff. Got a few people out, lost a few too. Ugly."

"Pretty bad here, too."

"Yeah. Listen, I'm sorry but we're heading back out again in a few minutes. Not sure for how long. I wanted to touch base."

"Okay, just text me when you can. Where are you heading to?"

"Same area we were yesterday. Aiden came up with a tactic they want to try out. According to Ozzy, Mosul is wrapping up and they'll be able to start moving west. How about you? Did Aiden's buddy ever show up?"

"Yeah, Jake. Dr. Lyons, that is. Ton of experience, great teacher."

"Same as you."

"I guess. But I'm just putting out fires mostly. Made a few friends though."

"Good." Porter paused. He could see Aiden and the others patiently waiting for him to finish. "Well, I need to get moving."

"Okay. I love you. Be careful."

"Careful doesn't keep you alive in this kind of place."

"Well then, do whatever keeps you alive."

"Copy that. I love you too. Call you soon."

Porter hung up and secured his phone. He assessed his replenished gear one last time. *The thing that keeps us alive is firepower.* Porter picked up the rifle and checked it. *And this doesn't cut it.*

Jake and Jen made eye contact and she knew he'd overheard the conversation.

"Porter," she said, putting the phone in her pocket.

"Yeah, I gathered. They alright?'

"Sounds like it. But he'd never actually tell me if they weren't."

Jake smiled. "Yeah. We're kinda programmed that way."

"Oh, I know. I've been married to the SEALs since I was twenty. Well, sorta anyway."

Jake nodded.

"You call your wife recently?" she asked.

"Yeah, every time I get a chance. Texting at least."

"And what do you tell her?"

He laughed. "That everything's alright."

"Of course." Jen smiled.

"Did he mention Aiden?"

"Yeah, says he's doing Aiden stuff."

"So in other words, running recklessly into the thick of it."

"Is that what he does?"

"All my life. But he always gets 'em out of it, too."

Jen nodded but didn't answer, and hastily left the room.

Allen McCoy leaned in close to his mom. "Am I supposed to drink the tea, too?"

"Yep, you'll like it," Ginger whispered back.

Allen took the glass mug and sipped, then gently put it back down, careful not to let his feet touch the beautiful embroidered food mat. His eyes widened as Renas set down a large plate loaded with flat bread, and her father motioned for the Americans to eat.

Jake dove in but Jen hesitated, following the cues of the family. She took the bread and tore off a piece, then used it to pinch up a portion of the rice and the accompanying dish, a stew of chicken, vegetables, and spices. Shiloh made eye contact with Renas' daughters and smiled, her initial discomfort long since melting under the smiles and camaraderie of young girls happy to entertain a guest.

Allen devoured the flatbread, looked skeptically at the main dish, and soon regained a hearty appetite upon the arrival of a large plate of pastries.

"It's called *klecha*," Renas said. "Do you like it?"

Allen nodded until he could speak. "Yes, ma'am."

"Good, because you must eat the entire plate," she teased.

"Uh…" Allen grinned sheepishly.

"Everything is delicious," Jen said. "Thank you for inviting us."

Renas translated for her father and husband. Her father replied in Kurdish, and she translated again.

"He says we are blessed to have you as guests." She lowered her voice. "But I suspect they're just happy for the excuse to have their favorite dish."

"All men are," Ginger agreed.

The men sat with their backs against cushions along a wall in the largest room. With five years of deployments in Iraq under his belt, Jake could stumble through the conversation but needed digital translator apps to fill in the gaps.

Renas handed a dish to Ginger to dry. "I was not aware that Dr. Lyons and your husband were acquainted."

"They grew up together. In fact, Jake became a PJ because of Aiden."

"What is a PJ?"

"Pararescue jumper. It's the Air Force's version of Special Forces."

Renas nodded. "I assumed he was trained as a surgeon from early on."

"PJs get as much training as medical students."

"In less time," Jen added, "and while also jumping out of airplanes."

"And was your husband doing this with Dr. Lyons?" Renas asked Ginger.

"No. Aiden served in Afghanistan until he lost is leg. Never deployed to Iraq, but he did visit twice as a counselor."

"And your husband was also a soldier, here?" she asked Jen.

"Iraq, yes, but really all over the world. He was always getting deployed, never wanted to get married while on active duty, so I waited."

Renas was confused. "So…when did he get out of the military?"

"Five years ago."

"And you didn't get married till just recently?"

"He was chicken," said Ginger.

"Yeah," Jen laughed.

"How long did you have to wait for him to…not be chicken?"

"Fourteen years."

Renas mouth hung open.

"I know." She shook her head.

"But he was only chicken about getting married," Ginger quickly added. "In everything else he's…" she glanced at Jen, "he's as heroic as they come."

Jen nodded. "He's kind of a stud, when he wants to be."

"Yes," Ginger said. "He is that."

Aiden paused in the dark, hoping he had the right tent.

"Ginger! You in there?"

All three McCoys looked up at the sound of Aiden's voice, then poured out and hugged each other in the darkness.

"We just broke away for a few hours to see you guys. Heading back out late tonight or early tomorrow morning, I suspect."

"Where?" Ginger asked.

Aiden hesitated, so Porter answered. "The old city."

"They're dug in pretty tight there, right?"

"Yeah," Porter said. "Iraqis are making a big move on it. Ozzy asked if we'd come along."

Ginger nodded. "Are you going to have time to go see Jen?" she asked Porter.

"Spoke with her earlier. I texted her but she hasn't responded."

"They're working almost all the time," Ginger said.

"I'll see her soon. We'll probably only be gone for a few days."

A few hours later, Aiden and Ginger sat with their hands locked together. "I don't have to go, really."

Ginger looked down, and he felt a coldness in her body language. Not anger, but fear. He put his arm around her and she nuzzled closer, closing her eyes.

"When I think about the crash all I can see is smeared images, like a bad wiper obscuring the view out of a windshield, then a jolt. Part of me wants to get up in the air and see this place from a different angle. You know, to see it like I remember it. Down here on the ground it all seems so different."

"You want to leave?"

"Yes. But that's mostly fear." She kissed him. "Watch out for those guys. And bring yourself home, too. You copy?"

"They don't need me to watch out for them, it's more like the other way around. I feel like an out of shape old man out here."

"I doubt that. Just do what you do."

"You too."

"Good to go?" Porter asked.

"Hundred percent," Aiden said, hunching up his backpack straps, then picking up the rifle. "You?"

"Just a walk in the park, Kazanski."

Guy gave them a questioning look.

"It's from a movie," Porter offered.

"I know. I have seen *Top Gun*," Guy said, walking past them, the first to get in the vehicle.

Aiden patted Ehmed on the back. "Ready to roll, chief?"

Ehmed hesitated. Hozan kicked the ground with the toe of his boot.

"Are you sure you want to go there?" Hozan asked. "It is the most dangerous area in Iraq."

"I know," Aiden said, placing a hand on his shoulder. "Keep close to Ginger for me. Okay?"

Hozan nodded. The one-legged former PJ climbed into the Humvee and went off to war once again.

19
Audibles

Syria

The overhead drones and the CIA officer on the ground confirmed what Mario hopped was true: The landing zone was secure.

The Chinook swooped in fast and low over the razor fencing and landed in the facility parking lot. Touchdown.

Mario rushed out of the helicopter and took a knee, his gun pointed at the man standing in the open, his hands held out in front as if he expected the SEALs to target him. Mario ignored a sudden burning in his knee and verified the man's appearance: aviator sunglasses, tactical pants, and a black nylon jacket, zipped up.

"That's our contact," Mario said in his mic as he stood. He shook off the tightness in his knee and quick-stepped to the man with his rifle pointed low but ready, just in case. When they were close enough to speak over the noise Mario spoke the countersign.

"Tannenbaum."

The CIA responded with the correct parole word. "Sapphire."

Mario lowered his rifle and surveyed the area. His men had already fanned out and in less than a minute, his radio crackled.

"Facility secured," Josh said.

"They're ready to go." The CIA officer motioned for them to follow.

"Where's your counterpart?" Mario asked as they walked. "There are supposed to be two of you."

"On his way, got delayed by something. Gonna be driving a black SUV to the north gate, so do me a favor and don't light him up when he gets here."

"Copy," Mario said, then he keyed his mic to speak to the Chinooks. "Rebel One and Rebel Two, this is Cyclone One. We've got a friendly who should be approaching in a black SUV through the north gate. Repeat, a friendly in a black SUV en route to the north gate."

"Roger that Cyclone, got eyes on it now," one of the helo pilots said over the radio.

Mario turned back to the officer. "Let's get your people on board."

"First we need to get the cargo."

Mario stopped short. "No cargo. Just the people."

"Negative, friend. Cargo first, then the civilians. Plans have changed."

Mario rolled his eyes and began to key his mic. "Cyclone Three, get me a relay to HQ on this, we've got—"

"Negative," the officer said firmly. "This doesn't get broadcast. We've got ten crates with diplomatic tags that don't exist. Do you understand?

Mario turned around to examine the facility again, thinking.

"I know it's a pain in the ass but I'm guessing you know the drill on this."

Mario shook his head and debated his bad options. Option A was to stand his ground and ignore the case officer's request, probably resulting in a dressing down by any number of superior officers and perhaps a demotion. Option B was to capitulate to the CIA officer on scene and perhaps incur the same result. Option C was to call it in for instructions and perhaps incur a completely different result he couldn't predict. He swore.

"Show me the cargo."

The CIA officer walked him to a grouping of ten large white suitcase-style crates with locks, nearly pristine except for small stickers that designated them as dangerous biohazards. Mario shook his head and swore again.

"Cyclone One, this is Rebel One. Your black SUV is approaching the gate. Two occupants."

"Rebel One, please confirm. Did you say two occupants?"

"That's affirmative, Cyclone One."

"Who's the passenger?" Mario asked the officer.

"No idea," the officer admitted. "But only I get to shoot him."

Hazail sat in the backseat, her eyes darting from the windshield to the side windows. The facility came into view and she saw one large helicopter sitting on the ground with its twin rotors spinning, another helicopter circling their vehicle, and a man standing behind a mini-gun pointed directly at her.

"Don't worry," Dominic said from the driver's seat, "they're expecting us." *Me, anyway.*

Hazail tried not to stare at the Chinook but found herself stealing glances and trembling.

Dominic's handheld radio crackled in the seat next to him. "Dingo, acknowledge."

"Dingo copy. I'm at the gate, black SUV. Female passenger in the rear seat. Tell 'em to let me pass."

There was silence on the other end of the radio for ten seconds.

"Dingo, why the hell do you have a passenger? Over."

He tried to think of a good reason. "Classified. Instruct them to let us pass."

Ten more seconds of silence.

"Negative, Dingo. Turn off your engine and exit the vehicle. They're gonna check you out."

He swore and tossed the radio into the seat.

"What is it?" Hazail asked.

"Nothing. But those soldiers are going to want to make sure we're not the bad guys. Come, we need to get out of the vehicle. Do exactly as I instruct you, keep your hands held high, and please, do everything slowly."

"He's supposed to be alone," the CIA officer said, annoyed.

"Of course he is," Mario rolled his eyes. "Cyclone Four and Five. Check them out."

"He'll be armed, pistol and submachine gun at the minimum."

"And the woman?"

The CIA officer shrugged.

"Exactly."

"Make sure they can see your hands," Dominic instructed as they got out of the SUV. "Put them on the hood, like this. And spread your feet apart, like this." He demonstrated with his own, and Hazail followed his instructions.

The gate rolled open to the left and two soldiers approached with rifles pointed at them.

"Easy there, boss," Josh said, recognizing the Syrian. "English?"

"Yes. Not her though."

"Tannenbaum?"

"Sapphire," Dominic answered.

"Copy that. At ease. Identify the young lady, please."

"She's with me," Dominic said, standing up straight. Hazail gave him a questioning look, and he spoke to her in Arabic. "You may let go of the hood, but move slowly, and keep your hands up."

She did so and the SEAL looked at her. "Need to verify no bomb vest."

"She has only underwear underneath. Can you pat her down instead?"

"Yeah, sure."

"But please be respectful."

"Of course."

"They won't hurt you," Dominic said in Arabic. "They just need to make sure you don't have a suicide vest."

She nodded and slowly lifted her arms at the SEAL's instruction. Josh ran his hands around her torso and back, then around her waist and legs before motioning her toward Dominic.

"We're walking back. I'll follow," Josh said. "He'll drive your car in after he checks it out."

"No problem." Dominic briskly made his way to the gate with Hazail close beside him.

Two SEALs finished loading the crates onto the Chinook while the others identified and escorted the fifteen civilians onboard. When everyone was stowed, the back ramp closed and Derrick keyed his mic while walking to the side of the helicopter.

"All set here, boss."

"Copy," Mario replied. "Rebel One, standby." The SEALs watched Dominic and the CIA officer in conversation from a distance.

"What's the holdup? They're going too, right?" Sean asked.

"I think they're arguing about the kid," Mario said. "Wasn't on the VIP list, apparently."

Hazail sat several feet away from them on a concrete step with her hands gently folded in her lap.

"Neither was the cargo. Whadaya figure's in those crates?"

"Nothing nice, that's for sure."

Mario gave his men a hard look. "What crates? I didn't see any crates."

The SEALs gave nods of understanding. "Copy that."

"Like hell."

"What will it matter? No one's taking an inventory of this bird's cargo," Dominic said.

"Eyes only, you damn well know that. She can't go where you're going. What did you think was going to happen?"

"Didn't have a choice. She stays with me then till I can get her back safe."

"Where?"

"Iraq."

"Where in Iraq?"

"Mosul."

"Get outta here," he said with a sarcastic flush. "And how do you suppose you're going to do that?"

"I'll figure it out."

"This is amateur…" He stared at Hazail with his hands on his hips. "You know how to deal with this."

"That's not an option."

"It's a distraction, and a security risk I'm not afforded to grant you."

"She's an intel source and needs to be delivered intact."

"You really think that will fly?"

"She doesn't exist then. Same as that cargo you just loaded up."

They stared each other down, both recalling missions and compromises over intersecting careers.

"You're on your own with this. I never saw her and I'm not pulling any levers for you on it."

"Good. I want this off the radar anyway."

"And if you screw your cover and get yourself captured, that's it. Nobody's trading to keep you alive." He looked at the Chinook still waiting. "We don't have time for this crap." He started to walk away but paused and turned back. "Dom,

I wish it were different, I do. Hand her over to some bleeding hearts or a journalist or something."

"I need to get her somewhere specific. Like I said, it's classified."

"So be it." The officer boarded the Chinook without another glance backward, and Dominic slowly walked back to Hazail.

"Where are we going now?" she asked. The SEALs were still watching them, waiting for him to join them.

"To take you back home." He removed a small duffel bag from the back of the SUV and walked over to the SEALs. Mario leaned in over the helicopter noise.

"Who is she?" he asked.

"An intelligence source. An important one."

Hazail, staying close to Dominic's side, tried to ignore the mass of large, heavily-weaponed men surrounding them.

Mario looked her over. "You say so." Once they were onboard the helicopter, he pressed further through the headsets. "So where are you taking her?"

Dominic laughed. "You mean, where are *we* taking her." The SEALs looked at him with a mixture of curiosity and skepticism.

"Don't worry about it, son." Dominic gave Hazail a wink, and closed his eyes.

20
CASEVAC

Old City, Mosul

Goriel's driver hit the gas as bullets peppered the side of the Humvee. The vehicle bounced over an obstacle in the road, deviated from the planned route and onto a dirt path. Wild transmissions in Arabic flowed through the radio and Aiden braced himself against the doorframe, the vehicle jarring violently over uneven ground.

The small convoy got through the hail of fire and all five vehicles halted to regroup. The soldiers dismounted and Aiden quickly made the rounds to see if anyone was hurt.

Goriel spoke into the radio and waited for the response while barking instructions to the others.

"What now?" Guy asked. "Are they going to assault?"

"No. Watch," Porter said, pointing to the buildings in the distance.

A jet they couldn't see screeched overhead and came into frame as a bomb loosed from underneath it. The buildings they'd just passed exploded with a force that shook the ground, followed by a fireball that quickly turned into black smoke. A few seconds later another jet dropped another bomb a short distance further along the street.

Most of the Iraqis cheered. Goriel and Aiden's team merely watched and waited for the dust to clear.

"We should check for civilians," Guy said.

"They were told to evacuate many times," Goriel explained. "We even dropped leaflets. Anyone still here is either daesh or too foolish to heed the warnings."

"What about the elderly?" Aiden asked. "People who can't move?"

"The daesh killed them all long ago," Ehmed said. "They're all gone."

"How can you be certain?" Guy continued.

"He's right," Goriel said. "They slaughtered everyone, or took the rest as prizes."

That afternoon they dismounted again. A short patrol resulted in a small exchange of gunfire, confirming the lines Goriel was already aware of. They holed up to await reinforcements, a pair of Russian T-72 tanks which rolled past and were also soon taking fire.

Goriel began issuing orders and Aiden crouched beside him as bullets rained in on the tanks from several directions, impacting the armor. The tanks paused, turned their big guns to point at the enemy positions; the lead tank fired a 125mm shell, destroying a building. The second tank maneuvered left with Iraqi troops behind it, fanning out to keep the machine between them and the concealed enemy.

Aiden heard yelling from a street behind them and saw two figures running away, civilians fleeing in the direction they'd just came from.

"Porter—" he started to call, but Porter, a short distance away, had taken a knee and was looking skyward.

"What is it?" Guy hollered, trying to see what had his attention.

Squinting, Porter watched something high overhead slowly move in and out of the blowing smoke, inching along. He lost sight of it and his gaze fell on the tank and the dozen Iraqi troops lining up behind it. Aiden and Ehmed were moving to join them.

Looking skyward again, he caught the black outline directly above the tank, high in the air.

"No, Aiden!" Porter shouted. Then to Guy, "Stand fast!" He ran and horse collared Aiden from behind.

"What the hell?" Aiden yelled, falling backward.

Porter yelled at Goriel's men. "Get away from the tank!"

Goriel paused and turned to face Porter, confused.

"Get your men away from the tank!" He pointed to the drone, hovering.

Goriel screamed to his men in Arabic. Most fled but a few stared as the drone dropped from the sky, perfectly into the tank's opened hatch, and exploded with a force that sent some men tumbling and tore others in half. Fuel ignited and tank shells popped off in secondary explosions. Cooked ammunition swarmed over the street, hissing and devouring the flesh of those caught in the blast. A wave of flame washed over the intersection, followed by thick black smoke forcing those still alive to close their mouths and clamp their eyes tight.

A silence followed and Goriel rolled slowly onto his side, blood splattered across him. Before he could pick himself up, Aiden was there.

"You hear me?" Aiden shouted.

Goriel nodded, dazed.

A quick glance told Aiden that the blood on Goriel probably wasn't his, but rather from the body of a soldier strewn in the dirt not far away. "Lie back and let me check you out."

"No," Goriel said, shaking Aiden off. "I'm good. Let's move."

Aiden scanned for other injured men while Goriel stumbled, disoriented. Porter grabbed him by the shoulder, helping him to his feet.

"There you go," he said, and ran to the other tank while searching the sky.

"Cut his armor off," Aiden said to Guy, assessing another casualty. He leaned in to speak with his patient. "Hey. You hear me?"

The soldier's eyes darted around.

"Just relax, friend. Ehmed, ask him his name. Keep him talking."

Ehmed spoke to the man who slowly began to respond as Guy got the body armor off.

"Penetration wounds," Guy said, "all along his left side."

Large caliber weapons pummeled the intersection all around the remains of the tank. The Iraqis returned fire from small arms and vehicle-mounted .50 caliber machine guns. The remaining tank loosed another round from its long gun before maneuvering away.

Porter ran back to Aiden, still near the destroyed tank. "We need to move him," Porter said. "You're sitting ducks out here." Aiden furiously finished packing the penetration wounds that were seeping blood.

"Okay," he said, grabbing the wad of remaining hemostatic gauze that wouldn't fit into the man's collar. He put pressure on it while lifting him below the arms. "Let's move."

They set him down behind a wall. Aiden listened to the soldier's chest and looked for another decompression needle but couldn't find one. Guy packed what he thought were the worst holes with Quick Clot until Aiden noticed additional holes in both sides of his chest. He tore open a chest seal and placed the pair of thin sticky squares on the front and back wounds of the right side of the man's body. Porter covered them as they worked, firing controlled bursts toward concealed shooters, conserving ammo and keeping an eye on his friends' lifesaving efforts. Aiden moved to the left side and realized he was out of chest seals.

"I need another —" he started to ask Guy, but instead took the package the chest seal had come in and tore it in two, taking surgical tape and fashioning a jury-rigged seal over the other lung with the square packaging. When his lungs stabilized, Aiden assessed the smaller wounds.

"He needs medivaced, go tell Goriel."

"Have to find him first," Guy said.

Aiden took in the chaos surrounding them. Only then did all four men realize that in the midst of the firefight, the surviving tank had moved off down the road in the opposite direction, taking the soldiers with them.

"Do you see Goriel anywhere?"

"I'll find him," Porter said, and made a dash to catch up. After a dozen feet, enemy fire tore across the lane that separated them from the column of infantry and armor moving away. He jumped back and swore, firing again while backing away from the lane.

"We're cut off," he said, returning to the others.

The sounds of battle followed the tank as it left. The street became quiet, and the four of them were alone with a wounded and dying soldier.

U.S. Forward Operating Base, Northern Syria

The Green Berets were perplexed to see the familiar Syrian helping a young woman out of the Chinook. The strange duo walked directly toward them, with the SEALs following close behind.

Dominic ignored the curiosity of the men flanking him on both sides as they passed. He kept a firm hand on Hazail's back, propelling her forward through the sea of elite soldiers.

A cold sweat gripped Casey Allen. Hatred mixed with confusion, and for a moment he wondered if the Syrian he'd long ago marked for a terrorist might actually be a prisoner. But he wasn't bound. And he had a girl.

Casey made eye contact with the man for the third time in as many months, and this time the eyes looked different; gone was the death-stare of the previous two encounters. These eyes communicated something Casey couldn't place.

The Syrian passed him and disappeared with the SEALs under an awning, leaving him to his speculations.

"Sit here," Dominic said to Hazail. "I need to speak with that man. Do not speak to anyone until I get back. I'll be right over there."

She nodded and folded her hands in her lap.

Dominic gave a pointed look at the SEALs, motioning toward Hazail with his eyes.

"Keep an eye on the kid," Mario said to his men, as he and Dominic walked over to the commanding officer, who frowned upon recognizing Dominic.

"That took longer that you planned," the colonel sneered. "And what's with the girl?"

"Change of plans. The girl is an intel source."

"Who is she?"

"I'm afraid that's classified."

"Well, I'm afraid I can't allow her on my FOB, then."

Dominic tried to hide his frustration. "Colonel, I'm asking for your cooperation on this. We both have our orders. I'm on a tight timeline, which is tighter now due to circumstances."

"Like a little girl tagging along on deep cover ops. For some reason I doubt Langley signed off on that."

Dominic decided to play a poker face.

The colonel turned his attention to Mario. "Talk to me."

"Op was successful. We evacuated the civilians. And..." he glanced at Dominic, "he informed us of his little add-on there."

"What did the other spook say about it."

"I wasn't privy to that conversation. He extracted with the Chinook as planned."

The colonel nodded, looked at Dominic. "So? What's your operational status?"

"Nothing changes. Need to leave tonight, destination Rabia, just across the border. After that I've got business in Iraq."

"I thought Rabia was in the southeast."

"Different Rabia."

"You do know the Russians and Iranian Republican Guard are all over Abu Kamal, right?"

"I'm aware there is a war, yes."

The colonel stared. Mario clenched his jaw to keep from laughing.

"We don't have orders to take this cargo into Iraq," the colonel said.

"Not the cargo, just me."

"You're gonna leave her in Rabia?"

"That's classified, sir."

"How are you going to enter Iraq?"

"I'll drive."

"Drive what?"

"I'll arrange my own transportation from that point. All I need from you is to get this shipment there as arranged. I really don't see what the problem is."

"When this operation came up nobody mentioned kids tagging along."

"Didn't know I'd have one. Sorry."

A tense five seconds passed. "Alright. I never saw her."

"Saw who?" Dominic shrugged and started to leave the tent, but paused. "Got a shower nearby, colonel? I could use a shave."

"What about your cover?"

"Time to change it." He addressed Mario. "You might want to get your men some rest, commander. We'll set out at 0300."

An aide walked in and spoke to the colonel. "Sir, priority communication for you on the line."

Dominic walked past them. "Never mind. I'll find the shower on my own."

From afar, several eyes watched Dominic kneel in front of the young girl. Mario redirected their attention.

"Refit your gear and then get some grub and shuteye. We're moving out in fourteen hours." He turned to the Green Berets. "Some of you too, I reckon."

"Where?" one of the SEALs asked.

"No idea."

"With him?" another asked.

"Them, apparently."

"Mission brief?" Casey asked.

"Later."

"What gear do we need beyond the ordinary?" another SEAL asked.

Mario turned and watched Dominic lead Hazail away.

"As much ammo as you can carry."

Guy and Ehmed stayed with the Iraqi soldier while the Americans surveyed the terrain. Aiden and Porter felt overexposed in the open spaces between buildings, hearing constant but distant bursts of machine gun fire, and they rushed back to brief the others.

"Let's carry him back the way we came in."

"How far?" Guy asked.

"Not sure yet. But we need to move."

Guy and Ehmed picked up the collapsible stretcher on which the IDF soldier lay and moved to a more sheltered area twenty feet away. Aiden dialed a number on his phone and waited for several rings.

"Aiden. I'm here," Ginger finally answered.

"Yeah, listen, we're good but we got separated from Goriel and his men. I've got a wounded IDF soldier who needs evac. I'll send you the pin of my phone location, I have no idea where we are."

"Okay." She paused. "Okay, I see the map. I'll try and get them to get an ambulance there."

"Hurry please. He's stable but severely wounded."

"Okay. I love you."

"I love you too." He hung up and checked the vitals on the soldier. "Any idea where we are?" he asked the others.

"Place all looks the same to me, man," Porter answered.

"I have an idea," Ehmed said, "but Hozan knows this area much better than I."

"She gonna get him an ambulance?" Porter asked.

"Said she'd try."

"We could take him back on foot," Guy suggested.

"It's a long way," Porter said, peering around. "Snipers could be anywhere."

"Maybe I should make a run up ahead and try to connect with Goriel?" Guy suggested.

"No," Aiden finally said. "Let's stay put and stay together. If something goes down, we're gonna need every gun we can get," Aiden said.

Rifle fire erupted again in the distance.

"Hello," Ginger spoke in Arabic to the IDF officer. "You have soldiers here," she pointed to her phone, "wounded. They need an ambulance."

The officer waved his hands, speaking too fast for Ginger to follow. He pulled out a tablet and turned it so she could see it, pointing to the screen and waving no.

"Hold on. Hozan! Aiden needs an ambulance, here." She showed him the map on her phone.

Ginger waited while Hozan tried to explain, but the officer became even more dismissive and stormed off.

"They don't have any available."

"Okay," Ginger relented, thinking. She dialed Aiden.

"Hey, it might take some time to round one up. Everyone here seems busy with other matters."

"Copy that," he said. "Understand. We'll make do."

She hung up and put her phone back in her pocket and looked for her kids.

"Now what?" Hozan asked.

"I don't know." On the sidewalk Shiloh and Allen were helping Gary and Linda distribute food to an unending line of grateful people.

"We could go," she said. "In the Land Rover. It's not that far."

"Yes, we could. The route from here to there should be cleared, but you never know."

Ginger walked over to Shiloh and Linda.

"Hey."

"What's wrong?" Shiloh asked, reading her mother's look.

"Dad's got a soldier who needs an ambulance. There aren't any available."

"Where are they?" Linda asked, handing a bag to the next child in line.

"Not far."

"Critical?" Gary asked.

Ginger nodded. "Aiden wouldn't have called for help if it wasn't." She hesitated. "We were thinking of taking our rig and picking him up ourselves."

"Yeah," Shiloh said. "You should go help him."

"It might be dangerous." Ginger looked at Linda, silently asking her a question.

"I'll look after them," Linda said. "Go ahead. Lord be with you."

Aiden's phone chirped with a text:
Stay put. Evac inbound. Call if you need to displace.

"Looks like we've got an ambulance on the way."

"Better hurry. I don't like sitting around like this," Porter said.

Ginger drove around obstacles in a desolate, quiet street, squeezing though the narrow spaces at varying speeds, accelerating when able, never stopping.

"Looks deserted," Hozan said. "But you need to watch out for IED's or boobytraps."

"Yeah, I know. Although Ozzy said this passage was recently cleared."

"That was days ago. They can re-mine it overnight."

Ginger focused on the road. "I know what to look for."

"Have you ever been in combat?" Hozan asked, his rifle in a ready position across his chest, pointed out the window.

"Once or twice."

Another series of gunshots.

"Getting closer," Aiden said.

"Yeah," Porter agreed.

"Maybe Guy's right. Maybe we should start him on foot. Meet the ambulance halfway?"

Porter pondered the idea. "Negative," he said finally. "Too many hidey holes along the way. Better to stay put and get him out by vehicle. We'd move too slow otherwise."

"Sorry for getting us in this," Aiden said. "I couldn't leave this guy."

"It's why we're here."

"Yeah."

The sound of a vehicle's engine caused them to scramble for cover. Porter and Aiden took up firing positions and centered their sights on the front grill of a Land Rover speeding and bobbing their way.

"Civilian?" Aiden shouted to Porter across the narrow street.

"Maybe a V-bed!"

The Land Rover slowed, seeming to sense its danger. It came to a stop several dozen meters away and flashed its headlights.

"What do you make of that?" Guy asked.

Everyone heard Aiden's phone ringing but kept their weapons on the Land Rover. Aiden steadied the rifle with his right hand, taking out his phone with his left and saw

Ginger's name flashing on the screen. He ignored it but it continued ringing, and still the Land Rover stayed put with its engine idling.

The ringing finally overcame his fear and he answered the call, keeping his eyes on the vehicle.

"Not a good time, babe," he said, about to hang up.

"It's us."

"What?"

"In the Land Rover. It's us. See me flashing my lights?"

Aiden gasped. "Hold your fire! It's Ginger!" He released the grip on his AK and stood up with one hand waving, the other still holding the phone to his ear. "What are you doing here?"

"We're the ambulance you called for. And sweetie, please tell Porter not to shoot us."

"Alright, easy now." Aiden helped Hozan pull the soldier into the back of the Land Rover. "Just keep him as still as possible and turn him over to their medics as soon as you come across one. I wrote down everything here but you may need to translate it for them."

"You're not coming, too?" Hozan asked, concerned.

"There's nothing more I can do for him out here. He needs surgery. Just try to protect him from too much bouncing around. And make sure nobody shoots my wife."

"Yes, please," Ginger said from the driver's seat.

"Drive smart," Porter added.

"I got it," she said, putting it in gear. "What are you going to do?"

"Press forward and try and reconnect with Goriel," Aiden answered. "See what we can do along the way."

She nodded. "Alright, my ears are on if you need us again." She backed up the Land Rover, spun it around, and was off again in a cloud of dirt.

When it was gone, they all stood staring at the spot they'd last seen it.

Guy asked finally, "Where to now?"
A sustained exchange of gunfire sounded in the distance.
"I guess that way," Porter motioned.

21
Delivery Vehicles

Northeastern Syria

Dominic rode in the passenger seat up front, with Mario driving. Hazail spoke to him from the rear of the vehicle where she sat uncomfortably between two soldiers who had initially tried and failed to appear non-threatening..

"How long will we be driving?"

"For several hours still," he answered in Arabic. "You should try to sleep." He turned to face her, now with a mustache instead of a beard. "It may be some time before you get another opportunity to rest."

She leaned her head back and closed her eyes.

Dominic met the gaze of one of the soldiers who quickly turned to look out the window into the nothingness of the pale desert.

The questions Mario had wrestled with since he first set eyes on Hazail now surfaced in the quietness of opportunity.

"Does she speak any English?"

"No."

"So, what's her story?"

"It's classified."

Mario rolled his eyes. "Fine, but why is she here with us, on this op? You spooks may have pull over our chain of command, but all I care about are these guys. And I need to know how she's a threat to our mission."

"You should've taken that up with your CO."

"I did. He told me to piss off."

"She doesn't threaten your mission."

Mario silently pondered his next inquiry, and was surprised when Dominic continued the conversation for him.

"I wouldn't put your men in undo jeopardy. She's just cargo, and it's what I do — shuttling people here and there, shipments here and there, packages here and there. She's just another parcel."

"No, I've been doing this too long. You could get her wherever you wanted pronto with a phone call." He paused, thinking. "So she's either bait, or it's something personal you want to keep off the radar. Is that it? Are you off the reservation?"

Dominic said nothing, and it was clear that every ear in the vehicle was paying attention.

"Whatever," Mario said. "Not my business, but she better not get dumped into some pervert's lap."

Dominic's eyes were closed now. "Or what?"

None of the soldiers knew how to respond, and therefore didn't. A half-mile passed as the question hung in the air. The SEALs meditated on unsaid responses that ranged from rage to confusion.

"She's going home," Dominic said finally, "if she has a home left. I know who her father is. And I'm trying to get her back to him." He stared back at Mario. "Off the reservation. That good enough for you?"

"You really must not want the Agency to know about this. Couldn't you get her a VIP flight into Mosul with one call to Langley?"

"Maybe. But I don't have time for that. And she stays with me till I do."

"You don't trust them," Mario said, stealing a glance.

"I don't trust them."

"Just like that bioweapons facility was supposed to be destroyed, instead of pilfered. Right?"

"Nobody destroys anything of value here."

"What's the Agency's angle on that…since we're being honest."

Dominic said nothing for a minute, and Mario figured the conversation was over. As suddenly as he'd clammed up, Dominic restarted the conversation.

"Have you ever heard of Smedley Butler?"

"Someone named their kid Smedley?" Mario asked with a chuckle.

"Marine. One of the most decorated soldiers in U.S. history. World War One, double Medal of Honor recipient."

"Damn," Mario said.

"In the thirties a bunch of fascists tried to recruit him to create a shadow government controlled by foreign bankers. He toyed with them a while, got the intel, then turned them all over to Roosevelt. Know what FDR did?"

"Had him killed?"

"Nothing. Not a damn thing. Know why?"

"Why?"

"Because Roosevelt knew that those who profit from war are way more powerful than presidents and prime ministers. It's the same reason why he didn't force Henry Ford to stop making all the German Army's trucks, why GM kept supplying the Luftwaffe with replacement parts, why Standard Oil helped make Zyclon-B gas. And it's the same reason why you all just smuggled a crap ton of Lord knows what out of Syria. The people who fight wars don't start them. The people who start wars don't care a dime about ISIS, or Al Qaeda, or communism, or Nazis. Maybe once upon a time they did, but I haven't met many in fifty years of doing this. It's just another market to them. Have you noticed how many people want a piece of Syria? Well, everyone is getting some. It's just how it works. It never ends."

"You're a cynical old nag," Mario laughed. "If that's true then why take a ton of guns to people who'll just use them against us someday? Why don't you just hang up your shoes and tell them to take a hike?"

"Because regardless of the money men and their agenda, these bastards — the ones who sold that little girl in the back seat for less than your optics kit — are evil, and someone needs to kill 'em. That's us."

"Been here a long time and haven't been doing much of that. Pretty much just helping out guys like you. Maybe I ought to retire myself."

"Yes, you should. And soon."

Rabia, Syria

His family had been warriors, and no one knew for exactly how long. Elders had told him they were warriors from the beginning, direct descendants of Sassanids who took on the Romans, usually on horses, and honored as those who faced death over the centuries but lived to pass on the tales.

In the First World War they took the saddle again for the Ottomans, then afterward at the behest of the British, and though no longer mounted, they were no less effective. Whatever regional power sought to control their small but strategic position on the map found them invaluable.

Historically speaking, Iran and Iraq were next up. His family fought for and against both countries during the decades before he was born, losing too many husbands and uncles for anyone to remember.

Then, the Americans.

Pasha never quite understood why his family loved the Americans. His father respected them after meeting them on the quickly overrun battlefields of the early 1990s. Sadaam Hussein unleashed hell on his people after the ceasefire that ended that war. Yet his father remained one of their most prominent supporters when the Americans returned a decade later.

His uncles considered the American's hasty withdraw a betrayal to the Kurds, but his father disagreed; having seen the child prisons and rape rooms up close, he knew Sadaam better than they. He stood by the Americans right up to the end, when both he and Pasha's mother were murdered in the same month — she by a bus bombing along with a dozen of his classmates, his father beheaded as a warning to collaborators.

Those acts might have deflated the warrior zeal in others. They had the opposite effect on him and his grandfather, who never missed an opportunity to remind him that though the enemies changed, his family did not. They would respond as they always had, with stubborn action onto death – theirs, or their enemies', or both.

That ethic cost Pasha's cousins their lives and his grandfather his business, his fingers, and later, his head. Pasha carried on in their place. Too young to join the Americans when they patrolled the streets in force, he had to make do with an ill-equipped Iraqi army when the daesh rolled over his country.

He hated that he was forced to flee, but fortunately it wasn't far to the arms of his people, the Peshmerga. They held when others hadn't and won their peoples' homeland back as their forefathers had done. And they would do it again, with or without the American airpower currently streaking overhead, or without the yet-undelivered heavy weapons promised months ago.

Pasha scanned the road and saw few vehicles, as usual.

"Nothing is happening, Pasha. Relax," the tired soldier said next to him.

"We're vulnerable and they know it. They will come. We need tanks."

"It's because they don't come that nobody will give us tanks. The tanks are for the Iraqis, not us."

"They provided mortars."

"A few. I'd rather have a paycheck than a few boxes of mortars."

"You need money to defend your country?"

"I need money so my family can eat. You don't have children to care for."

"No…I don't have anything."

The soldier knew Pasha. Knew he'd struck a nerve, yet dismissed it. Everyone here had a story and most of them were tragic.

"You have us."

"I'd prefer a tank," Pasha smirked.

"You don't need a tank. You need a wife. Come, dance with us tonight."

"Wives get killed. I need no wife."

"Then dance because you don't have a wife," he smiled.

"I will dance because you have a wife," Pasha smiled back. "But I still want a tank."

Al-Yaarubiyah, Syria

Casey slowed the Humvee to a crawl and the six-vehicle convoy continued for another thousand meters until the radio crackled.

"Hold up. Standby."

"I don't like this," Thrombull said, staring out the window as the early morning sky continued its transition from inky purple to dark orange. "Too exposed."

"This place is controlled by the YPG," Demarius said. "They're like the OG militia in this part of the world."

"More jihadies by another stripe," Casey sneered.

"That ain't true, Allen," Demarius said, "and you know it."

"Never heard of 'em," said Thrombull.

"No, how about the YPJ?"

"How about you YP your butt, Smith?" he snapped. "I don't give a rat's whisker about the little dudes manning those guns. Ain't another American within a hundred miles, except up there." He pointed to the sky.

"And you sure as hell know we don't have no QRF if that Agency spook up ahead leads us into a fight," another soldier chimed in.

"Well, I'll have you know, Clayton," Demarius said, "that the YPJ is an all-woman Kurdish force. Y'all about to meet a bunch of girls with guns, and more combat experience than any of us. Doesn't that sound worth the drive?"

"Not if they're the only ones who've got our six," Thrombull said.

"If they're even on our side," Clayton scoffed.

"I've got your six," Casey said. "We got each other. The rest of those sand rats can stuff it."

"Yeah," Demarius agreed, "plus we got a whole car full of SEALs up there, and an old man with a kid. What could go wrong?"

The checkpoint guards approached Mario's lowered window. A nearby .50 cal trained in on the convoy. Dominic exited the vehicle and walked around the front while a soldier peered into the rear windows. The SEALs on both sides of Hazail had their weapons ready, friendly forces or not.

"We are here to supply the forces across the border." Dominic spoke with authority and mild annoyance. "Your orders are to let us pass without delay."

"These are Americans."

"Yes, and you've got Germans, British, and Americans within your ranks, yes?"

"These are not conscripts, these are clearly American Special Forces."

"And you're holding them up."

"I must get approval."

"Fine. Take me to your commander."

"You'll need to wait until I can get him to speak with you."

"Fine. We'll wait." He got back in the vehicle.

"So?" Mario asked.

"Just a child. We won't be waiting long."

"Not a fan of sitting around."

"Relax. The real fun won't start till we hit the next checkpoint."

Mosul, Iraq

A long eruption of heavy weapons' fire caused Aiden and his friends to quicken their pace in the direction of the shooting. As they got closer they heard screaming, and the shooting intensified. Five men were dead in the road, at least a dozen others bled and limped toward them, clutching their injuries.

Porter examined the first man he came to. "Relax buddy. Sit down." He took out a dressing and packed it into the tattered flesh that had been the soldier's bicep and began wrapping it up.

Guy knelt over an Iraqi fighting to breathe and bleeding from the chest, his eyes rolling back into his head. "No, no, no! Listen to my voice. You're alive," he said, catching him as he began to collapse onto the ground.

Aiden, in triage mode, scanned the men surrounding him. A chorus of Iraqi voices shouted at one another, pointing at a bleeding man in the road, still moving. A soldier ran out into the open to grab the fallen soldier's vest but was shot in the head and fell dead next to him. The others took cover beside Aiden, who looked at the soldier in the open, alive and struggling. He noticed streams of cords hanging from the buildings and laying in the streets — old phone wires and electrical cables, long disabled.

"Let's use these as a lasso," Aiden said, yanking on a cord. "We can toss it to him."

The soldiers watched, and a few understood immediately. One Iraqi cut the cord with a combat knife and another removed his own tactical vest, taking out the magazines from its pockets, then fixed the vest with its Velcro straps to the end of the line. When it was ready, the

Iraqis hollered at the wounded soldier and tossed the vest so it landed on top of him. The soldier lifted his head slightly but his comrades barked at him to lay still and play dead. The soldier slowly slid his arm through a strap.

"Pull him quickly, he's pouring out blood," Aiden said. Several hands joined in to pull the line and the soldier slid along the pavement, leaving a thick trail of blood in his wake. In seconds he was behind cover and Aiden crouched over him immediately.

"What's your name, friend?"

The soldier only gave heavy breaths in response.

"That's okay, I just needed to know you're breathing." He quickly threw a tourniquet on the man's right thigh and visually inspected the rest of him while cranking it down, searching for other sources of blood loss. He commenced a blood sweep, raking his hands with sprawled fingers around the neck, back, and groin, locating bleeding from all three areas.

As the medics worked, a motley group of about twenty Iraqis gathered – crouching, standing, and waiting. They wore all manner of clothing and gear, outfitted piecemeal with whatever they could find; some wore mismatched uniforms, others wore t-shirts and tactical vests like the ones Ginger had purchased in Erbil. Nearly all had bandanna-style head coverings and a variety of weapons.

The hardened fighting men surrounding Aiden and his mates were grateful for the additional medics regardless of where in the world they'd come from. Some offered help but most simply stood expressionless, while further down the road Porter could see officers holding tablets and conferring. Ehmed spoke with one of the soldiers and the man became animated and loud, pointing east, as Aiden worked frantically to stabilize the patient they'd just dragged to safety while listening in to discern what he could of the conversation.

"Machine gun, that way," Ehmed translated, pointing. "Took out many men. It opens up whenever they try to cross this road."

"Airstrikes?" Porter asked. They waited for the translation.

"Says they've got some armor moving up here to provide cover. That's why the officers over there are waiting."

Porter made his way among the rest to the edge of the building they were using as cover. Some of the Iraqis gave him the side eye but most ignored him, opting instead to scrutinize Guy and Aiden as they moved on to another wounded soldier.

Aiden craned his neck to see the men lying in the open, hoping for any sign of life but seeing none. He patched up another soldier bleeding from the back of the head, shot through the eye but still alert in spite of the injury. He had to be convinced to lay down and Aiden quickly got a round, plastic disc out of his kit, placed it over the man's eye socket, and held it while wrapping a large bandage around his head, feeling the tissue damage on the back of his head. He hoped he wasn't pressing the man's brain, but he was pretty sure he was.

"Ask him how he feels," Aiden said. "See if he knows where he is."

Ehmed spoke and the soldier replied with a few words.

"Just rambling. Not making sense."

"Okay, tell his buddies to take his rifle and grenades."

Ehmed did and the man jerked back in protest when the other Iraqis tried to disarm him. They hesitated.

"They don't want this guy armed, believe me," Aiden said. "He's gonna be high as a kite in a second."

Aiden gave the man a shot and the patient calmed down and rested.

"Two of these guys need evac immediately." Aiden motioned for Ehmed to translate. He did, and the soldiers shrugged after a brief exchange.

"They're not saying anything," Ehmed said, frustrated. "No officers."

"Yell to the officers, then." Aiden motioned to the men across the way. Ehmed tried again, and was shouted down by an officer who waved his arms dismissively.

"He says they have wounded up the road, too. We're to wait for the armored vehicles."

"At least two of these guys are gonna be dead in an hour," Aiden said. "Probably three."

Porter returned after examining the tactical position of the machine gun with two of the ISF soldiers. "Can't see anything. Need to bomb it, or like he said, wait for a tank."

Aiden lifted himself up on his knees, wiped the blood from his hands onto the soldier's pantleg, and pulled out his phone.

"You gonna call her to come here?"

"They're gonna die if she doesn't. We can move them back to where she met us earlier, and secure that pick up location."

Porter swore and exchanged magazines. "Alright." He spoke to Ehmed. "Tell these guys we need to move their buddies for evac, and make sure this road is clear for the ambulance."

"Ambulance? You mean Mrs. McCoy?"

"I guess so."

Ehmed relayed the information to the Iraqis, who nodded and began spreading out to protect the road.

Aiden spoke into the phone. "Hey—" He was interrupted by a distant bomb blast, and waited. "Hey, it's me. We could use another extraction if you're able."

Rabia, Syria

The convoy moved slowly past the checkpoints, and at every marker young men and women peered into each vehicle. Shockingly, Casey saw curious looks from friendly faces. These soldiers appeared different from any he'd previously seen in this part of the world.

"Those your girls, Smith? That one looks about fifteen."

"That fifteen-year-old girl has been in more firefights than you have, Bianco," Clayton said.

"Or you," Casey added.

Pasha watched the vehicles roll past with eager eyes. The third and fourth vehicles were flatbed trucks with covered pallets of cargo. A 6-ton covered truck driving heavy on the rear axle followed, and another Hummer completed the convoy.

"I don't think they brought your tank today," his friend said. "Maybe we should tell them to send back whatever is in that truck, eh?"

"I'll take it, whatever it is," Pasha smiled. Several soldiers followed the vehicles, ready to help unload and distribute whatever new toys the Americans had provided.

Dominic stepped from the lead vehicle and was immediately embraced by a Peshmerga general who kissed both of his cheeks and spoke in friendly tones. After a brief exchange, Dominic introduced him to Mario in English.

"These men will unload these gifts with you," Dominic told the commander. "After that I will need to continue on to Mosul. Can you provide me a vehicle?"

"You want to travel to Mosul by yourself?" the commander asked.

"Me and another, yes. We have business in Mosul and must not delay."

The Peshmerga general examined the vehicles still running. "Come, let us discuss the matter over a chai. I will see what I can do to assist you." He motioned for the Americans to join him inside, and Mario and another SEAL went in with the Green Beret lieutenant while the rest of the Americans either took up defensive positions or assisted with unloading the trucks.

Hazail hesitated a few feet behind Dominic, like a child by her parent in a strange environment.

"You will need to stay here," he said, turning to her. "I will be just in there."

"I understand," Hazail nodded, lowering her head, ready to stand as a statue for as long as necessary.

Dominic noticed three female soldiers watching them, and waved them over. Hazail's eyes darted to the women who approached with quizzical looks. They were older than her, but not much.

"This is Hazail. Please show her kindness while I meet with your commander."

"Certainly," one of them answered. Dominic nodded and went inside.

"You look very tired," the soldier said to Hazail. "Would you like to sit down, perhaps take a rest?"

Hazail looked over the women, their weapons, their clothing, their hair. She turned to look at the men unloading the crates from the truck, saw others standing nearby with weapons at the ready. One of the SEALs noticed and gave her a friendly wave while chewing on an energy bar.

"Yes…I would like to lay down, if it's safe to do so." She had never seen a woman holding a rifle before, nor dressed for battle. They exuded a confidence that she only remembered as a distant memory from earlier times. She had lived among strong women her entire life, and seen many of them die because of it. These women were strong in an entirely different way and had lived because of it.

"Yes, dear, you will be safe with us. Come."

Mosul

Ginger brought the Land Rover to a screeching halt at Porter's feet in the center of the road. She rolled down the window as he came around to her side.

"You came in like a bat outta hell. You good?"

"Saw some guys back there I didn't like the look of, need to do this fast. Where you need us?"

"Here's fine, but turn it around and get ready to roll. We'll load 'em in the back."

A few seconds later Aiden directed the men in loading the injured. An Iraqi medic went in first holding an IV bag; he attached it to one of the interior roof handles while others hoisted the first man across the folded rear seats.

"Maybe I should go with her," Porter offered.

"No room. Gonna have to pack 'em in like sardines," Aiden said. "Besides, Hozan may need to lead her around obstacles."

"I don't like it, man. She's a primo target in this thing."

They fit all of the non-walking casualties plus the Iraqi medic who would try to keep them stabilized on the bumpy ride out. Aiden closed the rear door and went to Ginger's open window.

"I'm sorry to keep you at this. It was either that or let 'em die."

"It's why we're here. I'll get 'em out."

"I love you."

"I know." She gunned the accelerator and was off.

He watched her disappear down the road. Another noise soon replaced it as the tread of a large-tracked vehicle approached.

"Looks like they finally got that armor," Guy said.

"She seem alright to you?" Porter asked, concerned.

"Yeah," Aiden said. "She'll be alright."

The familiar whining sound repeated somewhere overhead, and Porter said what they were all thinking.

"Another drone."

22
Those Who Face Death

Jarabulus Corridor, Southern Turkey

A chain of large vehicles suddenly slowed as they approached the checkpoints right on time. The American-trained Turkish border security watched them on the cameras, anticipating what would come any second now.

And then it happened. The radio crackled with the coded phrase:

"Lights out."

The men followed their orders as usual, and looked the other way as the vehicles passed uncontested and unmolested into Syria.

Mosul

A young man lifted his forehead up from the prayer rug, stood, and walked briskly to the opened door of his waiting vehicle. The older man who held it open embraced him and kissed his head before ushering him into the driver's seat.

Welders quickly secured a plate over the door, the young man sealed inside never to be seen again. All he had to do was steer and keep his foot on the gas.

From a nearby rooftop a man examined the aerial view of the city on his tablet, afforded through the lens of his drone hovering nearby. He flew it slowly, maneuvering to a better location where he could observe the crowd of soldiers along a street, but with enough obstacles between it and them to hopefully avoid detection long enough.

"Here," he said to his companion.

"Excellent," the man agreed, noting the coordinates. He placed a phone call.

"Tell them to hurry," the drone operator said, noticing the battery waning.

"Get a closer image. He wants to know the troop strength."

He decreased altitude and inched closer. "Two groups of…at least two dozen soldiers each. They're not moving. An armored vehicle just came into frame."

The other man relayed the details into the phone. "It's a prime target. Do not delay or we will not be able to maintain visual."

The young man's earpiece directed him again. "Stop…very good. You must back up and take the next left turn you just passed. And do it very quickly."

Hammam Al-Alil, Iraq

Jake could feel the phone vibrating in his leg pocket, but with his hands inside the chest cavity of a bombing victim in his sixth surgery of the day, the call would have to wait. A second later he heard the chime, the special sound reserved for Cynthia's texts. If it was an emergency, she would keep calling.

Rabia, Syria

"Have I ever dealt with you in a disingenuous manner?" Dominic asked.

"No. I trust you fully, but you are not the country you represent, and America is not invested in the security of my country."

"I don't deny that. But what do you call the truck loads of weapons we just gave you?"

"And to our enemies."

Dominic had nothing to say to that, and didn't try. The general continued.

"And what you previously sent us, Russian jets just bombed out of existence."

"My country's not at war with Russia."

"Neither are we, supposedly. But the bombs drop. And somehow this American air superiority seems unable or unwilling to support us. Forces slip down from Turkey or Jordan, with American weapons and training, I might add. What can we do against them with M-16s and a few mortars?"

"We've had this conversation before, friend. That's why my men are unloading machine guns as we speak. I can take them back," Dominic bluffed.

The general held up his hands. "Light machine guns. We need force projection vehicles. Tanks, helicopters, and training to use them."

"Again, we've had this conversation before. If it were up to me I'd get you your whole shopping list, but I can only get you what's authorized by the suits in D.C., and tanks aren't exactly easy to procure or deliver."

The Kurdish general nodded. "Well then, how about you arrange for us to get them from the Russians. Friend."

Mario and the Green Beret lieutenant sat up straighter. Dominic pondered the question.

"I might. But first I'll take your request back to my superiors. In private they say they support a free Kurdistan."

"And in practice they profit from all sides and care little or nothing about us. Right?"

"Maybe. But I do care."

Pasha gathered with the eager crowd as the first crate was opened by one of the Peshmerga soldiers. Casey, Demarius, and most of the Americans looked on from a distance as one of the SEALs began a brief rundown of the light machine gun, also known as the Squad Automatic

Weapon, or SAW, to their new owners. He was just getting to the interchangeability of magazines and his interpreter struggled to keep up.

"The SAW can either use 30-round or larger drum magazines, or can be belt fed if—"

Shots rang from the checkpoint gate nearby. Every soldier shouldered their weapons in that direction, then recoiled when a massive explosion filled the air and shook the ground. Screaming and shouting followed. Darting figures ran toward them through the smoke.

One wearing a bulky jacket ran at top speed toward the back of the truck Casey Allen was using for cover. Casey opened up from sixty yards and cut him down but another running next to him managed to push a button in his hand, detonating a suicide vest and almost taking out three Peshmerga soldiers barely out of range. One of them recovered fast enough to fire, attempting to disable a vehicle that was trying to exploit the hole made by the first explosion.

Hazail jumped, her terrified eyes opening wide. The women around her leveled their guns and flew out the door.

"Stay here," the last soldier barked, "and lay on the floor!" She made it to the doorway and turned to see Hazail trembling, a trickle of liquid generating a pool underneath her. The young woman mumbled something to herself, still pointing her weapon out the door, and slowly backed up to Hazail, softening her tone.

"I will be very near. Right outside, but we are under attack and I must fight. Do you understand?"

Hazail nodded, then noticed the urine and began to cry. "I'm sorry."

"There is no time to be sorry. You must be ready to fight, too." She pointed to a collection of duffel bags in the corner. "There are clothes in there you may change into."

Hazail looked and nodded.

"Do you know how to use a gun?"

She shook her head. The soldier nodded and pulled out her combat knife.

"Then here, take this."

Hazail took the weapon and stared at it. The soldier glanced out the door and lowered her weapon, annoyed. She put both hands on Hazail's shoulders, remembering the way an older woman had once taught her.

"You must become fierce. Fierce! Never let them take you alive. If you must die, take them with you. Never surrender to them. Do you understand?"

Hazail nodded again, crying.

"Sister, be brave. I must go now."

Dominic fled the meeting and caught a glimpse of the last woman exiting the building where he'd left Hazail. She had her rifle poised and made eye contact with Dominic, his pistol in hand. He ran to her.

"Where is she?"

"In there, I have to go."

"Yes, go. I'll take her."

The woman hesitated. "I gave her a knife."

"Good."

The soldier ran toward the distant firefight. Dominic entered and smelled the urine, saw Hazail kneeling in a corner with the knife in one hand and searching for clothes with another.

"Hazail."

She jumped and turned to him, dropping the knife.

"I'm sorry," he said, noticing her condition. "Change quickly, I will be right outside. Nobody will enter this building without my permission." He quickly stepped out, closing the door behind him.

Another explosion shook the compound and Dominic knelt, removed his magazine to verify it was full, tapped it back in and pulled the slide back just enough to verify he had a round chambered. He made a quick sprint to the nearby Humvee, retrieved a discreet duffel bag from the front seat, and ran back to the door of Hazail's barracks, removing a Sig Sauer MPX machine gun from the bag.

He unfolded the stock, took off his jacket, and slung its shoulder strap around his neck and right arm, then backed up into a shadowed crevice. With a good line of sight in three directions, he crouched low, checked his watch, and waited.

Mosul

The armored personnel carrier slowed to a stop and the Iraqi soldiers shouted to one another. Ten men assembled near the right side of the vehicle. It lurched forward, and as it moved the men moved with it, using its bulk as cover. A machine gun peppered its exposed side and the vehicle increased speed, forcing the soldiers to speed up with it. In a few seconds the ten soldiers safely crossed the expanse.

The vehicle backed up and was soon ready to make another run with another ten soldiers beside it. On the second run, the machine gun was silent as it passed.

"They're not shooting at it this time," Guy noticed from a block away.

"Conserving ammo?" Porter asked.

"Why waste it on an APC?" Ehmed said.

The vehicle came back for a third run and they hurried to join the group huddling beside it, keeping their heads down as it moved along. They were almost past when an explosion rocked the street ahead of them. Then another, then a third.

"Mortar attack!" Porter yelled as the soldiers scrambled, keeping their heads down. He took a position along a wall and his party followed. Cracks of rifle fire filled the air and the armored vehicle maneuvered out of the road and down a side alley with soldiers behind it, firing wildly down the street. Another round of mortars fell, and Porter and his men held fast to the wall. He surveyed the position and his fields of fire with his AK.

"Let's stay with them," he said, leading them toward the vehicle.

"Copy. Guy?" Aiden turned, looking for him.

"I'm on you," Guy nodded. "Go, Porter."

They moved with rifles pointed out and upward, quickly attaching themselves to the Iraqi squad. A technical sped by a parallel street on the left and the Iraqi soldiers unloaded on it before it slipped out of sight. Several ISIS fighters followed, running, only to be cut down immediately by the Iraqis and Americans.

"Move!" Porter yelled to the driver. The vehicle had stopped with them huddled in the open behind it. "We're too exposed here!"

"Fall back," Aiden said from behind him. The four ran back to the spot they'd previously occupied, fifty meters away from the vehicle that was currently absorbing fire from two sides.

"Why the hell isn't he moving?" Porter growled.

"Probably doesn't know where to go," Guy said.

"Anywhere's better than standing still in the town square!"

An RPG slammed into the tracks of the vehicle and several soldiers scattered away from the explosion, some injured and crawling away. Other Iraqis rushed to join their comrades in the fray, using the remains of the APC as cover, and the street was engulfed in a full-blown firefight. Porter glanced back at Aiden and shook his head. Aiden shrugged, searching for targets and a next move.

An Iraqi screamed, triggering his attention. To his right, four civilians fled down the street in the same direction Ginger had driven.

That Others May Live.

"Let's move, back that way," he pointed to the civilians.

Porter nodded.

Rabia, Syria

Casey Allen hit them with bursts from his rifle, taking down each assailant but still they came. A 6x6 truck slammed through the broken remains of twisted fencing and men ran behind it with guns. The volume of fire increased in both directions as the Americans and Peshmerga displaced to concentrate their fire on the breached gate.

Derrick slapped Casey on the shoulder and pointed.

"Look, they're moving within the fence line." Three men with vests and rifles ducked behind a building and ran into the shadows. "They're gonna flank us. Come on!" he yelled, running left.

Pasha and three other Peshmerga soldiers watched the Americans moving left. He knelt near the trucks with his men, returning fire with careful aim. The attackers advanced again and again, and neither Pasha nor any of the others had given an inch of ground to either the suicide-vested daesh or the charging vehicles. But to their right, other attackers seeped through.

He glanced at the opened crates of fresh weapons near them.

"Load two of those."

His companions went to work on the machine guns while Pasha and another kept a steady rate of fire in the center of the breech. Soon both of the new guns were operational and the men lay down on the ground behind the truck with the bipods extended. Another wave of ISIS tried to enter the gate, and as the SAWs opened up on them, the sound caught the attention of several nearby.

"Stay here. Own this corridor and keep hitting them." Pasha slung his rifle across his back, taking a SAW with a drum magazine for himself. "You, reload for him and keep hitting that center. Constant fire."

"Where are you going?"

"Left. They're trying to flank us." Pasha ran off.

Casey crept along with his rifle raised, knowing their foes would emerge from the shadow at any moment. Two SEALs joined them and they paused, acknowledging each other and waiting, ready for the daesh whenever they crossed into the open.

From around the corner they heard screaming in Kurdish, followed by an explosion that took out the wall next to them and threw everyone off their feet.

Casey rolled, ears ringing and his head in a fog. He slowly got to his knees but a sudden blast of machine gun fire knocked him out of his daze, and he was suddenly alert and searching for targets.

Two figures advanced at full speed through the smoke. Casey got off a three-round burst, then, *click*. He swore, knelt, and removed a magazine. A bullet grazed his helmet, another tagged him in the arm, and third struck his chest plate, knocking him to the ground.

"Allen!" Demarius called to him. "Allen, you hit?" Their men were spread out, taking cover and returning fire, mostly hugging the ground. Casey rolled to his left and felt blood and a searing pain under his elbow as he worked to reload his M4.

"I'm good!" he shouted, racking a round into the chamber and getting to his knees again.

Clayton tossed a grenade, stopping three men but the incoming fire continued from farther back. Casey moved right and crouched behind a mangled filing cabinet that had blown out of the building from the suicide bomber's detonation. He sensed someone approaching him from behind and turned in time to see Pasha lay down not far from Demarius and open up with the SAW in bursts.

He needs more ammo. Casey studied the soldier, then his eyes darted to his own men – Smith, Thrombull, and Clayton

– shooting at fighters who were clearly trained better than they had been taught to expect.

"Smith!" he said.

Demarius looked over. "What!?"

"Instruct that shooter to pace himself," Casey gestured to Pasha. "I'm going for more ammo."

"Copy!"

He ran back toward the trucks and heard shooting in three directions – left, in front, and to the right. *Good, they haven't surrounded us yet. We need to contain them ahead of us. We've got good interior lines.* He grabbed two cans of linked 5.56 ammunition to belt feed into the SAW and ran back. Demarius was kneeling beside the Peshmerga gunner, keeping a consistent rate of fire to cover his flank.

"I'll feed you," Casey said, opening the ammo can. "Here."

Pasha fired another burst as the drum went dry, and worked with Casey to reload the gun.

Far to their right on the opposite side of the compound, Peshmerga fended off attackers who used the same tactics — a man would dash forward, get as close as he could, and detonate a suicide vest. Directly behind him, others would try to exploit the disoriented soldiers, racing forward en masse while shooting. The rushes intended to scare the defenders into falling back, but they didn't; they stubbornly held their ground even as the attackers reached within feet of them, calmly and rapidly reloading, or moving sideways or even forward to meet them head on, men and women alike.

An hour into the firefight, mounting casualties were almost entirely on the attacker's side. They abandoned the rushing tactics but continued a consistent rate of fire. It was a matter of who would run out of ammunition first.

Dominic listened to the shooting intensify and then wane, back and forth like gusts of wind. He could easily see the SEALs coordinating the battle from the nearby headquarters building, but he kept his position beside Hazail's bunker. Eventually Mario noticed him and ran over.

"What the hell are you doing?" Mario asked. "You gonna get in this, old man?"

"Negative."

"They keep trying to exploit the breech, trying to get around us from within the fence line. But I think we've got 'em pretty well pinned where they are."

"All right, I'll be here."

"The girl, right," he nodded. "We called in air support. Smash 'em from the air. They can't keep up this assault for long."

"Good, I need to get to Mosul."

"Now?"

"I'm not going to find you to say goodbye," he smirked. "Gonna slip out as soon as I –"

He was cut off by two medics running, carrying a screaming woman toward the barracks and Dominic made way to let them pass. They could see it was a YPJ soldier with bleeding wounds in the neck and side of the chest.

Mario shook his head. "Do what ya gotta do."

They put the woman on the cot next to where Hazail stood, dazed by the activity. The soldier gritted her teeth and writhed in pain, tilted her head back and took deep breaths. She met Hazail's gaze and her lips quivered as she let out another cry.

One of the medics knelt and placed bandages on her stomach, and the other cut away her clothing with scissors to get a better look. He noticed Hazail staring.

"You!" he barked.

She straightened and looked at him.

"Take her hand. Speak to her."

Still she stared.

"Time to grow up now!" the female medic snapped at her. "Speak to her. I need her to fight."

Hazail nodded slowly and took the wounded woman's hand. She looked younger than the one who'd given her the knife, but similar, just a few years older than Hazail was.

"What…what is your name?" she asked timidly.

The woman closed her eyes and cried again.

"I'm sorry. Please…" She couldn't think of what to say.

The medics administered morphine and dressed her wounds as she took fast shallow breaths with wide eyes. The drugs calmed her but she continued biting her lip, wincing. Her mouth opened as if to scream but no sound came. Again her head tilted back.

Hazail held her hand firmly, tears streaming down both their faces. Slowly the soldier's grip lessened, and then went limp.

"No, please don't—" Hazail gasped. She put her other hand over her mouth to stifle a cry.

The medics exchanged quick words she barely heard and rushed back out, leaving her alone with the deceased soldier as gunfire echoed from outside.

From the shadows of the barracks, Dominic spotted a group of men sprinting toward him on the right with their heads down. When the lead runner was fifty yards out, he fired his first three shots, then quickly three more, all of the bullets hitting the first two men before they knew what was happening. The third aimed his weapon at the bunker but was also met with a wave of 9mm. The fourth got a burst off in Dominic's direction before falling dead; a sharp sting gripped the muscle of Dominic's left thigh and he fell to the ground.

He had the wherewithal to put an extra round in each body before releasing his grip on his weapon, sitting up with his legs in front of him. Dark red blood soaked his pants and he reached under his thigh to find the exit wound.

He removed his blood-covered hand and reached into his chest pocket for a bandage, pressed it under his thigh, and shifted his weight to hold it in place. He tore open the front of his pants leg to see the entry point, felt his pockets, and swore to himself.

"Hazail!" He called out and waited. "Hazail!" he said again.

The bunker door opened slowly and Hazail looked around. Dominic waved her to him.

"I'm injured. Not bad but I need you to get a first aid kit. Did you see one in there?"

She recoiled at the puddle of blood forming under him but quickly recovered.

"Um, yes, let me check." She ran back inside and he waited with his weapon ready, a fresh magazine inserted. The partially-used one went in his jacket pocket. She returned with a large wall-mounted first aid station, the plastic backing cracked.

"I'm sorry, I had to break it off the wall."

He chuckled to himself. "That's fine. Go back inside." She hesitated though, watching him rip open a roll of combat gauze with his teeth while holding the entry hole with his left hand, then start packing the wound with the length of gauze.

She knelt next to him. "Can I help you?"

"No, please take cover. They may make another run at us," he said with labored breathing, and then swore as he looked at his pants. "Actually, cut away this pantleg so I can wrap it. Take those scissors there."

She cut it off, unconcerned with the blood and working faster than he expected.

"Pick up your weapon," she said. "Let me do this." She wrapped the bandage around his thigh, secured it tight with the Velcro strap, and briefly admired her work. "Is that good?"

"Yes." He said, testing his leg while attempting to stand.

"Are you going to be okay?"

"Yes, yes. Go back inside unless I call you again." She obeyed this time, and he took several deep breaths, wincing from the pain, but shouldered his weapon again.

"We need to move. That way," Casey said to Pasha.

Pasha agreed and picked up the machine gun, running to where the Americans were reestablishing.

"This is a better field of fire," Casey explained. "Keep it hot and don't shoot us. We're gonna advance right and try to bottle these guys up into your line of fire. Do you understand?"

"Yes. Go, go!" another Peshmerga answered for Pasha.

"Good. You're doing good. Keep this lane closed, nobody gets through here. Just keep reloading him." He ran off with the others.

The Peshmerga soldier looked at Pasha, annoyed. "Do they think this is our first battle?"

23
TCCC

"Taking fire," Hozan said, as pings struck the Land Rover's front right fender. Ginger barreled down an unfamiliar street he had detoured her onto, and sketchy figures darted across the way.

"Faster," he said. "Plow through this intersection."

She slowed to avoid hitting a passing car, then gunned it through.

He relaxed a little in his seat, then turned to the men in back. "Hang on, we're almost there." She let off the accelerator, more cautious of the people populating the streets.

"Excellent driving. That was close."

"Thanks."

"Let's take them all the way to the hospital. It's not far."

"Just tell me where to go."

Within minutes they were there, and they helped the Iraqi medic unload the wounded soldiers. Then they stood alone, staring into the back of the blood-smeared cargo hold.

"Thanks for navigating," she said, quickly texting Aiden a sitrep.

"I grew up in the Old City." Hozan took a drink of water and gestured to the area they'd just come from. "It was once a normal place. With families, and life." He shook his head in disgust.

She nodded. "I need to check on my kids."

"Of course."

She texted Linda, then began wiping out the back of the Land Rover with paper towels and baby wipes.

Just got done. Are you and the kids still there?

The reply came back almost instantly:

No. We went back to the compound to rest. We'll stay here till you can get back.

Okay. Thanks. I'll likely be on my way there soon.

"What do you think?" she asked Hozan. "Can we run that gauntlet again if they call?"

He peered in the direction of the city, thinking, and shook his head.

"No. I'm surprised we made it that time."

Ginger ran her fingers across the bullet holes along the door as she used to do with her Apache after hairy missions.

"Yeah. I believe you're right."

"They good?" Porter asked, inching around a barricade to see if the way was clear to advance.

"Yeah, took a few rounds on the way out but they're back safe."

"Don't call them again."

"Agreed. That what's I told her."

The four of them huddled low, wondering which way to move next when two trucks tore down the street a hundred feet away. A column of soldiers up ahead sprayed them with bullets but had to duck when the daesh unleashed an RPG, the impact sending rocks everywhere.

"Guy, you're hit," Aiden said, noticing minor lacerations from the debris.

"So are you," Guy replied. "It's not bad." From his vantage point, he could see several wounded soldiers in the open. He rolled over and took aim from a laying position and began firing. Farther back, Aiden and Ehmed traded shots with fighters down the street.

Porter, crouched next to an abandoned vehicle, scuttled over to a small group of Iraqi soldiers and tapped one on the shoulder. The man turned, and Porter gestured for them to follow him to flank the attackers.

He led his adopted squad of three into the building to his right. They ducked through, using the furniture as cover, and reached a corner window with a view of the enemy fighters' exposed right. Porter pushed out the side door and popped off six rounds in succession, killing two. Another turned to fire but Porter cut him down as well as others ran to the building across the street. He inched forward, searching for targets as the Iraqis filed in behind him.

A sharp, familiar, whining noise loomed overhead.

Aiden rolled over and spotted the hovering drone. From down the street he heard Iraqis shouting. Two emerged into the open, followed by Porter, who turned toward him and gave a half-hearted thumbs up.

"Look up!" Aiden shouted. "Drone!"

Through the drone's lens the operator examined the corner. Soldiers congregated, twenty at least, three directly in the center with others nearby and closing. It wasn't a perfect target, but it would have to do. He gave the code word.

Aiden heard the vehicle's engine rev but he never saw it. All he saw were the Iraqis shouting, then shooting at something downrange. Porter raised his rifle and fired on full auto, then just as abruptly released his grip on the weapon and turned to sprint toward Aiden. He got three strides away before the entire intersection exploded, catching him and all the soldiers in the blast.

A cloud of dust enveloped Aiden. His ears rang and he clenched his eyes tight as the shockwave settled, then opened them to check but the dust still hadn't cleared. He rose, coughing, and started searching for Porter among the destruction and gore.

Porter's filthy Red Sox ball cap was still tight on his head and Aiden stopped short. Porter's head, chest, arms and legs were intact, but his midsection was sliced wide open. Aiden froze.

Fear gripped him, a fear he'd only known twice in his life — once as a child watching his first hero bleed out in front of him, the second high on a peak in Afghanistan, when he'd met Porter face to face. He was lost. There seemed nothing he could do but stare and panic.

God, what do I do?

Guy shoved past him and knelt by Porter's head.

"He's still breathing," he said, examining Porter's injuries, his organs exposed, his intestines leaking out.

"Aiden!"

Why did we even come here?

"Aiden! He's still alive! Help me."

That others may live.

"We need to pack him up," Aiden said, taking command. "Quick, but gentle." He crouched down, and thousands of hours of training, from backcountry courses to PJ school, through combat in Afghanistan and Africa, all came rushing in to fill the vacuum that fear left in its wake.

Penetrating abdominal trauma. Work the problem.

Guy watched as Aiden took out the largest dressing in his pack, opened it and sprayed it with a sterile saline solution.

"What are you doing?"

"We have to keep the organs wet. Check his vitals while I pack him up."

Jets screamed overhead, soldiers stumbled around, orders were barked in the distance, but Guy focused on training his ear to Porter's chest and felt a barely functioning lung take a shallow breath. There was hardly a pulse.

"He's breathing but going into shock."

"I know. We've got to get him packed up and warm. Get the ReadyHeat blanket. No! First, here." Aiden handed the saturated dressing to Guy as a mother would hand a baby to a friend. "Hold it closed for a second, make sure it's clean, we can't let any dust touch it." He donned a fresh pair of gloves, then paused, looking at the bloody mass in front of him, anatomy schematics playing in his mind's eye.

Never put the organs back in the cavity. Cover them. Let the surgeons do the repairs.

He gently worked to get everything in as neat a pile as possible over Porter's open wound.

Your greatest secondary danger is infection. Keep it as clean as possible.

"Okay," Aiden said, unsure of himself. "Let's cover it, slowly."

Guy laid the moist bandage over Porter's abdomen. Ehmed was now there, watching them and the courtyard simultaneously. They placed a second and a third bandage over the first and secured it as much as possible with tape, fearful of making it too tight.

"We need to get him wrapped up and warm," Aiden paused. "And medivaced."

Speaking the word made him realize the futility of the suggestion. There was no helo coming for them like they'd had in Afghanistan. No medical Stryker enroute or a radio call away. No QRF to call for…

A voice spoke in Aiden's head. *Call her.*

Ginger. I can't risk her coming a third time.

Call her. She can get him to Jake.

Jake? It's too dangerous for her.

That others may live.

Okay, God. Okay.

"We need to get him to Jake," Aiden said. They lifted him onto a thick blanket reinforced with a warming agent designed to stave off hypothermia.

"What about his other injuries?"

"Deal with those while we wait for the ambulance."

"You're calling her back again?"

"If we don't he's dead in less than an hour." Aiden removed his bloody gloves and took out his phone, looked at his watch while dialing the number and noted the time.

Clock's ticking.

The phone just rang and Aiden didn't leave a message. He texted instead:

Porter injured severe need evac stat.

Ginger was driving back to the compound when she got the call.

"Can you answer that?" she asked Hozan.

Hozan took the phone from her leg pocket as it stopped ringing. "Missed call from your husband."

The text chimed.

"Mrs. McCoy." Hozan's voice changed.

"I can speak to the generals," Ehmed offered. "They have casualties, too."

"He won't be a priority for them," Aiden said, looking down the intersection at the officers trying to reestablish order. The Iraqi medics were busy patching up the walking wounded. Many others lay dead across the intersection. "Besides, I don't see any triage happening. Or any other survivors."

A jet overhead released a bomb a distance away, but the soldiers were unfazed.

Aiden's phone chimed:

On our way. How bad?

He replied:

Bad. Blowed up but still alive. Pray.

Ginger spun a U-turn and accelerated, throwing Hozan against his seat.

Lord, protect them both…all of them.

She swerved to avoid a bus and gunned it through another intersection.

"You don't have to come with me. I can let you off if you want."

She swerved again to avoid a broken street lamp she'd almost hit on the first run, mentally checking the waypoints she'd memorized after the second pass.

"No, I'm with you," he said, bracing himself against the door as she bounced over a curb to avoid a new obstacle that wasn't there earlier. "But shouldn't you go a bit—" she lurched the vehicle forward "—slower?"

"I'm good. Text him back."

Hozan struggled to hold her phone while bouncing around in the racing swerving vehicle.

"Okay. Go ahead."

Aiden's phone chirped with the notification:
ACKNOWLEDGED. INBOUND HOT. SITREP?
He managed a smirk.
That's my girl.
He fired off a reply:
Stable but critical. LZ HOT. Be careful.

Hozan typed her dictated reply:
COPY. ETA TEN MIKES
Chief Warrant Officer Genevieve Cooper had flown over the same streets in hundreds of missions a dozen years and half as many surgeries ago. The castoff, barely-running Land Rover was an inadequate cockpit compared with the Apache she once dominated, or the Little Bird she'd mastered after a few days, but it would suffice today. Ginger swerved, steered, sped, and prayed, focused solely on the current mission, bombs and bullets be damned.

24
Sunsets

Rabia, Syria

Casey took a knee and fired nine shots in quick succession. Beside him, Demarius and the SEALs moved to their left and threw grenades over the sandbag barricades at the concealed fighters. A second after the explosions, three figures streaked to the left. Pasha cut them down with the SAW.

Mario sighted the man in the chest, but noticed his bulky vest and shot him in the head. He pivoted his scope left and fired, dropping another, then right and eliminated a third. To the left, one of his men let off a burst from a .50 caliber machine gun.

"Apaches inbound," his comms man said.

"How long?"

The whooping of helicopter rotors answered for him, followed by a burst from the helicopter's 30mm chain gun. The enemies' advance went up in a cloud of rock, dust, and flames.

Mario scanned left again, catching movement in his peripheral vision. "They're running. Left flank!" He turned, running to gain cover so he could fire in the other direction, but on the fourth stride felt a major pop in his right knee, dropping him to the ground. He swore, got on his elbow and tried to stand but the pain seared when he put weight on it.

He laid down on his left thigh, propped himself on his elbow again and pulled his useless leg along as he slithered toward the cover of truck's wheels. He used the big tire to pull himself up to a standing position, babying his knee and hobbling to get in a shooting posture.

"You hit?" Derrick said, running to join him.

"Negative, damn knee went out."

"Okay. You're good here. Just stay here."

Mario checked his targets, his weapon, and his world, saw his own men cut down the figures who'd squeezed loose of the Apache salvo.

The Apaches circled in wide trajectories around the border checkpoint, searching for additional targets. As the frantic pace of the battle waned, the pain increased in his knee. He swore again and pounded the steel of the trucks wheel well with the flat of his fist.

The Green Beret lieutenant waved for his men to advance, and Casey and the others moved as one toward his position. A fighter popped up, screaming, and again Pasha hit him with a burst before he could detonate the vest.

Casey and Demarius ran within range of the sandbags and tossed two more grenades over, ducking as they exploded. Casey rose to peer over the edge of the sandbags and saw twenty dead or dying men, their desire to kill mitigated by the combined airborne and ground level firepower.

"Hold your fire!" Mario said, hopping on one leg toward them.

Casey started to climb over the sandbags to inspect them but a Peshmerga captain stopped him.

"No, no!" he said in English. "They may have wired themselves." He examined the men laying in the depression, then sprayed the pile of bodies with his rifle.

"Cyclones report in," Mario said into his radio.

"All good."

Mario turned to Casey. "Your guys good?"

"Affirmative."

"Affirmative my ass," Mario said, noticing Casey's bleeding. "You're wounded."

Casey looked at himself and saw the blood. "It's nothing."

"Sure, let's check you out anyway. D?" he barked to Derrick.

"Yeah?"

"Collect our guys."

"Copy that."

"And, D."

"Yeah, boss."

"Find me a pair of crutches, will ya?"

Casey sat on the ground while the SEAL medic wrapped up his gunshot wound.

"First time in combat?"

"Yeah."

"What'd ya think?"

Casey watched Pasha and several of the Peshmerga soldiers securing the base entrance and deploying to remove the obstacles. Pasha made eye contact with him, and each nodded to the other before Pasha walked off.

"Not what I expected."

"Never is." The medic finished bandaging up Casey's arm. "You're good."

Dominic limped to the door of a civilian SUV and inspected the interior with a quick glance. He tossed a radio and his duffel bag into the passenger seat and placed the small machine gun in the console.

"Get in," he told Hazail as he got behind the wheel and started the engine, then caught a glimpse of two of the SEALs.

Mario hopped over. "You still here?"

"Yeah, leaving now."

Mario noticed he was sweating and pale, and pointed to his leg. "You look like death, man. You're injured."

"I'm fine. We need to leave."

"You're no good if you keel over behind the wheel, bro."

"I'm fine," he said, putting the vehicle in gear.

"BS." Mario held himself up by the car's side mirror. He looked around, then down at his knee. "We should go with you."

"No. You're injured, too. Also, you don't have orders for that."

"Our orders are to protect you and the supply transfer. I'd say that's still in play."

"No," Dominic shook his head. "As much as I'd love the extra firepower, I'll get through better on my own." He held out his hand. "It's what I do."

"You spooks are a breed of mutts." Mario shook his hand. "Glad I was finally able to meet one I can respect."

"Get your men home, sailor. That's all that matters."

Mario nodded.

"Oh," Dominic added, pointing upward, "if you could radio those birds and tell them not to light us up, I'd appreciate it."

"You got it. I'll even tell them to cover you for as long as they can stay with you."

Dominic waved as he raised the driver's side window, and the other SEALs walked up to Mario as the car pulled away.

"Where's he goin'?"

"Finish his mission."

"So what's our next move?"

"Find me a damn chair to sit in."

Mosul

Goriel jumped out of the Humvee and made his way straight to the highest-ranking officer he could find.

"Where is General Abdelhossein?"

"In there, I believe," he answered, pointing to a building.

Goriel hurried past and found his father looking over papers, accompanied by two of his aides. A smile cracked on Ozzy's face at seeing Goriel unharmed, then his expression changed to alarm.

"What is it?"

"You heard about the car bomb?"

"Yes. You're alright?"

"I've lost them."

"Lost who?"

"Your Americans."

"They're dead?" Ozzy asked, paling.

"No. I mean, I don't know. We were separated long before that. I searched for them but we kept getting engaged every block. I don't know where they are."

Ozzy nodded, seemed lost in thought for a moment. "I see. You're alright, though? You?"

"Me, yes. My men have taken heavy casualties. I just thought you'd want to know about the others. What would you like me to do?"

Ozzy sat for a moment pondering, remembering Porter and his own time serving with him on countless missions.

"Nothing. Unless we know where they are, they're on their own. They can handle themselves."

"Damn," Ginger said, slowing the vehicle for two men in the middle of the road. They were armed, and when they saw her they turned and started shouting. She pulled her pistol and shifted it to her left hand while still driving.

"Good guys or bad guys!?"

Hozan raised his rifle. "Bad."

Ginger gunned the gas and held the wheel steady with her right hand. With her left hand she ripped off a few shots out the window in their direction. Hozan extended his rifle out his window and let off a burst. The men scrambled for cover as she passed them. From behind, bullets hit the back tail gate just as they cleared what looked to be the start of a roadblock.

"Did you see that?" Hozan asked.

"Yes."

"They're going to try and stop us on the way back."

"Yes. Gonna have to fight through them, I guess."

"Maybe not. I know another route. Maybe I can lead us through."

"Just tell me where to go. But first we get our men."

Aiden finished packing up Porter in a tight wrap to maintain body heat. Then he waited, wondering if he could help others, but saw only dead bodies and angry soldiers, oblivious to them.

"Here they come," Ehmed said, holding his rifle ready, barrel pointed down-range toward the speeding vehicle, waving with his other hand.

This time it didn't slow at all. Ginger came in hot and slid to a sudden stop mere feet from him, maneuvered a fast three-point turn, leaving her tailgate facing Guy, who hurried to get the door open.

Hozan popped out of the passenger door. "We need to move!" he said. "There's daesh converging."

Ginger opened the door and glanced at Porter, then at Aiden, who shook his head at the whole situation.

"There." He pointed to Porter's tactical vest and rifle, laying in a pile. "Put those on while we load him up."

She strapped on the vest while Aiden, Guy, and Ehmed lifted Porter into the rear of the vehicle. Hozan stood guard with his rifle raised.

"Movement!" he shouted and tore off several shots, moving to the open passenger door as cover.

"Gentle does it, guys," Aiden said, bracing Porter's lower back and rear, trying to ignore the shooting while securing his patient. "Hold him steady."

Ginger crouched and picked up Porter's AK-47, aimed and fired from the knee, then moved to the car, using the engine block as cover. Two fighters lay dead and it was quiet again for a moment.

Guy secured the IV bag to the roof handle and checked Porter's vitals again. "Yes. We're ready," he said, taking his rifle and propping it on the lowered rear passenger window. Aiden ran around and tapped Ginger on the shoulder, his own rifle at the ready.

"Loaded, let's go!"

"Affirmative. How is he?" she asked, putting the rifle in the front seat next to Hozan and getting behind the wheel.

"No change. Need to get him to Jake STAT," he answered, running to the back of the vehicle.

"We can't go back the same way. It's too hot."

"You have another route?"

"Hozan does. Take care of Porter, I'll get us there."

Aiden noticed the bullet hole in the rear passenger door as he boarded and slammed it shut.

"Which way?" she asked Hozan.

"Same direction, but instead take your first left up there," Hozan said, pointing.

The vehicle lurched forward and tore down the narrow streets of the war-ravaged city. Aiden took out his phone, scrolled to Jake's number, and dialed him again. As before, he got no response.

Come on, Jake. Answer. He swore and hung up again, struggled to administer another injection into Porter as the vehicle swerved.

"What's up?" Ginger called from up front.

"Trying to prep Jake. We need to get him into surgery as soon as we get there, but he's not answering."

"Call Jen, she's with him."

"I…alright, but I don't have her number."

"I do. Hozan, give him my phone."

Jake again felt the phone buzzing in his pocket as he sutured up the wound. He made another mental note to check it in twenty minutes when he was finished.

Jen heard and felt her phone ringing in her pocket. Jake noticed and briefly lifted his eyes to her, silently wondering why both their phones were suddenly chirping.

"Dr. Lyons, are you okay if I check this?"

"I can finish up," Renas said.

"Go ahead," Jake said.

Jen removed herself from the operating room, removed her gloves, and saw Ginger's name on her screen.

"Hello?"

"Jen, it's Aiden. I need to speak with Jake asap. It's an emergency."

"Yes, he's just closing up a patient. What kind of emergency?"

"It's…"

"Porter?" Jen asked, her voice cracking.

"Yes. He's alive but we need to get him to surgery immediately. We're transporting him now."

She let out a barely audible gasp as fear overwhelmed her, and she started to sink as her legs lost their strength.

"Jen?"

Stand, daughter. With supernatural assistance she regained her foundation. *Fight for him.*

"Yeah, Aiden." Twenty years of training kicked in as the veteran nurse alter ego wrenched command from the terrified war widow. "I'll get him."

She hurried to the plastic window on the operating room door and tapped it rapidly, startling those inside. Making eye contact, Jen shook the phone and motioned for Jake to take the call.

"Please finish this up for me." Jake handed the suture instruments over to Renas.

"What?" he asked, coming out.

"Aiden." She handed him the phone, then turned and covered her mouth.

Jake put the phone to his ear. "Aiden, this is Jake."

"Porter's injured, we're bringing him in. Car bomb. Penetrating abdominal trauma and multiple impacts. Going into shock."

Jake turned to see Jen's back toward him, shaking from barely stifled sobs. "How long ago?"

"Thirty-seven minutes."

"Any foreign objects in the cavity?" He asked, watching Jen. She turned to face him, but her eyes were closed.

"I – I don't know!"

"Aiden. Breathe, brother. Focus."

"I don't think so," he said, in a quieter voice. "Jake, I had to scoop up a handful of his guts. He's breathing shallow. Weak pulse. I just don't know, man."

"Did you give him blood?"

"Don't have any."

"Drugs?"

"Dopamine. I bandaged it up and wrapped him to keep him warm. Hemodynamic instability."

"Peritonitis?"

"Yes."

"Okay. Forty minutes…approximately?"

"Yeah. I think so."

"Okay." *Still inside the Golden Hour.* "Just get him here as fast as you can."

"Working on it, coming in hot. Anything else I can do?"

"No. We'll be ready for him." Jake hung up.

Jen faced him with red eyes. "Let's get it ready."

"You don't need to. We've got plenty of people who can assist."

"No!" she snapped, then regained herself. "I'm going to help you. Please."

"Alright," he said, putting a hand on her shoulder.

"Damn it!" Ginger slammed the brakes, sending everyone airborne inside the vehicle. The intersection was blocked, and she put the vehicle in reverse to back up.

"No!" Hozan said, "Go around it. Don't go back."

"You sure?"

"Yes, go quickly."

She put it back in gear and swerved left to avoid the vehicle in the street. The tires bounced over broken concrete and an old sign as she maneuvered through a barely-wide enough gap between the wreckage and a wall, scraping the driver's side door against a street pole and busting off the rear-view mirror on that side.

The windshield fractured in three places, splintering what remained of it and distorting the view.

Ehmed, in the seat behind Ginger, spun around and fired a burst through the open back passenger window, five o'clock of the vehicle's center.

Aiden glanced at the shattered windshield. "Ginger! You alright?"

"Yeah, but I can't see hardly where I'm going!"

"RPG!" Guy said as a streak shot toward them from the left as they barreled past and the explosion rocked the street just behind them.

Porter sat bolt upright. "What the—" He screamed profanities, trying to move his arms while Aiden pushed him down. More expletives. "Get me out of this!"

Guy helped Aiden hold him down while Ehmed and Hozan fired out the windows and Ginger accelerated to sixty.

"What are you doing, Aiden!" Porter yelled, trying to get free.

"You're injured. Stay the hell down!"

"What are you talking about!?" His head swiveled, searching to make sense of it all.

"You're gut shot. Just lie back or you'll kill yourself."

He let out a long, painful groan, followed by rapid breaths, and fell backward.

"Porter?" Aiden patted his sweaty face, listened to his breathing, put his ear to his chest, and heard a sudden, rapid beat. "Cardiogenitic," he said to himself. "Porter, stay with me, here. Need you to chew these," he said, searching his med kit.

Porter blinked his eyes open, confused. "What? Where'd those guys go?" he said, weakly raising up his head. "Where's Jen?"

The vehicle swerved. More shots pinged off the car.

"Turn up here now," Hozan instructed. "Right! Here! Here!"

The vehicle lurched right on two wheels.

"Guy, get me some Aspirin."

Guy fidgeted in his pack and pulled out a bottle. "Here." He handed it over and picked up his rifle.

"Now, through here, through this alleyway," Hozan instructed. The vehicle took a hard left, then accelerated in a dark corridor of the rapidly darkening city. Aiden spilled pills all over the interior but managed to get two into his hand.

"Here," he said to Porter, "chew these."

"What?"

"Just chew 'em, you're having a heart attack."

Porter obeyed and moaned again, chewing slowly while his head drooped lower and lower.

"Porter?" Aiden slapped his cheeks. He had passed out again.

God, help me.

Jen cupped her hands over her eyes to shade the glare of the setting sun, and noticed how incredibly quiet the front gates were. In both directions she saw only a few people instead of the usual hordes, and they were casually administering aid to mild cases, mostly malnourishment. She heard no aircraft, saw no clamor. She sat on a plastic chair staring at the road.

God. I can't do it again.

She listened for an approaching vehicle that still did not come.

"Jen," Renas said, softly coming up from behind, lowering her voice to almost a whisper. "Doctor Lyons asked me to find you." She pulled another plastic chair over and sat, putting her arm around her.

"I don't—" Her voice broke in sobs. "I don't know if I can be in there. I don't even know if I want to see him when he arrives. I can't…"

Renas held her. "You don't need to. I will take care of him." They sat in silence as a minute passed.

"No," Jen said, getting up slowly. "I need to be in there. I can't just wait around while others do it."

Renas nodded and managed a weak smile. "Then go scrub in. I'll wait for them." She took her hand. "Strength, Jennifer. Hope."

Rabia, Syria

Pasha and his companion approached the Americans and sat beside Casey and Demarius. Several of the Peshmerga soldiers danced and sang around the flames as the visitors watched from a respectful distance.

"You should join us," he said. "The victory is yours as well as ours."

Casey glanced at his sergeant, who watched with growing interest.

"You lost men today," Casey said, more as a question.

"A man and woman. Soran and Medya."

"So why are you throwing a party?" one of the SEALs asked.

Pasha translated the exchange for his mate, who replied rapidly before standing, bowing, excusing himself to dance.

"He said, we don't…party…as you call it," Pasha explained. "We celebrate the victory. It belongs to Soran and Medya, as well. And you."

"Then why don't you dance with your boys?" Demarius asked.

"I don't dance."

"Why not?"

Pasha scraped the ground with his heel.

"He don't dance, either," Demarius said, referring to Casey. "Too much hate. Right, Allen?"

Casey said nothing, but watched as two female Peshmerga came over.

"He says you are too scared to dance with us," one said to Demarius in English.

Demarius looked at his captain, who grinned.

"Hell, I'll dance with you," Demarius said, standing rapidly. "Comin', Captain?"

"Negative, Smith," he said, shaking his head.

"I'm with ya." Josh stood to join them. "Besides, you don't want to see an old white dude like him dance. It ain't pretty."

Casey and Pasha smiled inwardly as they left with the women. After watching them for a minute, Casey spoke.

"Thanks for watching my six."

"We have the same enemy," he said, staring toward the fire.

"Do we?"

Pasha looked at him. "The daesh killed everyone I ever loved." He turned back to watch the others dancing around the fire. "Anyone who kills daesh is my friend."

Casey pondered the thought, then said, "In my country we'd say that anyone who fights my enemy alongside me is my brother."

"Then I guess we are brothers," Pasha said.

"I guess so."

A Peshmerga soldier plopped down next to Pasha, patting him on the back.

"There now, my friend. That was a different day, no?"

Pasha smiled, and his friend leaned in and pointed to the SAW.

"Would you still rather have a tank instead?"

Casey raised an eyebrow.

"Yes," he smiled at Casey, "but this will do for now."

25
Transports

Porter rose from the surf, his feet finding the sand in waist-deep water as he waded ashore. He wiped the water from his hair and face and only then noticed the beauty of the tropical beach, the pure blue sky, and the scent of the sea mixing with nearby flowers and trees.

He noticed several figures lounging shirtless in the sand near the tree line. Most had their heads tilted back, soaking in the sun, a few with their arms clasped behind their heads.

Only one of them seemed to notice Porter, and he raised his head and smiled as Porter advanced to join them.

Northern Iraq

The SUV swerved slightly to the highway's edge, and Dominic jerked the steering wheel to get back on the road.

"Are you alright?" Hazail asked.

"Yes," he answered.

She glanced at his leg again before looking back out the window.

"Where are we?"

"Not far now from Mosul."

"Why Mosul? I know nobody there."

"I can hopefully establish contact with your father there. And perhaps take you to him."

He calculated the various routes and scenarios. ISIS and Iraqi soldiers were the least of his worries now. Nor was he much concerned with the simple danger of driving through a warzone. He knew all of those matters well enough, had mastered them over the course of decades operating in this part of the world. What worried him now was the troposphere teeming with American and Russian aircraft raining down pinpoint destruction on men like him frequently, and with good reasons. And along with this threat from above was his increasingly painful, throbbing leg, and the bullet within it.

"Hello?"

"What?" he said, startled again.

"I asked if you have any idea where my mother might be?"

"I'm sorry. No."

"Or my brother?"

"No."

"You look very sick."

"It's painful. But we cannot stop even if we wanted to. There is no one here who can help us."

Hazail leaned her head against the window.

"If your brother serves under your father, they're likely to be near one another."

"I hope so." She looked at the small machine gun again.

"Do you know how to use it?"

"I've never touched one. My father always warned my brother and I to never touch a weapon. We would sometimes find them in the streets where we grew up. After shootings or bombings. Even his own rifle, he never wanted me to touch it."

"Do you know why?"

"So nobody would think we fought with them," she said. "They paid children to place bombs. Deliver weapons. I knew some of those children."

"He is a good man, your father. Smart."

"I never wanted to touch one, anyway. My brother did. Our men fight, but our women don't, I suppose."

"I suppose."

"But those women back there, they fight."

"Yes, they fight very well."

"I'd like to be like them."

"Perhaps you will, someday. I suspect your father would agree with that now."

Porter took shorter steps as the wet sand transitioned into hot dry pits. He recognized these men, all of them, in the same brown UDT shorts he'd once seen them in. All had once lain under the lid of a casket Porter had hammered a SEAL trident into; Tanner was there…so was Jerry, and Geno…Shep, and…Porter stopped, his shadow draping across Gator's legs. Gator raised his sunglasses.
"You're blocking my sun, jerk."

Ginger hit the brakes and laid on the horn. No vehicles gave way and she inched forward, nearly getting clipped by a speeding bus as it passed by.

In the back Aiden listened to Porter's shallow, almost non-existent breathing. Guy hovered over him as well, watching, feeling his weakening pulse.

Ginger saw a break in the traffic and gunned into it.

"Take the next left at this exchange," Hozan said, finally lowering his rifle and relaxing a bit. "Do you know where you are yet?"

"I think so."

"Here. Now right, here."

She took the sharp right turn onto the connected highway.

"Now you will need to go through the roundabout coming up. Mosul General Hospital is to the left, go through it and veer left."

"No," Aiden said, "take us to the field hospital in Hammam. I need to get him to Jake."

"It will add another twenty minutes at least," Hozan said.

"Ginger, make it there in half that."

She nodded. "On it. Is that your roundabout?"

"Yes."

"Hold on, everyone."

The beat-up Land Rover swerved through the roundabout at 60 mph and pinned its occupants to the right-side doors. Aiden and Guy braced Porter.

"Left, left, left!" Hozan shouted. "There, go there!"

Ginger took the left turn and saw the busy hospital out her side window as she passed. The vehicle straightened out with the taillights of many cars and trucks clustered on the highway ahead of her. "You sure, Aiden?" she asked.

"Yes. I want Jake to do this."

"It's a mostly straight shot now," Hozan said, bracing himself as the Land Rover increased to 80 mph and started to rattle.

"Gonna have to weave through this traffic," she said. "And pray the tires hold out."

"We trust you, babe. Just a walk in the park."

Guy checked his watch, felt Porter's wrist again. "What else can we do?" Guy asked.

"I don't know," Aiden said. "I don't think there's anything we can. How much longer?"

Hozan and Ehmed held the door handles as Ginger flew through the traffic, maneuvering swiftly and gaining speed.

"Not long at this speed," Hozan said, wiping the sweat from his face. "So long as we don't crash. Twenty kilometers. Ten minutes perhaps?"

Ten minutes. Aiden said to himself. *And not a thing you can do during it.*

Ginger slowed as the congestion intensified, a weigh station across the highway bringing traffic almost to a standstill.

"I wish I had a siren. Should I lay on the horn?"

"No," Hozan said. "That will make us a target. We're almost there. Take the next left, just as we clear the awning."

Aiden checked Porter's vitals again. *Heart Rate, 122, too fast, faster than it was earlier. Blood pressure, decreased. Arterial pressure, decreased. Respiratory rate, up, nearing 30.*

"How's he doing?" Ehmed asked.

"Decompensated shock."

"What does that mean?"

"It means his body can no longer compensate for his injuries," Guy said. "He'll die of shock if we can't get him treated soon."

"What about his injuries. His organs?" Ehmed asked.

"I have no idea," Aiden said. "That's Jake's expertise. Won't matter if his heart and brain stop working, though."

Ginger met Aiden's eyes in the rearview mirror. She made the turn and gunned the gas.

Hammam Al-Alil, Iraq

"There it is. Slow…there," Ehmed said.

Ginger slowed but still aggressively maneuvered into the receiving area. The armed security waved and shouted but Ehmed and Hozan jumped out of the vehicle before she fully stopped it and rapidly conversed with them. She threw the transmission into park, bolted for the rear, and opened the tailgate.

"Go in and tell them we're here," Aiden said. "And bring back a gurney."

"On it." She hurried past the Kurdish troops who were now more interested than annoyed. She came face to face with a nurse and spoke in Arabic. "We have a man who needs immediate surgery. I need to see Doctor Lyons or Nurse Dawkins."

"Mrs. McCoy."

Ginger turned saw Renas.

"We're ready for him. Where is he?"

"Right out there, we need a gurney."

"Easy, keep him wrapped up tight and don't jostle him," Aiden said as they slid Porter incrementally out of the back of the ambulance. Two men assisted to get him on the gurney and secured to move.

"We will take him to surgery immediately," Renas told them in Arabic. "Doctor Lyons is ready, the O.R. team is standing by."

"What did she say?" Aiden asked Ginger as they walked alongside the gurney.

"She knows. Jake's waiting for him."

They burst past the busy receiving area and went briskly through the tent city, past artificial flood lights as Aiden spoke to the attendant nurses.

"He's got a penetrating abdominal wound." Ginger translated for the others as he continued. "Exposed intestines, may be damage to the organs. I couldn't tell." Aiden speedily threw out a litany of numbers and medical terms to explain Porter's condition. "Ginger, tell them."

"I—"

"Tell them, they need to know," Aiden said, impatient while continuing to stare at Porter's whitening face.

"I don't know how to say all of that."

"It's okay," Renas said. "We understand."

"Stage three shock. Heart rate was at 140, respiration increasing, blood pressure falling off."

"Up here, turn," Renas instructed.

They turned the corner and Renas stopped them. A surgical team tried to take the gurney from Aiden but he held fast.

"Where's Jake?"

"He's in the OR, waiting for us. Jennifer is in there too. Please. You must let us take him from here."

He looked over her shoulder, trying to get a glimpse of Jake.

"Aiden." Ginger put a hand on his elbow.

He let go of the gurney and stepped backward, shaking.

The nurses whisked Porter through plastic, swinging double doors, leaving Aiden and Ginger alone in the silent, sterile passageway.

His arms dropped and he turned around. Ginger's hands shook as she clutched the sides of her head. Their watery eyes met and they grabbed each other, tears streaming down both faces. Aiden wept and clutched Ginger as tight as she had once clutched Porter's vest many years ago in a place not very far from where they now stood.

"I love you," she said quietly.

"I'm so sorry," he said weakly, staring at the ground. "There wasn't anything I could do for him." His words choked him. "Why did I even bring us here?"

Ginger held him tightly. "God brought us here."

"Can you hear me? Porter?" She leaned in. "It's me, Jen."

Porter's eyes were open but his stare was a mile long.

"He's in shock," Renas said, gently removing the top portion of the Redi-heat blanket and hooking up the patient to monitors by the arm.

"Non-responsive. May be losing brain function from loss of blood," Jake said. The nurses worked to get him blood. "Let's intubate him, nurse?" Jake said to Jen.

"Yes," Jen said, and began sliding the tube into her husband's mouth and throat, something she could normally do blindfolded. "Remember how many times I threatened to do this to you, babe?"

"Nice work," Jake said.

With all the tubes connected and monitors beeping, Jake took in the data. "Okay, let's remove the blanket and see what we're dealing with."

The team began peeling away layers of wrappings and clothing, much of which was stuck by clotted blood to numerous superficial lacerations. Soon he was naked except for the mass of large bandages covering his abdomen.

"Okay, let's take this easy. Gentle does it," Jake said, still watching the vitals and grateful he was now fully sedated.

They removed the bandages and were struck by the enormity of the wound. Jen shuddered and had to briefly look away.

"Okay, folks. I know it's hard, but try not focus on the organs. Our first priority is to make sure the cavity is clean. None of what we do will matter if we have contamination. Let's rinse and check for objects and fecal matter. We'll deal with this one step at a time. Copy?"

"Yes doctor," several voices affirmed in turn.

Jake made eye contact with Jen. "You good to go?"

"Yes," she nodded. "Let's do it."

"Slow and steady," Jake said. "This is gonna take some time."

"Where are the kids?" Aiden asked after they had sat for several minutes, collecting themselves.

"They're with Linda. I should call them…but what to say?"

"Just tell them we're on the way. Let's just get there."

"How is he?" Guy asked, waiting at the Land Rover.

"Don't know. It's gonna be a while, I imagine. We need to go to our kids, let 'em know we're alright."

"I will stay here, and text you when we know something," Guy said.

"So will I," Ehmed offered.

"I will drive you to them," Hozan said. "Ma'am," he said to Ginger, "you were amazing today."

She tried to smile, and quietly got into the backseat.

Dominic slowed as the city structures became more condensed, the war damage more prominent, and the looks from drivers more intense. He passed by them without making eye contact but spying everything, his darting eyes assessing every detail and his internal GPS ticking off the remaining miles. He turned and cringed at the pain in his thigh, weary from stress, exhaustion, and blood loss.

"Are we safe now?"

"No."

Hazail closed her eyes but opened them a moment later when the vehicle suddenly lurched to a stop.

"What is it?"

Dominic stared out the window. A sudden flurry of military vehicles sped across the intersection in front of them. He waited, the engine idling, and lowered the window to hear not too distant gunfire. Flames filled the night sky behind a building less than a mile away. Another series of airstrikes took out two more targets farther on.

"Where are we?"

"Mosul."

"Is my father here?"

"I believe so." He closed his eyes and saw stars.

"How do we find him?"

He was jolted back and opened his eyes. "I'm not sure."

Hazail noticed his squirming. "Is your injury bad? You seem in much pain."

"It's nothing," he said, and put the car in gear.

An officer approached and saluted Ozzy. "Sir."

"Yes?"

"I was told to inform you that the American was just taken to one of the field hospitals."

"Which one?"

"Which field hospital, sir?"

"No, which American?"

"One named Dawkins, sir. One of the ones attached to your son's squad, I believe."

"What happened?"

"I don't have the details, sir."

"Okay," Ozzy sat down. "Anything else?"

"No sir."

"Thank you."

Ozzy turned to look out the window. He closed his eyes and remembered Porter. *When, God? When will you stop taking them away?*

Porter took a step backward in the warm sand, examining the row of men before centering again on Gator. He knelt and scooped up a handful of sand.

"You know, if you're gonna get salty with me I might just shove this down you drawers, frogman."

"Try it."

Porter laughed and dropped the sand, still squatting next to his friend.

"So, what now?"

26
Waiting Games

Chugiak, Alaska

Abigail was two sips into her morning coffee when she opened her email. The sender was expected, the headline was not.

From Mosul: URGENT PRAYER REQUEST

She hurried to open Aiden's email with mug still in hand.

Thank you for continuing to pray for us on this mission in Syria and Iraq. I will give a more detailed update later but I ask each of you to pray for the life of my friend and ministry partner, Peter "Porter" Dawkins. He was gravely injured this morning in Mosul and is currently undergoing emergency surgery in critical condition.

Please pray for a miracle for our friend.

Aiden and family

Abigail set her coffee down and quickly picked up her phone. She rattled off a text to Aiden asking if there was anything specific she could do. When no response came she texted Josiah, then remembered he was currently in-flight and would be home that evening. She then sent a series of texts to friends and acquaintances, and finally settled back in her chair, closed her eyes, and prayed.

Mosul, Iraq

Ginger stared out the window from the back seat. Beside her, Aiden pocketed his phone and made a feeble attempt of policing his gear. In frustration he set aside his med pack without closing it. He noticed his AK-47 sitting idle in the back of the Land Rover and wondered if he should ready it, just in case, but didn't have it in him. Instead, he simply took Ginger's hand.

"Who did you send it to?" she asked, still looking out the window.

"Everyone."

They could both hear his phone buzzing with replies. Soon after, Ginger's did the same. Neither bothered to answer any of them.

Shiloh and Allen were at the window upon hearing the vehicle approach, and outside the house as soon as they saw their parents get out of it.

"Hi," Shiloh said, but immediately noticed her mom had been crying. "What is it?" she added, her eyes widening.

"Porter." Ginger tried to remain composed. "He was injured."

"Is he okay?"

Ginger paused.

"We hope he will be," Aiden answered for her.

Gary and Linda came out to join them. "Wow," Gary murmured at the sight of the vehicle, bullet-ridden, nearly every window cracked or broken, the front left tire barely holding enough air to drive on.

"Where is he?" Linda clasped her hands and moved closer to Ginger.

"At the field hospital," Aiden said. "In surgery, with Jake."

"What happened?" Gary asked.

Aiden glanced at Shiloh and Allen before answering. "Car bomb," he said. Ginger closed her eyes.

"Took out a whole squad of Iraqi troops," he continued. "Porter…I patched him up as best I could. Rushed him to the hospital." He forced his voice to sound positive and tried another weak smile. "Jake can patch him up."

He knelt down to Allen and Shiloh, leaning in to hug them, but they stared at his shirt and pants. He looked down and realized for the first time his clothes were stained with Porter's dried blood. He was fumbling for something to say when they threw their arms around him.

"Is it really bad? Is he going to be okay?" Shiloh asked through tears.

"We won't know for a while," Aiden said. "Yes, it's bad, but he's alive. They're going to have to do a lot to keep him that way."

Gary inspected the vehicle while Hozan watched in silence. "This wasn't from a bomb blast," he said in a low voice. "You guys were in a firefight."

"Yes," Hozan said. "We made several runs acting as an ambulance. Mrs. McCoy drove through it all. On the last run we were under fire for most of the way."

Linda hugged Ginger. "Are you okay?"

Ginger shook her head. "No."

"Can we go to the hospital?" Shiloh said.

Her parents shared a look of uncertainty. "Maybe," Ginger said, "but we won't be able to see him for a while, even if he's out of surgery, which I doubt…it will be several hours before we can sit with him."

"What about Jen?" she asked.

"I don't know," Ginger said. "I know she's there, though."

"I need to be there," Shiloh said with stern insistence.

"Okay," Aiden nodded. "I'll take you, but we need to give them some time to work."

Several transfusions later Jake was relieved to see Porter's blood platelet level above 50,000. Still a far cry from the normal level of 150,000, but getting there, slowly. They had worked to control the internal hemorrhaging and fluid leakage from numerous sources, including the rectum and pelvic walls. He had already made two trips to the operating room to stabilize Porter and had yet to even address the spinal fluid leak, but had just finished a twenty-minute consultation with a stateside neurosurgeon he'd interrupted on his way to bed.

"So we need to transport him, then?" Jen asked as he hung up the phone.

"He doesn't think it's wise and may not be necessary."

"Easy for him to say."

"I agree with him. The more immediate concern is finding all of the foreign bodies, and removing them and the rectal contamination. We need to do that now."

"Okay, so another surgery now?"

"No, first we get more images. I don't want to miss anything."

Jen was frustrated. "Every time we're in there we're exposing more of him to infection and all it takes—"

"Believe me, I know but—"

"—I know, I know," she said, waving her hands and pacing. "He could get closed up and die from infection a few days later."

Jake pursed his lips and looked away. "Maybe you need a rest?"

"Maybe *you* need a rest."

"Yes, I do. But there's not many people here I trust for this. Besides, it's what I do."

"It's what *I do*, too."

"I know. But we've been at this for" – Jake checked his watch – "ten hours, almost."

"I'm fine."

"There's not much you can do in this round, Jen. And we're going to need you rested when he wakes up."

"If he ever wakes up," she said quietly.

"Have hope. Don't make me order you to bed. Maybe you can give his parents an update."

"Okay" she relented. "I'll take a little break."

"And please sleep. Even just twenty minutes, okay?"

She nodded and walked out.

Jake sent a hurried update to Aiden.

EYES ONLY: Stable, finally. Real possibility of long-term neurological damage. Wait and see. Going back in.

Hours later, he closed up the final incision. He stepped back and surveyed his patient, assessed the monitors, racked his brain for the thousandth time for anything he might have missed. Reluctantly he turned a page in his mind.

"Okay, that's all."

The OR staff, seven in all including Jen and Renas, waited as if Jake had another instruction. When he didn't, they slowly began cleaning up the room. Jake examined Porter's body, his head swimming and eyelids heavy.

"You've done all you can do," Jen said softly. "It's your turn to get some sleep."

"Yeah, maybe."

"Doctor." Jen put a hand on his arm. "Jake," she smiled, "Go call your wife."

He nodded slowly and walked out.

Jen leaned in close to her husband – his breathing tube removed, still unconscious, his body warm, too warm despite the drugs pumped into him and the cooling methods trying to manage the fever.

The other nurses tried to ignore her, tried to give them a moment of privacy as she whispered to him.

"You're a fighter," she spoke a level louder. "I need you to fight…Porter."

The nurses stopped the clinking and gathering of equipment, cognizant of something terrible and beautiful in front of them.

"I never gave up on you, you jerk. Don't you dare give up on me."

Jen stood and Renas put her arm around her. Together they rolled Porter to as private an area as could be granted, and nobody called it a recovery room.

Jake scanned the intake screening area and found Aiden, who waved at him. Guy, Ehmed, and Shiloh also stood.

"How is he?" Shiloh blurted out.

"Jake, this is my daughter, Shiloh."

"Hello," he said, with a compassionate nod. "He's alive, breathing on his own but still unconscious, still dealing with a fever."

"What else needs to be done?" Aiden asked.

"He's going to need more surgery but not here. Not yet. We need to wait and see if he regains consciousness after the sedation wears off, wait for his fever to break, and make sure he's got adequate brain function."

"What does that mean?" Shiloh asked.

"Let's sit," Jake said, ushering her into a chair and sitting next to her. "He lost a lot of blood, and because his heart stopped so many times for so long, he may not have gotten enough to his head."

"So," Aiden explained, "he might have some brain damage."

"He's also fighting an infection," Jake added. "There was just so much in there. We have to wait and pray he pulls through it."

"And when he does?" Guy asked.

"Then he'll need to be transported. Either Europe or stateside to a neurosurgeon for additional surgery. I've already spoken with two and they agree we need to wait to see if it's necessary."

"Why wouldn't it be?" Ehmed asked.

"Because if he's already lost brain function," Aiden said, "then according to them, there wouldn't be a point. Plus he could die from the infection long before that, anyway. Right?"

"That's right," Jake said softly. "I'm sorry. We just have to wait and see."

"Thanks," Aiden said. "You probably need to get some sleep, huh?"

"Yeah. I'm slated to head back home the day after tomorrow."

"Then you really need to get going. Gonna get thrust back into the fire as soon as you get home, no doubt."

"It's how it goes."

"Talk to Cynthia recently?"

"Not in days."

"Then get out of here. And be sure to tell her I said thanks for sharing you with us."

Dominic was sweating, blinking to stay awake. He drove slowly now, through crowded streets wondering where to begin. For the hundredth time he considered his options. For the hundredth time he almost reached for his radio to communicate with his contacts, and for the hundredth time decided he couldn't do that to her, that she would be cast away, never to be heard from again.

"Are you sure you're okay?"

"I think…" Dominic blinked hard to keep his eyes open. "I think, maybe I need to find a doctor. I'm sorry."

27
Good And Faithful Servants

Ginger put a gentle hand on Porter's left arm, trying to get out words but finding none, and she pulled her hand away slowly. On his other side, Shiloh continued to stare at his face, silently praying for his eyes to open. Jen stood in the corner, trying to be brave.

"Is there anything we can do for you?" Aiden asked her. She shook her head.

Aiden held Allen tight in his arms and noticed other patients nearby with glazed expressions, family members and their loved ones with the same hopelessness Aiden now fought.

"Perhaps we should go? Give Jen some space?"

Ginger nodded and took Shiloh's hand.

"I'd like to stay," Shiloh said anxiously.

"No, sweetie," Ginger said. "There's not enough room for us to wait here the whole time."

"It's okay if she wants to stay," Jen said. "I'd appreciate the company." She held out her hand to Shiloh, who took it.

Ginger nodded. "It might be a long time till he's awake."

"I know," Shiloh said. "I just want to stay with him."

"We'll stay onsite," Aiden told her. "Maybe see if we can lend a hand. Just text us."

"Okay." When they were gone, Jen sat with Shiloh.

"You know, he thinks you're the coolest girl he's ever met."

"He thinks I'm a dork."

"What?" Jen actually laughed. "No, he doesn't."

"You've heard him. He says it all the time."

"Yeah, but he doesn't mean it. Not really."

"It's okay. When he first joined up with Dad, he used to see me reading all the time and he'd tease me about it. My dad told me to call him Froggie. It's kind of our thing." She looked down. "I'd always tease him for smelling bad."

Jen allowed herself another laugh and put her arm around her.

"Yeah, I know what you mean…but when he recovers, I won't let him call you that anymore."

Aiden tried to muster up the energy to treat patients, or minister to them, but all he could do was sit on a folding chair and wait. He closed his eyes, trying not to focus on recent images that were too vivid, memories too sharp — a snowstorm on a nameless mountain in Afghanistan, jokes with other Alpha males on fishing boats, a brief firefight in a wadi in Africa, guns and trucks and helicopters and barbecues.

He remembered the ceremonies and the funerals, the awards and the nightmares. He recalled conversations over lunch plates and coffee mugs, the challenges, and victories, and losses. He and Porter had fired bullets and spilled blood, theirs and others.

Why did I bring them here, God?

The voice answered, *He chose to come. They all did.*

They followed me.

No, they followed Me, as did you.

Aiden went over his actions of the previous day, replaying them repeatedly – coulda, woulda, shoulda.

It doesn't matter now. I was foolish to bring them here.

No. He did his duty. He's always done his duty.

Aiden was afraid to ask the question that had been on his mind ever since the blast…

Is he going to die?

Yes. Everyone dies.

That's not what I meant.

That's not what you should be asking.

Aiden thought about what Porter would tell him. He thought about what his father would tell him, his grandfather.

What next?

That's better. Pray. And call your brother.

Chugiak, Alaska

Abigail McCoy was startled by the music playing from the nightstand. She sat up and searched for her phone, pulling it close to read the screen without putting her glasses on first.

"Aiden?" she answered. "I'm so glad to hear from you. Are you okay?"

"Most of us. Did you get the email?"

"Yes, Josiah and I both tried texting you."

"I got them. I just didn't have any news and I've got so many texts to sort through."

"I can pass on an update if you'd like. I put the prayer request out to everyone I could think of as soon as I got it. What's the latest?"

"He's not good, Abby. We won't know the extent until he wakes up, if he wakes up. They're treating an infection too so it's pretty hairy right now."

"I'm so sorry. What can we do?"

"Just pray. I tried calling Josey but he didn't answer."

"He's flying. May be landing soon, I'm not sure what time it is. I was asleep."

"I know, sorry for waking you."

"Oh no. It's good to hear from you. Can you tell me what happened?"

"If you're up for it."

"Buddy, getting up in the middle of the night praying for you and your brother has been my life sentence."

Aiden smiled. "I'm glad you answered, sis."

Hammam Al-Alil, Iraq

Jen stood in front of the hospital window, the stench of disinfectants around her. She placed her hands in the pockets of her old blue hoodie, rekindling the silent debate she'd had so many times before. She'd cried for so long, and so many times over that same question: *Can I let him go?*

So many friends and family over the years had suggested she should. Now there was only silence. She turned toward the bed. Shiloh was asleep in the chair beside him, finally.

Good. It's your last chance.

Jen pulled over a stool on the other side of him and put her lips close to Porter's ear, wanting desperately to climb into the bed with him.

"Peter," she whispered. "If you can hear me, it's Jen." She choked up trying to get the words out. "I just want you to know…that it's okay." Tears flowed and she paused, hanging her head low. "You don't need to be in pain. You can go if you need to."

She laid her head on his chest and waited, listening, hoping.

"Do you remember what you said to me when Chris…afterward? You told me that sometimes the hero dies. I wanted to punch you so bad. And if you hadn't looked so pathetic, I would have. But you were right."

She stared into space for a long time.

"I always knew it would probably end this way. I never wanted to admit it, prayed it wouldn't, but I knew."

She cried harder now and spoke through tears.

"You were just too damn good at war to die from something stupid like old age. But it's okay. I'm not mad…I'm…I'm okay, if God wants to let you rest now."

She leaned in farther and kissed him. "When you see him, tell him I wasn't mad at either of you. I loved you both."

She stood and walked back to the window.

Under the lengthening shadows of a war-torn city, one of the first Medal of Honor recipients since the Vietnam war sat with his wife, herself a decorated combat aviator. Together they each wrapped an arm around their son and prayed.

Nearby, a former Pararescue jumper and current trauma surgeon closed his eyes and said a brief prayer for the man he'd spent the last day and half trying to resurrect.

Miles away, General Abdelhossein, the most influential and powerful officer in Iraq, slowly moved to a discreet corner flanked by aides and American military liaisons. He got on his knees and bowed his head low. Some backed away. Those who knew the general's routines whispered quiet explanations to the unenlightened newcomers. As the general was known to pray for his family and his men, he now prayed for his friend.

Next to the bow of an old wooden fishing boat in Boothbay Harbor, Maine, a retired Coast Guard captain scraped paint from sun-stained wood and prayed for his son. Down the lane and across the street, his wife watched the ocean waves from her favorite vantage point. From here she'd prayed her boy through the Naval Academy, and later across two wars and multiple continents, and he'd always made it back.

Six hundred miles south, the current U.S. President said a silent prayer for a man he knew only by reputation, but whom he had always intended to meet.

Several states away a different U.S. President set down his pen, cupped his hands over his page, and prayed for a sailor he once happily pinned a Silver Star on.

In Virginia Beach, a group of beefy men in shorts and blue t-shirts locked arms in a circle, took a knee in the sand, with confused young SEALs looking on from a distance. They lowered their heads and prayed for the man who'd put most of them through hell.

On Coronado Island, three men ran alongside cadres of miserable sailors holding logs high above their heads. They remembered the man who made fun of them, the beer they drank, and the way they failed to live up to his expectations. They silently prayed for their brother between barking orders to wet and sandy trainees they hoped would someday follow in his footsteps.

In a pristine auto shop in Palm Desert, a man sipped his coffee as the sun shone through the window, reflecting on the morning's email. In resignation he closed his eyes and offered up one of only a handful of prayers he'd ever spoken to a God he didn't really know, every one of which was because of his daughter.

In a dimly lit, silent sanctuary in Kentucky, a pastor gathered his small church staff to pray for the man who'd brought his favorite white girl back to life.

In five buildings across a compound in the heart of Africa, three dozen former child soldiers of all ages knelt with their teachers, sobbing and praying for the man who first encountered most of them as he looked down the barrel of his gun.

And in a hotel room in Portland, Josiah McCoy sat in a cheap chair, remembering the man who once shoved him into the snow to keep him alive while taking on a mountain of enemies.

Josiah rubbed his eyes, praying, shaking, and wishing he could stand alongside Porter's bed, or at least alongside Aiden, making a difference. He stood and opened the hotel's mini bar, examining its small variety of lackluster beers. He closed the fridge and prayed for one more chance to share a real beer with his second favorite hero.

"Up to you, bro."

Porter looked up and down the row of men.

Gator put his sunglasses back on and lay his head back in the sand.

Suddenly from behind, Porter heard screaming. He turned to the ocean and saw a woman far from shore behind the wave crests, flailing. The screams grew fainter as the figure was dragged further out to sea. Porter stepped closer and the person disappeared below the water, the next wave obscuring the view. The figure surfaced again and a scream rang out louder than all of the others that had proceeded it.

"Get on with it," Gator said.

Porter ran to the ocean and splashed through the low surf till the water hit his knees. He dove ahead into the rough sea, thrusting with powerful strokes and kicking his legs, fighting against the current. A seven-foot wave crested and crashed, tumbling him in the whitewater. He reoriented. Feeling the surge of the next swell, he dove deep and swam till he felt the wave pass, then surfaced for air and caught a small glimpse of the woman. She waved her hands and fell below. Another swell took him up and he had to decide, over or under.

He dove deep, kicking and swimming harder than he'd ever swam in his life, harder than in BUDS, harder than the time he swam with one arm dragging a nearly dead and mortally-wounded brother to a waiting submarine, harder than the laps he'd pounded out in the pool every day for weeks after Gator had died.

He tried to surface but couldn't. The light faded and he seemed to sink further no matter how hard he kicked. He lost all sense of direction in the darkness of the cold sea.

He had nothing left. He could not rescue her, or himself, and he blacked out.

Diffused light pierced the darkness and he tried to take a breath, but he couldn't open his mouth. His eyes were shut tight and he realized he was no longer cold, no longer tumbling in the currents of the sea, but laying still, warm, and quiet.

Porter tried to use his hand to wipe the water from his eyes but his arm didn't respond, his breathing was shallow and difficult; his tongue and mouth were dry, his eyelids heavy.

Suddenly he remembered the truck bomb, the street, the war.

Get in the damn fight. Open your eyes. Where's Aiden?

The muscles around Porter's eyes pried their lids open a sliver, revealing a blurry scene. The image cleared some and he could make out Aiden sitting in a corner, staring at the ground. Porter tried to turn his head but only his eyes responded. Hospital equipment filled his vision — his arm covered in tubes, a blanket over his body, more instruments to his right and then, close enough to touch her if he could move, Shiloh McCoy leaned against his bed with her eyes closed.

He tried to speak but no sound came. With a mighty second effort he inched out a weak word.

"He…ey."

Shiloh opened her eyes.

"Hey…dork."

Aiden stood, his eyes wide.

Porter lifted his head an inch and examined Aiden from afar. He cocked his head and spoke in a louder voice. "Man…you look…like hell."

Shiloh smiled and teared up. "Hi…Froggie."

"Hey girl," Porter rasped. He laid his head back and closed his eyes. He shifted his right arm toward her and she took his hand.

Aiden moved closer, grinning.

"Tell your old man," Porter said slowly, "that if he ever…shoves aspirin in my mouth again…I'm gonna…kick his ass."

28
Departures

USS Dwight D. Eisenhower, Arabian Sea

"Torn anterior cruciate ligament, I'm afraid," the ship's doctor said. "Gonna need surgery."

Mario absorbed the news from the exam table.

"Alright, do it. When can I get back to work?"

"Easy there, son, it's not gonna happen right away. Gonna take some time to get back to an operational level."

"Sure, I get it. How long we talking?"

The doctor sat down. "An average person, at least a year. An NFL running back, eight months minimum." He could see the SEAL thinking, and smiled. "Of course with you guys, there's no telling, maybe less. Don't sweat that though till after your surgery. Nothing you can do about it till then."

"I here ya, Doc." Mario got up and negotiated the pair of crutches.

He made his way past busy sailors of every station and style, all stealing a quick stare. He got a large energy drink, placed it in his cargo pocket, and sat alone at a table, wondering if he wanted to use the crutches and get himself some food. He stared out a window toward the sea, debating his next move.

"Hey there," Birdie Allen said from behind him.

Mario smiled weakly. "Ma'am."

"What, no lame pick up lines this time?"

"I guess not," he smirked. "Sorry, I'll think up something witty next time."

She nodded. "Sorry for your injury. Is it bad?"

"Naw," he said, getting his swagger back. "Just a hiccup. I'll be back out there turning you on soon enough," he winked.

"Ahhh, there he is," she laughed. "I noticed your team left."

"It's how it goes."

She placed her plate of food in front of him. "Here. I'll be right back."

He stared at the plate with a bagel and cream cheese, yogurt and fruit.

Birdie went through the line again and filled a plate with chicken tenders and french fries. She sat down across from Mario and ate a fry while he looked at the yogurt.

"I thought you were getting that for me?"

"Nope. Go get some yourself, big boy."

He smiled and ate the bagel.

"Called my bluff," she said, and switched trays with him.

She ate quickly and made a little small talk. When she was done, she handed a piece of paper to Mario. "When you get stateside, look me up. Maybe when this deployment is over I can watch you in a wheelchair race or something."

"How about instead, I just whisk you off to Jamaica for a week on the beach?"

"Not a chance," she stood, "but we can start with coffee." She arched an eyebrow at him and walked away.

Mario smiled and fiddled with the paper.

"Hey!" he called after her, turning several heads. "We already had coffee once!" He held out his arms, palms up.

She came back and leaned in, her face close to his.

"It's gonna take a lot more coffee than that, Chief."

Hammam Al-Alil, Iraq

Ozzy and Goriel led the small entourage of military officers through the crowd of curious, onlooking medical personnel, who parted for them. He found Aiden at the entrance and embraced him.

"So, he's alive, well?"

"Not well, not yet, but he'll get there."

Ozzy grinned. "The man is too stubborn to die. Please take me to him."

"Of course." Aiden led the general down the corridor, leaving Goriel and the other officers at the entrance.

Dominic parked the car and hobbled out, leaving the weapons locked inside. He limped toward the entrance with Hazail trying to support his arm. As they approached, soldiers sized up the pair. Dominic was careful to avoid eye contact as he limped past them into the intake waiting area. Hazail helped him to a chair while a French volunteer knelt in front of him with a clipboard.

"I have a gunshot wound," he said.

"Yes, I see that. Do you feel sick?"

"No. I just need it cleaned out and re-dressed and I'll be on my way."

"We have many people here. I will find a doctor to see you as soon as one can. You will be cared for." She smiled and left.

Dominic scanned the area, focusing on the Iraqi officers. "Hopefully this won't take long," he said to Hazail, already making up his mind to leave quickly.

Hazail's eyes went from person to person. She felt pity for them, felt their pain. She tried not to stare at the soldiers by the gate, but three of them came around a corner and she focused on the one in the center.

Her eyes widened. "Goriel?"

She stood, took a step closer, spoke aloud. "Goriel?"

He looked toward the small female voice.

"Brother!" Hazail ran to him.

He was stunned, his hand moving by instinct to his pistol when he realized what was happening. He caught his sister as she threw her arms around him.

"Hazail? Oh God! Oh God!" He pulled her close and wept. "How?"

Nobody noticed Dominic Reyes stand up and slink away into the shadows. No one ever did.

"Hazail…" Goriel held her at arms' length and looked at her. "Are you okay? How did you get here? Is Mother with you?"

Hazail shook her head, still brimming with tears. "No. Mother was taken long ago. Months and months, I think."

"How did you get here?"

"A man brought me." She turned back to the empty chair. "I—" she looked around, "I don't…" She pulled away from Goriel, but he followed her and reached for her hand.

"He's gone!" she said, panicked. "He was here. He was shot. We were in a battle…" she began to cry. "He saved me!"

Goriel saw several men with gunshot wounds. "We'll find him later. We must get you to Father."

"Father is here?"

"Yes," Goriel smiled. "He's here."

"The man who saved me. He was trying to find him."

"Then he succeeded."

Dominic moved carefully in spite of the pain, as an expert who doesn't want to be noticed can. He found himself near garbage dumpsters piled high, several aid workers smoking cigarettes a short distance away. They paid no attention to the man who sat heavily on the edge of an empty concrete flowerbed. Wincing, he grabbed his wound and tried to formulate his next plan as he wiped the sweat from his brow with his sleeve and blinked to keep his eyes open.

"You're injured, friend," Jake said in English, putting away his phone.

"Yes," Dominic nodded.

Jake inspected the bandages, partially soaked through with blood. "Field dressing looks good. Gunshot?"

"Yes."

"You speak English?"

"Yes."

Jake looked at Dominic's face. He seemed familiar. "Who dressed this wound?"

"I did."

"Yourself?"

"Yes."

"Are you a soldier?"

"No."

He nodded and pursed his mouth in approval. "Well, you did a fine job. You look like you're struggling, though. May I take a look at it? I'm a doctor."

"Yes."

"I can get a wheelchair."

"I can walk," Dominic said, standing.

Jake helped him to his feet, and put his arm around his back to brace him up. "Well, let me help you at least. Is there anyone here with you? Anyone you can contact?"

"No. I'm alone."

"What's your name?" he asked as they walked together into the building.

Dominic noticed the tattoo on Jake's bare forearm, two green footprints, the Jolly Green Giant tattoo of an Airforce Pararescueman.

"If it's all the same, doctor," Dominic said, switching to his natural American dialect, "if you could just patch me up and get me out the door, I'd appreciate it. If you know what I mean."

Jake whispered. "On a business trip?"

"Yeah." Then he switched back to a Middle Eastern accent. "And I'm already pretty late."

Jake smiled. "Copy that, boss. Get you back in the game in a jiffy."

"Papa!"

Ozzy heard her from a distance, and turned to see Hazail running to him.

"Hazail?" He dropped to his knees as his daughter flung herself at him. "Oh Lord, how? Thank you! Thank you! Thank you!"

His soldiers and Aiden stood aside as the realization crept upon them.

"Glory of glories. Is your mother here?"

"No. I don't know where they took her," she said, her head buried in his chest.

"You found her?" he asked, looking up at Goriel.

"She found me…us," he answered, still in unbelief.

Ozzy looked at him with tears. "We will find your mother, too. Of that I am now sure."

SEATAC Airport, WA

Josiah's phone chirped as he walked along the terminal. He saw it was Aiden and ducked into a chair at an abandoned gate.

"Hey," he answered. "What's the latest? How's he doing?"

"He's going to be alright, we're pretty sure. Jake's gonna escort him and Jen to Germany in a few days. He still needs more surgeries but not here. He should be able to fly stateside within the month, hopefully. Long recovery so he won't be returning to Africa with me, maybe for good. We'll see."

Josiah took a deep breath. "That's great. It really is. How are you doin'?"

"Tired but dealing. Been worse."

"And Ginger, your crew?"

"Drained. All of us, especially Shiloh."

"I'll bet."

"Gonna take it easy for a few days. Recalibrate. Then see what God wants us to do next."

"Like maybe take a vacation? A real one."

"That'd be nice. Maybe later. Still a lot of need here, and we aren't scheduled to fly out for a few more weeks."

"You never let up, do you?"

"I just follow orders."

"Yeah, well, speaking of doing illogical things in undesirable places…I was hoping to get to talk to you. I want to run something by ya. Maybe you can talk me off the ledge."

Erbil International Airport, Iraq

Five days later Jen held Porter's left hand while his right shook hands with several others in turn.

"Don't let him get lazy and soft," Guy said to her. "Americans get lazy when they no longer have to work for a living."

Porter pointed at Guy. "I'll run you down. Don't think I won't."

"You couldn't even run as fast as Aiden on your best day, much less run me down."

Porter smiled. "Yeah, I know. Tell those kids I'll see 'em again soon."

"I will tell them. Bless you, friend."

"Gentlemen," Porter said, wheeling left to face Hozan and Ehmed. "Thanks for getting me outta there," he nodded at the McCoy's, "and for protecting my family."

"You are our family as well," Hozan said. "All of you."

Porter and Jen went through the security gate. Jake nodded to Aiden before following them and passing through.

"You guys promise me something," Porter said. "If I ever hint at coming back to this country again, shoot me."

"You know," Jake replied, "I said the exact same thing on my last deployment."

Porter laughed. "So did I."

29
Resolved

Bethesda, Maryland

Mario sat in the hospital bed waiting, bored, and anxious to be released. He attempted to get up but the tenderness of his post-surgery knee told him to lay back and relax. He scrolled through his phone and saw several emails, including one from Birdie Allen. He read it and set it down, smiling.

An hour later, notifications began popping up in quick succession.

"The hell?" he wondered aloud as the door to his room opened and a SEAL Rear Admiral walked in.

"Sir," Mario said.

"How you feeling, son?"

"Ready to go, sir."

He nodded. "Good to hear that."

"Sir, is there something going on?"

"Yes. I hate to have to tell you this, but your team was on a mission in Syria. Their Chinook crashed. No one survived."

Mario glanced at his phone, text messages still flooding in. "Why did it crash?"

"Hard to say for sure at this point. The initial word is instrument failure."

Devastation enveloped him. In a flash he saw his friends, their families, wives, children. He recalled their homes, their trucks he'd ridden in, the jokes they'd told, vulnerabilities they'd shared with each other and no one else.

He wanted to cry but would compartmentalize that for later. Instead he tilted his head back, staring at the ceiling, remembering his last mission…their last mission. He recalled Dominic's history lesson, and his warning.

"Instrument failure, my ass."

"Excuse me?" the officer said.

Mario shook his head and closed his eyes. The pain of loss gave way to a silent rage that boiled within him.

Northern Iraq

Durwa moved along slowly amid the throng of dispossessed women and children. They ran the gamut of people groups, from tired and grateful non-combatants to viscously angry ISIS brides, true believers to desperate victims, all hungry.

She waited as Iraqi soldiers patted them down before allowing them near the food lines, searching for suicide vests. It didn't concern Durwa now; a bomb blast would be a welcome conclusion to what was left of her life.

As she got closer she noticed many of the aid workers were Western. A woman serving rice caught her attention, her chestnut hair flowing out from underneath a ball cap. Durwa watched as the woman excused herself from the serving line to attend to a young boy, and another woman and a teenage girl took her place.

Speak to her, a voice in her head said.

Durwa paused, feeling the compulsion to run to her. It overrode her agonizing hunger and she stepped out of line to make her way to the woman in the ball cap, who noticed her and smiled.

"Hello," Ginger said in Arabic.

"Hello," Durwa replied in her native tongue.

"Are you hungry?" Ginger continued in Arabic.

"I was but now…I'm not."

"Is there anything I can do for you? Would you like to sit with us?"

Durwa nodded and they sat, and she smiled at Allen. "Is he your son?"

"Yes."

"Hello," Allan said in Arabic. Then in English, "That's about all I know how to say." He shrugged with a toothless grin.

"He's still learning your language."

Durwa nodded awkwardly.

"Where are you from?"

"We lived in Tal Afar. In Iraq."

"You and your family?"

"Yes, for a time." She took a breath to say more, but stopped.

"Would you like to tell me what happened to you, and your family?"

"We were separated. I was sold to become a man's wife in Palmyra. He beat me very severely. I was later sold to another man. I don't know where I was after that. I was kept as a housemaid and slave, then I was sold again."

Ginger took her hand.

"You're safe now."

She shook her head and looked away. "Nowhere is safe."

"How did you get here? Do you have any idea where the rest of your family is?"

"The village was liberated, and we were told to come this way for food and safety. I don't know where my family is, but my husband wouldn't want me now anyway. Not after this."

Ginger swallowed hard, struggled to get words out. "It may be like that. That's true. But it might not. Will you believe me if I tell you that I know what it's like? To lose everything…to them."

"Do you?"

"Yes." Ginger pointed to Shiloh. "Do you see her?"

"Yes."

"It was terrible what the daesh did to me. But God carried me out of it. As He has carried you out of it. And God gave me her as a gift. He brings beauty from ashes."

"What is her name?"

"Shiloh."

"I have a daughter, Hazail. And a son, Goriel."

Ginger started at the name. "Is Goriel a common name among your people?"

"Yes." The brightening of a proud mother showed in her eyes. "He is a soldier, like his father."

Ginger's heart raced. "I know a few Iraqi soldiers." She treaded lightly with her next words. "Has he ever trained with the Americans?"

Durwa nodded, a hopeful pleading in her eyes. "Yes. Many."

Ginger smiled. "Would you like me to contact them for you? Perhaps they know of your son, Goriel."

"Yes, please. I would like that very much."

Ginger pulled out her phone and scrolled for Hozan's number. "I'm so glad you came to talk to me."

Langley, Virginia

The woman at the large oak receptionist desk hung up the phone. "You may enter now," she said with a professional smile.

Dominic walked into an opulent office he had never been in before. It was filled with mahogany furniture surrounding a small man in a pristine dress shirt who frowned and didn't rise.

"Reyes," he said, barely glancing up from his work. "Good afternoon. Have a seat."

"I prefer to stand, sir."

The man lowered his reading glasses to the rim of his nose, then took them off and leaned back in his chair. He chewed on the end of his silver pen, eying his underling.

"If I were in your shoes, I'd be happy to take a load off once in a while. You've been going solid in the field for," he looked at the papers on his desk, "damn. Since as long as I've been here."

Dominic said nothing.

"So, you're finally ready to retire?"

"I've already done so, sir."

"On paper, yes. But have you considered what you'll do afterward? Assuming I can't talk you out of it?" He followed with a supercilious grin and a fake chuckle.

Dominic stared at him.

"Let me put it this way, Reyes. If you were interested, we could find a more," he tilted his head back and leaned it one way, then the other, searching for the right word, "*pleasant*…assignment. Maybe overseas, maybe right here. Pretty much anywhere you'd like."

"Thank you, sir. I'm not interested."

The younger man picked up a few papers and flipped through them. "Your retirement package isn't all that impressive, Mr. Reyes…yet. What do you say about a couple of years at a posh duty station, maybe do some consulting, diplomatic relations, heads of state stuff, that kind of thing? It would quadruple this measly nest egg, I could promise you that."

"No."

The man behind the desk turned and laughed to himself. "Sooo," he took on a mocking tone, "what are you going to do next?"

"Not this." Dominic took his CIA credentials out of his jacket pocket and set them on the man's desk.

"You've had your meetings with legal, I take it. Signed all the necessary paperwork. Non-disclosure agreements and whatnot?"

"Yes sir."

The man rose and extended his hand. "Then good luck, Reyes."

Dominic shook his hand but held it longer and firmer than the man expected, and said, "Pity about those SEALs, eh, sir?"

The man looked confused, noticeably uncomfortable with Dominic's grip.

"Which SEALs?"

"Surely you're aware that we just lost an entire team," Dominic released his hand, "in a helo crash."

"Oh, yeah. I heard about that. Terrible tragedy."

"They were good men, sir. They all are." He turned to leave.

"I wasn't aware you were acquainted with them."

"Yes, you were," Dominic turned back. "And don't ever speak to me again."

Down in the parking lot Dominic called a number.

"Hey, Dad. Did you do it?" his daughter asked.

"Done as Dillinger."

"Awesome. So, what are you going to do now?"

"I've got an idea I've been thinking over, I'll tell you about it over dinner next time I'm in town. Not over the phone."

"Mysterious. So, you can take the guy out of the spy agency, but…"

"Still a lot of scumbags out there. I'll talk to you soon, sweetie."

Al Qa'im, Iraq

Pasha pulled himself up the wall and onto the roof. He took a hard look at the hated black and white flag before walking up to it and wrenching the pole from its rusty hinges. He went to the edge where a few dozen soldiers stood below and threw the flag and its pole down to the street. Soldiers across the rooftops nearby cheered, some danced, many sang.

Men stomped, spit, shot at, and urinated on it. Eventually someone doused it with gasoline and set it ablaze. There it burned until nothing was left but a charred pole in the street.

Pasha took a deep breath, stood tall, and held his head high.

"We won, grandfather."

Epilogue

November 2018
Anchorage, Alaska

Josiah tapped his leg anxiously. Abby picked lint off his shoulder and smoothed his jacket with a gentle hand across his chest.

"There," she smiled, "now all you need is a target on your back and some sweat on your palms, and you'll fit in perfectly."

"Last chance to bail out."

"Oh no. You own it, general. You got us into this mess, now you better drive it home, straight down their throats, or I walk. We had a deal."

"Yes ma'am." He looked at Stacy in her stunning dress. "Thanks for coming. You ready?"

"Sure, I guess," she smiled. "But then, I'm not the one jumping into the shark tank."

"You sure you don't want to move down there with us? Better weather."

"Nope. Not a chance."

"I guess it's just you and me then," he said to Abby. "Okay, let's get it over with."

The three of them walked into the crowded downtown pavilion amid cheers, red, white, and blue balloons, and dozens of waving signs with Josiah McCoy's name plastered on them.

"And here he is," the TV reporter announced over the live feed as Josiah made his way through the throngs of people shaking his hand, "Senator-elect McCoy, lifelong Alaskan, decorated retired combat pilot turned commercial airline pilot, will now return to public service to, in his words, 'Bring some integrity back to a government known for compromise and cowardice.'"

Another reporter chimed in. "Yes, few people knew his name even a year ago, but Senator-elect McCoy is just one of a small handful of highly surprising wins tonight across the country, almost all of them by highly decorated veterans, all answering and echoing the president's call."

"Yes," the other reporter crooned, "the president made that plea a year ago, and make of that what you will, nobody can doubt it had a resounding effect on voters in those districts. Senator-elect McCoy and these others shocked the pollsters, garnering overwhelming election day numbers over unpopular incumbents in the primaries…"

Hours later, Abby lay with him in a top-floor hotel room they couldn't afford, both too exhausted to undress any more than merely taking off their shoes. They stared at the ceiling.

"What have I done?"

"Nothing smart," Abby chuckled.

Josiah's phone chimed for the hundredth time. He peeked at it, then smiled and read it.

"Aiden."

"What's he say?"

He held the screen so she could read it.

Congratulations Bro. I guess you're part of the problem now.

Abby put her head on her husband's chest. "Better not be."

Palm Beach, Florida

Jen sat with her feet in the sand, her blue Florida Gators hat shading the book in her lap. She looked up to see Porter rising out of the water and walking toward her. As he got close he shook as a dog does, spraying water everywhere.

"Hey, stop it! You're getting my book wet!"

"Aw come on, why are you reading on the beach, anyway? Here, you need a hug?"

"Don't," she pointed at him, "take one…step…closer, or I'll end you."

"Bleh." He plopped down on the towel next to her.

Jen gazed at his torso, at the long scars across his abdomen. Then she went back to her book.

"I forgot to tell you," he said. "I heard from Guy this morning."

"Yeah?"

"Yeah. He asked when we're coming back."

"What did you tell him?"

"I told him I'm still trying to talk you out of it."

"It's not up to me."

"It's up to us."

She looked at her book. "We'll need to let Aiden and Ginger know soon, either way."

"Yeah…but not today," he said, putting on his sunglasses and basking in the sun. "I just want to be lazy today, and hang out at the beach with a hot girl."

"If you want this hot girl to stick around, you better not spray water on her books anymore." She kicked sand at him.

"I'm not afraid of you."

"Yeah, you are."

Sarasota, Florida

Teddy leaned into the microphone. "Thanks for joining us again folks, and as promised we're gonna make this one worth the price of admission. Today — the long awaited return of not one, but *two* previous guests who individually knocked our socks off the last time they were each here, but together they're like Wonder-Twin-powers-activate kind of badassery. Air Force Pararescueman and Medal of Honor recipient, Aiden McCoy, and retired Apache driver and Chief Warrant Officer Genevieve 'Ginger' Cooper McCoy. Friends, it...is…an…honor."

"Thanks for having us, Teddy, Ray," Aiden said. "It's our honor to be here."

"No, thank *you* for coming. Now let's not waste any time with the chit chat because we could talk for hours and not even scratch the surface of what our listeners need to know about your journeys. And I know Ray-Ray's itchin' to ask you the first question but I outweigh him so here's what I want to start with, and this is for either of you: You've both seen the reality of war from all sides — from the view afforded to top-tier operators in Afghanistan and Iraq, with all the tech and advantages money can buy, as well as down at street-level war from the civilian angle in both Africa and just recently on the ground in Mosul, with nothing more than a black market med kit and rickety old AK-47s. Through all of that…at this point in that…evolution, what is your take on the need to confront evil, and what is our part in that as oxygen breathers?"

"Is Ray's question shorter?" Ginger asked.

"Yeah, you can take a pass on his if you want," Ray said.

Aiden and Ginger silently questioned each other, and Aiden motioned for her to start.

"The first thing that comes to mind," she said, "is that you just see a need and meet it, no matter who or where you are. Yeah, in war you're duty bound to do your job. But in every facet of life that's also the case. I could be on the way home from grocery shopping or in the middle of a battlefield and if someone is desperate for help, I'm gonna have a hard time not helping them. I think we 'oxygen breathers,' as you say, need to ask ourselves if there's anything we can do in those moments to help. And there were a few times in the cockpit as well that I had to make tough choices about stepping in when I had every justification not to. Those decisions are risky, and sometimes lives are on the line.

Maybe we can't step in all the time, but more often than we like to admit to ourselves, we *can* do something. Even if it's just staying around and holding someone's hand till help arrives, or offering to pray with them."

"And you did a lot of that in Mosul, no doubt."

"I met a women in Iraq who'd been abducted by ISIS for several years, sold into a harem of sorts, raped, abused. Some of these women were just so broken. I mean *broooken*-broken, and all they wanted was someone to love them without hurting them. Having been in that place myself, I know God brought me to some of those encounters, which wouldn't have happened had I ignored the call to go back to Mosul."

"I like that take on it," Ray said. "I can't tell you how many times we've heard the same refrain from heroes, and I know that word makes some of us uncomfortable because to us we're just doing our job or honoring the code we signed up for, but really your actions are heroic because maybe nine out of ten people didn't answer that call, or they wouldn't if given the opportunity. But then you see that recognition of your actions in the faces of the people who would otherwise be dead – or still broken or wandering, and looking for comfort – if you hadn't. Right?"

"Many people rightly refer to my husband as a hero. And every one of them is right," Ginger smiled at Aiden. "He's saved more lives than anyone will ever recognize him for, and I think that anonymity is just fine with him."

"What do you say about that, Aiden?" Teddy asked. "How do you reconcile the call to save lives with the necessity to take out some really bad dudes in war? Or, not even in war, but just in dealing with a messed up, dirty world?"

Aiden closed his eyes, thinking. "Happy would it be for mankind," he began, "if the prevalence of Christian principles might ultimately extinguish the spirit of war, and if the ambition to be great might yield to the ambition of being good.

"That's a quote from Noah Webster's original definition of war. Webster went on to delineate between offensive and defensive war, and how we as Christians need to understand the difference. Which is all well and good when we have civil magistrates…leaders, that is…who know right from wrong and who follow a proper ethic when making decisions about how and when to fight evil. But rarely is that the case.

"Usually we have external forces driving those decisions — emotion, corporate interests, sometimes propaganda, contracts and alliances, politics — so the warriors like us end up having to make decisions in the field about how best to accomplish good in an evil environment.

"And make no doubt about it: pure evil exists everywhere. Right here in Florida, in Syria, and across the globe in ritzy, exclusive clubs just as much as in urine-soaked shanties. Evil doesn't play by civilized rules. And I agree with my wife. When we see it, no matter who we are or where we are, it's our duty – and I go it a step further and say it's our *privilege* – to serve our brothers and sisters by confronting it on their behalf."

"Just like any of us would if someone tried to harm our own kids, right?" Teddy agreed.

"People harm their own kids all the time though, or sit back while others do so," Ginger said. "Who will go to the mat to stop that? Who will have the guts to say 'Not on my watch' and put themselves in that arena? We can go along or try to ignore it all we want, but unless Christian men and women are willing to get a little uncomfortable, get over not being liked by the world, and call evil 'evil,' then people die."

Aiden waved his hands. "Look, I hate violence. I really do. But what's worse is seeing innocent people hurt and killed, especially kids. Sometimes we can't do anything about that. The world is messy, right? But sometimes we can, and sometimes violence is the only available option to save lives. But the thing that the pure pacifists forget in that equation is that our motivation in fighting is love. It's love that runs toward the gunfire. It's love that that holds those hands, and it's love that refuses to let others be victims. Warriors need to stand in that gap, often with a weapon…to protect the sheep from the wolves."

Tal Afar, Iraq

Ozzy placed his hand on the small of Hazail's back. "Here," he said, using his other hand to steady her outstretched arms, "don't anticipate the bang. Just pull the trigger, slow and smooth. Lean into it, get aggressive."

It seemed strange to hear the words coming from her father's mouth.

"Okay," she said. Hazail took a deep breath, lined up the white dot on the end of the pistol with the two on the back, centered in the chest of the paper target, and slowly pulled the trigger. The weapon recoiled and reloaded.

"Breathe. Go slower, we've got plenty of time."

She slowly aimed and took several more shots until the weapon's slide locked back.

"Good, it's empty now. Release the slide lock, like I showed you. Now ease it back into the holster."

"It's terrible," she said, examining the target.

"You hit the paper. That's a start. It takes repetition, stance…it all takes time to master. You'll get it."

Hazail nodded, chewing her lip. "Okay. Can I try the rifle?"

"Yes, but later."

Ozzy turned to his wife and looked at her tenderly. "Are you ready?"

Durwa took slow steps to the line. "Yes, I suppose."

"You don't have to," he said gently.

"I don't *want* to," she said, eying the target, but remembering a thousand abuses, the stench of evil men, the dead bodies, the screaming, the pain.

"Okay," Ozzy said. "We can wait."

"No," she relented. "We need to learn this. Who knows what might happen next?"

He stepped up to her and kissed her on the top of the head. "Then let's get started."

Emmett, Idaho

Dominic sorted the remaining ten emails into their corresponding files. He took a drink from his coffee mug and drained the last few drops onto his tongue, then got up for more when his phone started buzzing on his desk. Not recognizing the number, he decided to let the voicemail get it and left to refill his mug. When he got back, he checked the recording.

"Good afternoon, Mr. Reyes. My name is Hector Galindo. I'm a police officer outside of San Antonio and I was given your number as a possible contact regarding a case I'm working. If you wouldn't mind calling me back…"

Dominic wrote down the number, then did a quick internet search and found service records for a Hector J. Galindo, Air Force Pararescueman, retired, that seemed to fit the bill. After reading through a few site pages, Dominic called him back.

A voice on the other end of the phone answered. "Galindo."

"Afternoon. This is Dom Reyes calling you back. I got your message. How can I help you?"

"Thanks for returning my call, Mr. Reyes. It's my understanding that you're in the business of assisting with operations involving human trafficking. Is that correct?"

"Yeah, we've been helping out departments recently. What do you got?"

"Yep, I saw your website. My friend, Aiden McCoy, is an associate with one of your guys, Randy."

"Oh yeah. Randy was a cop down in Arizona for a long time."

"Well, Mr. Reyes—"

"Call me Dom."

"Well, sir, I'll be honest. I feel a little over my head in this. It's not my expertise, not by a long shot. I kinda stumbled into something and I'm not…I'm not getting the investigative support I expected. I'll put it that way."

"Not surprised, Officer Galindo."

"You can call me Hector."

Dominic took a sip of coffee. "Well, Hector," he opened a spiral notepad to a blank page and leaned forward with his pen poised. "I'm listening."

The Willard International Hotel, Washington D.C.

Allen opened the door of the suite and beamed at his grandparents, standing in the hallway.

"Hey there, you," Mrs. McCoy said, bending down to absorb the eight-year-old's hug before walking in.

"Welcome to D.C.," Josiah said from behind the collected group — Ginger, Shiloh, Abby, and Stacy, all dressed formally, and Aiden in uniform.

"Thanks," Mr. McCoy said. "Swanky joint you big-shot politicians get, eh?" They hugged.

"Fun fact: This is the very hotel that Grant was in when he coined the term *lobbyists*."

"Fitting. But it is nice, nonetheless."

"Thanks for arranging the ride down," he said to Aiden, handing him a polished oak box. "There you go, straight from the study wall."

"Thanks for bringing it," Aiden said, opening the box.

"Yeah, no problem. I keep saying you should keep that with you."

"With the places we travel, it's not worth the risk of losing it. I'd hate to have it lifted by some opportunist."

"Maybe," his father agreed. "You should have seen the Air Force crew who flew us down here. When they found out we had this as luggage they practically wanted us to sit in the cockpit. Talk about VIP treatment. I think I might start taking you up on those friends and family perks more often."

"I've been telling you…" Josey said.

"He's too stubborn," their mom said.

"So is Aiden," Ginger said. "Won't take the free travel unless it's for this kind of stuff, official government or military speaking engagements."

"If I gotta come to D.C. because of *this* guy," Aiden slapped Josiah hard in the chest, "then Uncle Sam can pay for it."

"When was the last time you attended a Medal of Honor gathering?" his mom asked. "Ten years ago? More?"

"Something like that," Aiden shrugged, trying to attach the medal behind his neck. Ginger stepped behind him, helping him with the clasp.

"I let the flight crew see it," their father admitted. "But none of them dared even touch the box. It was like the Ring of Power or something. I hope you don't mind."

"That's fine," Aiden said, and faced Ginger for final approval. "Good?"

"Man, that's sexy," she said, and he smirked.

"And what about you?" the elder McCoy said to Josiah. "Ready to become a Senator?"

"Let's just get on with it. Thanks for being here, all of you," he said to the group. "Even you." He slapped Aiden harder than he'd received a moment earlier.

"Staaaaap," their mom said, shaking her head and taking Allen and Shiloh's hands to leave. "*Boys.*"

"Excuse me…Senator McCoy, right?"

"Yes."

"My name is Ed Lewis."

The name registered with Josiah immediately. "Yes. It's great to meet you. Congratulations on your win."

"You the same," Representative Lewis said, shaking Josiah's hand.

Josiah leaned closer and lowered his voice as the cocktail crowd passed around them. "So, what do you think so far?"

Lewis spoke in the unapologetically brash voice of an Army combat veteran. "Biggest swamp I've ever been in." People in expensive suits gave curious and annoyed glances at Lewis before turning back to their business. "And I spent time eating snakes in Malaysia once upon a rotation."

"That's why I stuck to war from the cockpit," Josiah laughed, taking a sip of his beer. "I hear ya, though. I've already had about ten leeches approach me, trying to sink their teeth in."

"Is your family here with you?"

"Some of them. My parents took my brother's kids back to the hotel, but my wife and daughter are around here. My brother is probably somewhere nearby getting swarmed, no doubt."

"He is, I met him a little bit ago. I was acquainted with his wife from a few years back, she pulled me out of a tight spot once. You're a Hog driver, right?"

"Sure was."

"Always loved hearing you guys on approach. You saved our bacon more times than I can count."

"Glad to do it. Wonder if our paths ever crossed. We'll have to sit down sometime and compare notes, see where we may have overlapped." Josiah glanced around at the D.C. hobnobbers. "Maybe on other matters too, once this clown show gets rolling. There are a couple of other newbs around here you and I should hook up with."

"Sounds like a deal. I'll watch your six if you watch mine."

Josiah and Lewis shook hands again.

"You've got it. Just give me the nine line and I'll walk the rounds into 'em for ya."

"And I'll take 'em in the mud for ya, wing wiper."

Around 23:00, the five McCoys stepped out of the van in front of the hotel, exhausted and relieved to be done. They'd finished the official socializing with varying degrees of awe and disgust, and had to wait for everyone who wanted to shake Aiden's hand.

As they walked into the lobby, a few heads turned. Aiden was last in, still in uniform and wearing the ribbon around his neck.

A clerk behind the counter noticed him.

"Check it out," he said to the manager beside him, nodding toward Aiden.

The hotel manager, an ex-Marine, boomed out in the loudest voice he could muster.

"Ah teeeeen shun!" He gave a crisp salute to Aiden. "Medal of Honor recipient on deck!"

The McCoys paused as eyes around the hotel trained in on them.

From a chair nearby, a woman in a black business skirt and jacket paused her phone call, stood, and saluted.

A young man in a hotel uniform with close-cropped hair saluted Aiden from across the room.

Two middle-aged men in jeans and ball caps set down their bags on the marble floor, turned, and gave salutes as well.

And an elderly gentleman sitting in a deep chair near the window stood with great effort and obvious pain that he tried to mask. He raised a withered arm, giving a shaky salute over eyes that burned with pride.

Aiden looked around, his face ashen and serious.

Ginger let go of her husband's hand, turned to face him, and saluted as well, mouthing the words, *I love you.*

Abby nudged Josiah. Senator McCoy rolled his eyes and sighed, turned, and saluted his little brother.

"I hate you so much," he said with a slight grin.

Aiden winked, took Ginger's hand again, and led her to the elevator.

Acknowledgements

Thank you Jesus, for bringing this book to life and taking it to places I was unaware it needed to go.

Thank you to my wife, Shannon, who sat patiently beside me during the coffee-filled afternoon editing sessions, and never let an opportunity to slay unnecessary words go to waste.

To my older kids, thank you for the input and gentle course-corrections. And to the younger kids, thank you for reminding me why the things discussed in this book matter.

Thank you Bobby, for setting me straight on the details of combat aviation, and for all of the book recommendations. I'll get to them eventually.

To Joe Shinnick, thank you for fixing my dialogue and upping the intensity. And to Joe Paolilli, thank you for the years of encouragement and hook-ups with contacts and technical experts. You and your friends have made this series possible.

Thank you Robert, for watching my back on the medical side of things. I anxiously await getting to return the favor.

To subscribers and fans of the series, thank you for waiting through countless delays, and for standing for freedom while dark forces confront you daily.

And finally, to Dahojo, thank you for metaphorically rapping me on the head when I've gotten it wrong, and for watching over this endeavour almost since the beginning. I only wish Boss Mongo could have read the final chapter.

The Modern War Series

The Golden Hour: The hour immediately following traumatic injury in which medical treatment to prevent irreversible internal damage and optimize the chance of survival is most effective.

SEAL team Polaris is on a reconnaissance mission high in the Hindu Kush mountains of Afghanistan when they're led into an ambush. The A-10 fighter providing close-air support is shot down and Air Force pararescue jumpers, dispatched to extract the downed pilot, also suffer heavy fire.

As the clock ticks and casualties mount, the PJs join forces with Polaris – facing subzero temperatures, formidable terrain, and entrenched enemies – to rescue the missing pilot and get them all home.

Four years after a heroic rescue mission in Afghanistan, former Pararescueman Aiden McCoy continues to fight for the lives of veterans – this time at home, as they struggle with the physical and psychological effects of war.

Meanwhile in Iraq, Aiden's lifelong friend Jake Lyons impresses everyone with his combat rescue skills. As Jake's reputation grows, so does his exposure to the daily horrors of a chaotic war. Aiden must help his friend confront the challenges of trauma and get him back in the game.

Spanning two years in locations across the Middle East, American soil, and the shadowlands of intelligence agencies and special operations, *The Stars and Their Places* continues the tale begun in *Beyond the Golden Hour*.

Ginger Cooper, one of the best Apache pilots in the Army, engages in nonstop missions during the Surge of 2008. Her squadron, Pegasus, owns the skies over Iraq, supporting troops on the ground across the war-ravaged nation.

Porter Dawkins, a Navy SEAL, leads his counter-terrorism unit as they partner with the Army's elite Delta Force operators to target insurgent leadership in high-risk missions at a moment's notice.

As the insurgency adapts, Ginger and Porter need to overcome unit casualties and the ramifications of their personal choices as they work to defeat an increasingly creative and elusive enemy. When a top-priority target turns heads in Washington, the Delta Force and SEAL operators must combine with Pegasus for a critical mission, where failure could derail the entire war.

Also by Vince Guerra

The Dread Pirate Roberts is a fan-fiction sequel to *The Princess Bride.* It tells the tale of Trajan, a young Guilderian on a quest to avenge the death of his father who was killed by the current Dread Pirate Roberts. His efforts are quickly altered by Westley and other previous Dread Pirate Robertses, who decide to train and assist Trajan in his quest.

The Dread Pirate Roberts is available to read in its entirety for free at **vinceguerra.com/the-dread-pirate-roberts.**

About the Author

Vince Guerra is a writer, novelist, and homeschooling father of eight. He writes weekly about freedom, history, current events, and occasional nerd stuff on his website vinceguerra.com. You can subscribe to his writings at **vinceguerra.substack.com**.

He is the author of five novels: *Beyond the Golden Hour*, *The Stars and Their Places*, *Pegasus*, *Those Who Face Death*, and *The Dread Pirate Roberts*.

He lives in Wasilla, Alaska.

www.ingramcontent.com/pod-product-compliance
Lightning Source LLC
Chambersburg PA
CBHW021219310726

48971CB00006B/1622